Lucia's Lament

Coming Soon

by
EMILY DANIELS

A Song for a Soldier

Also from
Phase Publishing

by

Rebecca Connolly

An Arrangement of Sorts
Married to the Marquess
The Dangers of Doing Good
Secrets of a Spinster
The Burdens of a Bachelor

by

Grace Donovan

Saint's Ride

Lucia's Lament

EMILY DANIELS

Phase Publishing, LLC
Seattle

Text copyright © 2017 by Phase Publishing, LLC
Cover art copyright © 2017 by Phase Publishing, LLC

Cover art by Tugboat Design
http://www.tugboatdesign.net

Phase Publishing, LLC first paperback edition
May 2017

ISBN 978-1-943048-26-7
Library of Congress Control Number: 2017940523
Cataloging-in-Publication Data on file.

Acknowledgements

This book is dedicated to the real Ronald and Lucia, whose delightful love letters gave me the idea for this story.

I also want to thank my family and friends for their continued love and support as I wend my way through the craziness of the creative process.

Most of all, for my own sweet Ronald, who continually shows me what true love is all about.

Prologue
Embley Park, Hampshire
October 1854

Florence sat tall on the divan, her back straight, jaw set, and her grey eyes flashing with a determination that bordered on defiance. Her father sat across from her in his accustomed chair, his brown eyes unreadable. She knew her mother would not be pleased, and her sister would certainly object as they had when she decided to pursue a nursing career, but she hoped the man before her would support her in her desire to serve now. As she looked into his face, she couldn't tell what he was thinking.

He puffed on his pipe a couple of times, then spoke. "Is this that important to you, Flo?"

"It is, Papa," was her simple reply.

He sighed. "I suspected that it would be. Your Uncle Samuel has been here and spoken in favor of you going to Crimea as a volunteer with a nursing corps, and we received word yesterday that the government has entreated you to go help the wounded soldiers in the hospital at Scutari. I understand you will be superintending the nurses." His voice had a hint of pride in it. He puffed again and blew a smoke ring into the air, then continued. "Your mother and I will support whatever you decide."

"My mind is made up, Papa," Florence started to protest. "It is a *fait accompli*." Then she stopped and stared at her father. "Wait, what did you say?"

He smiled indulgently. "I said that your mother and I will support whatever you decide. We feel it is a great and noble work. All of your experiences thus far have prepared you for this and we are in full support of it."

Visibly relaxing, she smiled. "Thank you, Papa." It was so much more than she'd hoped, and had come so much easier than she'd feared.

Florence Nightingale was on her way to her destiny.

Chapter One

Lucia forced herself to stand still and not stomp her foot in frustration. How could her mother not see the importance of this call to serve? Those soldiers needed her, and Florence Nightingale herself had asked Lucia to go. How could she refuse?

Harriet Rix stared at the newspaper in her hands, the fear and anxiety etched clearly on her face.

"I knew that allowing you to attend that foolish Queen's Academy was bad enough, but your pursuit of nursing has simply turned your head to mush," she began.

Pointing at the newspaper, Lucia started to argue. "Mr. Russell says right there that the old pensioners, who had been sent out for such service, are 'not of the slightest use' and the soldiers have to 'attend upon each other'. They need nurses, Mama. I've studied and trained under Mrs. Fry and Miss Nightingale. I'm ready to go and be of use, as Mr. Russell says."

"I'm not arguing there is a great need for nurses in Crimea. After all, the newspaper says so, but why do you have to be the one to go? Your patients at the Institute for Gentlewomen need you here. If all the nurses go to war, who's going to tend to them?"

"There are plenty of nurses who are not going, Mama," Lucia was adamant. "Miss Nightingale is only asking for twenty to go now, and she has all of the nurses in London, indeed all of Europe, to choose from. I'm honored that she's asked me. You should feel honored, too, that your only daughter has learned enough to be given this great chance. Aren't you the least bit proud of that?"

Lucia watched the frustration on her mother's face. Her voice quavered a bit as she tried once again. "How can I give my blessing? You are twenty-five years old and haven't been seen in society enough to attract even one eligible suitor! You don't have enough life experience to truly know what is best for you. Therefore, I forbid it. You will stay here and make yourself available for this Season's events. You have agreed to sing at several parties in the coming weeks. They will be wonderful opportunities for you to meet some of the young men new to the area. Perhaps this year you'll find a husband."

Harriet's hopeful smile soon faded as Lucia gritted her teeth and clenched her fists. Her mother could be so infuriating. Social events. Eligible suitors. Singing at parties. How could any of those add up to the important work that waited for her in Crimea? She opened her mouth to speak her mind, but closed it again as her mother began wringing her hands and pacing the floor, her voice trembling with emotion.

"Are you going to forget your obligations? Are you going to abandon us all and run off to Crimea where there is war and devastation and who knows what other dangers? Has Miss Nightingale thought about how to keep all of the nurses safe from the war and the deprivation and the soldiers?" Her voice cracked a bit at the last word and Lucia knew her mother's imagination was running rampant.

"Stop, Mama," she cried, "you'll make yourself sick with worry. Miss Nightingale has thought of everything. She and her colleague, Mrs. Bracebridge, will be supervising us at all times. The government has asked us to go and help. Can I refuse our government's call for aid? I'm certain they have all manner of protections in place for us. Please. Say you'll permit me to go with your blessing!"

Surprisingly, her mother stopped pacing. Taking Lucia's hands in her own, she looked into her dark brown eyes, took a deep breath, sighed, and finally nodded. "I can see your mind is made up. What can I do but give you my blessing? When do you leave?"

Lucia squeezed her mother's hands, then let go and hugged her hard. "Thank you, Mama," she breathed. "Thank you."

The gray mare tossed her head, snorting, and whinnying her dismay at the way she was being treated. She was refusing to set hoof on the gangplank leading to the dock. The private leading her was obviously losing his temper as he brought the crop down hard on her rump. Still, the mare wouldn't move.

The young man stepped in front of her and tugged at the reins, trying to move her with sheer force. She simply tossed her head higher, nearly pulling the reins out of his hand.

Again, he brought the crop to bear, this time on her front quarters. This proved even more ineffective as she stepped backward, away from the offending crop. Truly angry now, the soldier swung the crop towards the mare's face, but was shocked when it was yanked from his hand. As he turned, he saw the crop fly through the air and land far below on the dock. Looking up, he yelled, "What…"

"Attention!" The single word was both order and warning. The private snapped to attention, but clung to the reins, the veins on his neck bulging with the rage that filled his mind.

The issuer of the order stepped forward and took the reins from him. His voice was low as he softly began humming. Ignoring the soldier at attention, he moved around him slowly, taking small steps toward the still-skittish mare.

It took a few moments for the horse to begin calming down, but then her head tosses grew smaller, her hooves stopped their stamping, her breath beginning to slow and soften. When she felt a familiar hand on her neck, stroking gently, she gave a great sigh and nuzzled the man's pockets.

The officer chuckled. "All right, Sophie. Just one, then we have to get you off this boat." He reached into his pocket and drew out a piece of apple. Feeding it to her, he pulled gently on the reins, leading her step by step onto the gangplank.

She balked for a moment when her hooves touched the less-solid footing, but he whispered softly to her and ran his hand down the length of her nose. Then he clicked his tongue and pulled gently on the reins again. She moved easily this time. When they reached the dock, he patted her neck, gave her another apple, and handed the reins to a soldier who'd been watching with great interest.

"Hold fast to the reins now, lad," the sergeant admonished him.

"Yes, sir!" he answered smartly.

The tall, red-haired sergeant picked up the riding crop in his large, work-roughened hand, then strode back up the gangplank, turning his attention back to the soldier still standing at attention at the top.

Nearing him, the sergeant noted the man's Adam's apple moving as he swallowed hard. His eyebrows were smashed inward, but they were raised, rather than lowered. His top eyelid was raised and the bottom one flattened out, rather than squinted in anger. The man's lips were thin, but not tight as they would be if he were angry. His shoulders were down and his hands were held close to his body, rather than having raised shoulders and clenched fists.

All these clues indicated that he felt more fearful than angry now. Good. Walking around him, the sergeant looked him up and down, disgust evident on his face. Completing his circle, he turned to face him. He slapped the crop into his own palm, the sound making the soldier jump.

Everyone within earshot seemed to slow in their duties, wanting to see how Sergeant Ferguson would handle this. Each man knew the young private was in serious trouble. The sergeant's temper had become famous during their voyage to Balaclava. It didn't help that the horse belonged to Lieutenant-Colonel Henry Griffith, their commanding officer, and that Sergeant Ferguson had full charge of the beautiful gray mare.

The sergeant's voice was quiet and the private felt somehow that this was a bad sign.

"Private?" The crop slapped into his hand again, a bit softer this time, but still threatening.

"Yes, sir?" he answered, swallowing hard.

"What just happened here?"

The private apparently thought a defensive posture would be effective. "I was ordered to help get the horses off the boat, but that stupid mare wouldn't step onto the gangplank. She's been on boats before and still hasn't learned how to behave. Someone had to teach

6

her some manners."

A sailor watching from his perch on the mast grimaced and looked away for a moment. Most everyone aboard knew that trying to excuse one's actions was a big mistake when addressing Sergeant Ronald Ferguson. He would have none of it. Better to admit your blunder, take your punishment, and be done with it.

This particular private apparently had not learned that lesson yet. He winced as the crop slapped hard against the sergeant's hand.

"Care to try again?" was the whispered invitation.

"I was having trouble getting the mare to move onto the gangplank," he started to reply, then his voice faded.

"So, you thought beating that fine mare would make up for your incompetence?" The question held more than a little threat.

"I wanted to encourage her to move," the man answered feebly. "I didn't know how else to do it."

"Perhaps you'd like a demonstration of the effectiveness of your 'encouragement' technique?"

The crop seemed to lash out of its own accord, hitting the railing behind the young man, as the sergeant moved around him. To his credit, the soldier winced but stood his ground. The next blow landed on a box to the private's right, splintering one corner of the wood. The third stroke nicked the toe of private's boot. Involuntarily, he moved his foot back.

"Stand still, or you will regret it!" the sergeant warned.

Four, five, six strokes, all cracking near the frightened young man, but none touching him. The seventh stroke took him by surprise as the tip of the crop landed hard across his backside. He yelped, then clamped his lips together waiting for the next stroke. The sergeant walked around behind him, stopped, and leaned forward to whisper into the man's ear.

"Private, horses are taught not by harshness, but by gentleness." He moved to face the trembling soldier.

"Look at me," he ordered.

The young man obeyed.

"You will never… I repeat… never treat another animal like that again. If you can't get a horse to move without beating it, you shouldn't be in the cavalry. However, since you are, we should further

7

your education in this regard. For the next two months, you will report to me each morning for instruction and practice on the care and handling of the horses. Every night you will muck out the corral and help with the feeding and watering. Is that clear?"

"Yes, sir," the private managed to whisper.

"Dismissed." The sergeant turned on his heel and strode back down the gangplank. Taking the reins from the soldier below, he led the mare away without once looking back.

Mr. Sidney Herbert's house was elegantly furnished. Lucia sat in the drawing room, awaiting her interview with Miss Mary Stanley and Mrs. Selina Bracebridge. Florence had said it was but a formality, since she knew how competent Lucia was, but still, the butterflies danced wildly in her stomach as she barely noticed the elegance around her.

What if Miss Stanley and Mrs. Bracebridge decided she was not worthy to go after all? Lucia was surprised at the intensity of her desire to be part of this expedition.

"It must be that there are wounded," she told herself. She'd always been drawn to help wounded things.

Lucia's mind wandered to a time when she was six years old and had found a baby bird that had fallen from its nest. It was chirping weakly and fluttering one wing, but was unable to fly because of the injury to its other wing. Lucia had carefully laid it in her handkerchief and cradled it in her little hands, walking ever so slowly home, taking care not to jostle the poor creature in her efforts.

When she finally arrived home, her mother started to chide her for "picking up that dirty thing", but her father stepped over to see for himself.

"It's not a dirty thing, Harriet," he'd said after examining the contents of the handkerchief. "It's a poor little bird with a broken wing." Turning to Lucia, he'd asked, "What would you like to do, Lucia *mia*?"

"I have to help it, Papa!" she'd exclaimed. "If I don't, it won't ever fly and it might even die!"

"Then help it, we shall," he'd smiled.

She and her papa had carefully splinted its wing, keeping it wrapped in a handkerchief so the poor animal wouldn't hurt itself while it healed. She fed it grubs and worms from the garden, despite her mother's protests at having such things in the house.

Her efforts were rewarded when, a few weeks later, she and her Papa agreed that it was healed enough to see if it would be able to fly. They carried it carefully out to the garden, placed it gently on a little tree branch and stepped back to watch. In a few moments, it began to sing, swaying back and forth on the branch. Little Lucia held her breath, watching for it to spread its wings.

When the song was finished, the little bird stretched its wings, leaned forward, and began to fall. Flapping wildly, it found the breeze and soared up and up, while Lucia laughed and cried, clapped her hands, and danced a little dance of joy. She raised her own arms straight out from her shoulders and began to run around in imitation of the little bird's flight.

"See, Papa?" she exulted. "It's healed! It can fly! Isn't it grand?"

Her Papa agreed that it was indeed grand.

"Lucia Rix?" a stern female voice roused her from her memory.

"Yes," she answered despite her dry mouth.

"This way, please," was the instruction.

She was led to a little office, where two women sat behind a large mahogany desk on pedestal legs with brass casters. It was stunning, as were the rest of the furnishings in the elegant office. The one on the left, she knew was Mrs. Bracebridge, a close friend of Miss Nightingale. The other, she assumed, was Miss Stanley.

"Please, sit down." Miss Stanley's voice was soft and full of invitation, settling Lucia's nerves quite nicely.

Lucia smiled at each of them and sat in the proffered chair.

"We understand Miss Nightingale has invited you to join her expedition to Crimea. Do you know why you are going?" Mrs. Bracebridge was all business.

Nodding, Lucia answered promptly, "Yes. There are wounded soldiers there who need nursing. This expedition is to fill that need."

"You have a good position at the Institute for Gentlewomen, don't you?" Mrs. Bracebridge inquired.

"I do," she replied.

"Why would you want to leave such a position to go to a battlefield hospital? Won't you miss your income? We certainly can't pay what you are used to from the Institute." Both women watched her intently and she realized the importance of her answer.

"The women I tend at the institute need some nursing, it is true. Mostly, however, they need rest in a quiet environment with their food and medicines administered to them regularly. The soldiers in Crimea need real nursing care. As I understand it, the surgeons there can't tend to their every need. They are too busy trying to heal the wounds and save the lives of hundreds of soldiers, each worse off than the one before. I can't stand the thought that they are suffering there when I have the means and knowledge to help them. How can I stay here in comfort and even luxury when they are in such need?"

Lucia became more passionate as she spoke. She didn't notice the sidelong glances Miss Stanley and Mrs. Bracebridge gave each other. She also didn't see their little smiles and nods of approval. She just kept talking and explaining her position, becoming increasingly animated with each sentence.

"When Miss Nightingale told me of their plight, I was horrified. If she hadn't invited me to go, I would have volunteered anyway. I have sufficient means to support myself, even without my income from the Institute. My father left me a sizable dowry when he died, and as I have no prospects for marriage at present, I see no need to deprive those poor lads of my nursing skill in hopes that some bloke will decide he wants to marry me someday. Besides, any man who decides to marry because of the size of his intended's dowry is not a man worthy to be married, in my opinion. So, you see, I am perfectly willing and able to go and be of some use in Crimea, if you'll have me."

With that, Lucia laid her hands in her lap, and looked at each woman in turn, waiting as patiently as she could for their answer.

Miss Stanley answered for both of them, "With zeal like that, Miss Rix, how could we turn you away? Can you be ready to leave on Saturday?"

Astonished and grateful, Lucia answered quickly, "Truly? I can go? I mean, of course, I can be ready whenever you say."

Miss Stanley chuckled. "We'll send over a list of items you'll be allowed to take. There won't be much room for personal belongings, and you'll need to save room for your uniform, which you'll receive on Friday. There will be a mandatory meeting here that evening. Mr. Sidney Herbert will address us and Miss Nightingale will give final instructions. Can we count on you, then?"

"Yes, of course!" was her enthusiastic reply. "And thank you!"

As Lucia was escorted out by the maid, Miss Stanley sighed. "At last. Here we have sat all day and only now found one worthy of this appointment. I wish people who may hereafter complain of the women selected could have seen the set from which we have had to choose. All London has been scoured for them. We have sent emissaries in every direction to every likely place. I am ashamed to have in the house such women as have come. Until now. She alone has expressed a wish to go from a good motive. Money was the only inducement for the others."

Mrs. Bracebridge nodded. "It is a sad commentary on the state of this city that women like her are so few. Miss Nightingale was wise in sending her over. I believe she will work out fine."

The young lady being discussed was at that moment having a hard time not skipping down the street. She was deliriously happy. At last, she would have a chance to truly serve, and her nursing training would finally be put to good use. This was what she'd been waiting for all her life.

Chapter Two

The makeshift tent hospital was filled with the muffled moans of wounded soldiers. Old pensioners moved among them, administering what little care and comfort they could. In a nearby tent, the screams of a soldier having his leg amputated seemed to silence those in the tents around him. Flies buzzed around untended wounds, as one red-haired sergeant lay white and still on his cot, still wearing the red uniform stained with his own dark blood.

"Be ye all right, Sergeant?" queried the young soldier lying next to him.

Sergeant Ronald Ferguson stirred, stifled a groan, then answered, "I'm as right as I can be under the circumstances, lad. Are ye needing tending yerself?"

The young man was quiet for a moment. "I don't need tending for myself, but the bloke next to me is struggling mighty hard."

Gathering his strength, the sergeant took a deep breath, then managed to sit up. He breathed shallowly through his nose as the nausea and dizziness threatened to overtake him. When his head cleared a little, he slowly stood up, wincing at the pain from the slash in his hip. He made his way around the boy's cot to check the soldier on the other side.

Lifting the blanket with his good hand, his face grew a shade paler. He covered the boy up again and reached for a rag on the floor beside the cot. Wetting it with a little water from the boy's canteen lying next to it, he wiped the young soldier's forehead and face.

The boy opened his eyes, but the sergeant could tell he wasn't looking at anything in this mortal realm. After a moment, his breathing just stopped. No gasp for air. No death rattle. He just stopped breathing.

Ronald mumbled a prayer for his soul, then returned to his own cot, collapsing with the added exertion of caring for someone else when his own wounds had not been tended to.

Later that evening, a surgeon finally made his way in to assess the soldiers in this tent. He had an old pensioner with him taking notes. As he stopped at each cot, he did a cursory evaluation of the occupant then mumbled something to the pensioner, who wrote furiously on his paper, and moved on.

Watching from his cot, the sergeant was not impressed with the lack of care being taken. When the surgeon came to the cot of the dead boy, he frowned.

"Why has this body not been removed?" he demanded.

"There's been no one to remove it, sir," the pensioner tried to explain. "The casualties were so heavy today that…"

"Stop!" the surgeon exploded. "I'm sick to death of hearing how heavy the casualties were today! Don't you think I know how heavy they were? I've been cutting into boys and men all day trying to save their lives. Now, I am required to make my rounds and decide which of these poor boys gets sent to the General Hospital and which must wait here until the next transport. The least you can do is provide someone to remove the bodies of the unlucky ones who die before I can get to them!"

The old man bent his head. "Yes, sir. I'll see to it."

However, the surgeon was already moving on. He glanced at the wounds of the next young man.

"Not critical. He can wait."

Then he approached Ronald's cot. Pulling back the ripped cloth of his pants, he gave a cursory glance at the slashed hip, then peered at the shoulder wound. He poked at it a bit, he asked, "Can you roll over, Sergeant? I need to look at your back."

Complying as best he could, he bit his tongue to keep from crying out as the surgeon poked at the exit wound in the back of his shoulder.

"Ball went through. Not critical. He can wait," was his cryptic verdict.

Without so much as a nod, the surgeon moved on, the old pensioner trying hard to keep up while writing.

Breathing a mental sigh of frustration, since physical sighs hurt too much, Ronald decided he was going to have to take care of these men himself. Apparently, the army surgeon was much too busy to care.

Lying in his bed, Ronald's thoughts returned to his childhood, to another time when someone was too busy to care. He and his mother had just moved into his mother's parents' home. He was vaguely familiar with the surroundings, as they had visited twice before in his young life.

It was a sad time. His father had died and his mother was sad all the time. She stayed in their room with the shutters closed all day, barely eating, and rarely speaking. His grandparents owned a small farm and were busy trying to keep it running. That left seven-year-old Ronald to explore the farm unhindered by adults looking over his shoulder.

He'd rescued a duckling whose mother had been killed by his grandfather's dog. He brought it to his grandmother, who was weeding the garden.

"*Seanmhair*, come and see!" he'd called before he reached her.

"What is it, Ronald?" she asked impatiently.

"It's a hurt duckling, *Seanmhair*," he called. "Come and see!"

Shaking her head, she declined. "I've no time for nonsense, Ronald. Run and play, now. I have work to do."

"But, *Seanmhair*," he implored, "it's hurt!"

His grandmother waved him off and went back to her weeding. Disappointed, he stopped and frowned. If his grandmother wouldn't help, who would? Maybe his mother?

Carefully, he carried the duckling back to the house, stepping quietly to the bedroom he shared with his mother. He opened the door a crack and peered into the darkened room.

"Mummy?" he called quietly.

No answer.

"Mummy?" he tried again. "Mummy, I have a hurt duckling. Would you help me tend it?"

No answer.

He tiptoed to the rocking chair where she always sat. She was there, with her eyes closed, her breath slow and shallow. He touched her hand softly. She stirred and opened her eyes.

"Mummy? I have a hurt duckling."

She raised her hand and touched his hair, stroking it once. "Mummy's resting now, little one. Come back later and you can tell me all about it."

Then her eyes closed and he knew she wouldn't help.

With tears filling his eyes, he left the room quietly and closed the door behind him. He knew it would be no good to talk with his grandfather about it. Ronald rarely saw his grandfather except at dinner. He was gone to the fields before sunup and returned from the evening milking after Ronald was in bed. There was no one who cared enough to help.

Sitting at the kitchen table, Ronald carefully unwrapped the injured baby. It moved and quacked a little, but couldn't seem to stand up. The boy sat staring at it, not knowing what to do. After a few minutes, he took a deep breath, nodded once decisively, and pressed his lips together in an expression so determined that no one could have doubted his intention if they'd been present to see it.

"Don't worry, little duckling," he said softly. "I'll tend you even if there's no one to help. I'll muddle through and figure it out. I'm going to get you well again. You just watch me!"

The next few days, Ronald experimented with different things he thought his duckling might eat, but nothing seemed to interest the little fellow. He seemed to grow weaker by the day and little Ronald was afraid he wasn't going to be able to make good on his vow.

One evening, his grandmother was cleaning up from dinner, watching him as he tried to get the duckling to eat some corn he'd saved from his dinner plate. There was no interest on the part of the duck.

"He canna eat that, Ronald," she said. "He be too wee to eat corn."

Looking up, he asked, "Then what do I feed him?"

"He be wantin' the same as his mammy fed him," she replied. Seeing the consternation on his face, she smiled. "But since you'll no' be his mammy, you can have a bit o' me corn to make him some warm duck mush."

Then next half hour, as she was mending socks, she instructed him in the making of "duck mush" made from cooked, mashed corn, a couple of fat worms from the garden, some tender grass from the pond edge, some hot water and just a dash of fresh milk. The mixture was boiled, then mashed until it was smooth, cooled, and then fed to the duckling from the tip of his finger. He giggled when the duckling first nibbled at the mush.

"It tickles," he laughed. His grandmother smiled and returned her attention to her work.

There was no other help forthcoming for the healing and raising of his new duck friend, but Ronald didn't seem to notice. He busily fed and watered his duckling, took him for walks and swims, and slept with him each night to keep him warm. It wasn't long before tiny feathers began peeking out from the duck down. After a few weeks, the sweet, fluffy duckling grew into a feisty, nearly adult duck who loved nothing more than to waddle into his grandmother's larder and steal her corn.

At that point, his grandmother said Ducky could no longer stay in the house, so little Ronald took him back to the pond, fearing all the while that the dumb dog would catch and eat him. He spent every waking hour by the pond, keeping watch, chasing the dog away with rocks when he dared come close.

The summer passed quickly, and fall arrived amid colorful leaves and cooler weather. That's when Ronald learned yet another life lesson. Friends sometimes move on. One crisp day, as he was laying on the grass by the pond, his duck settled happily by his side, he heard splashing in the pond. Fearing the dog might be looking for a duck dinner, he sat up, grabbing a handful of rocks he'd piled close for just such an occasion.

It wasn't the dog, however. Six ducks had flown in and landed on the water. They bobbed and dove, feeding from the rich store of algae and moss on the bottom of the pond. Ducky quacked once, then waddled into the water, swimming up to each new duck as if to say hello.

Ronald smiled, glad Ducky finally had some friends. His smile faded, however, several hours later when the new ducks suddenly took off, flying toward the southern hills. Ducky sat for only a moment, and then flapped his wings and churned his legs, ultimately taking flight after his newfound friends. The boy called after him, but his duck kept flapping and flying farther and farther away. In just a few moments, he was out of sight.

Tears streaming down his face, he ran to the house to find his grandmother, who was making bread.

"*Seanmhair*," he sobbed, "Ducky just flew away with some other ducks! I called and called but he didn't stop. He didn't even say goodbye!"

Without looking up, his grandmother answered, "Then ye did a fine job o' tendin' him, laddie. Ye can be proud o' that."

Little Ronald looked at her and realized for the first time that no matter what happened in his life, he would have to fend for himself, because everyone around him was too busy to care about what was important to a little boy.

Or wounded soldiers, Ronald thought sourly. So, if they are to be cared for, I'll have to do the caring. He glanced around and mentally made a list of the men in his tent and set about determining what he could do for them. They'll not go home thinking no one cares if I have anything to do with it, he vowed to himself.

Dear Mama,

Well, we are nearly there. Miss Nightingale says we should land at Scutari tomorrow. I am very anxious to begin our work, but let me catch you up on what's happened since I left London two weeks ago.

As you know, we met on Friday, October 20, at Mr. Herbert's home. He gave a very moving speech and we were all strengthened by his heart-stirring words. He told us that if any desired to turn back, now was the time of decision. No one moved. He impressed upon us that the work would be hard, but we are bound implicitly to obey Miss Nightingale in all things.

We were cheered no less by the sunny brightness of his presence than by his kindly and unfailing sympathy. We all left feeling excitement and anticipation for the journey and work ahead of us. Unhappily, the effect was not in all cases permanent.

I am much impressed by Miss Nightingale. Even more than I was before. As you know, it has been a privilege to work beside her at the Institute for Gentlewomen. She has such nerve and skill, and is so wise and quiet. Even during the preparations to board the boat, she was in no bustle and hurry. I'm certain it must be overwhelming to her at times, to have so much on her hands and such numbers of volunteers to attend.

I saw another side to her just before we boarded. Her family had come to see her off. I noticed her sister hand her something wrapped in white cloth. She opened the cloth and her countenance became so sad. I saw tears flowing down her cheeks and heard her say, "Poor little beastie, it was odd how much I loved you." I later learned that it was her pet owl that had died. Her family had brought it in order for her to say her final farewells.

We departed London with thirty-eight nurses; ten Roman Catholic Sisters, eight Anglican Sisters of Mercy, six nurses from St. John's Institute, and fourteen from various hospitals, including my friend, Jean. You remember her, don't you? She worked with me at the Institute for Gentlewomen. Miss Nightingale's friends, Mr. and Mrs. Bracebridge, have also joined us.

It is very hard for her to keep all of us in good humour, arranging the rooms of five different sects each night, before sitting down to supper. It takes a long time, but she bears all wonderfully. She is so calm, winning everybody, French and English. I don't know how she manages it.

Wherever she is seen or heard, there is nothing but admiration from high and low. Her calm dignity influences everybody. I am sure the nurses quite love her already, as I do. Some cried when she exhorted us after a little contention began to arise between the French nurses and the

English. When she was finished, all promised to behave well. Blessings on her! She makes everybody who joins with her feel the good and like it, rather than disposing them against it, as some well-meaning, oppositious spirits do.

Her influence on all, to captain and steward of boat, has been wonderful. She has breakfasted and dined with us each day, and she has had an amazing effect on some of the rougher hospital nurses. In fact, on the third day, after receiving all her attentions, all have become quite humanized and civilized. Their very manners at table have softened.

One of them, Mrs. Amy Wright, who is quickly becoming a dear friend, told me, "We never had so much care taken of our comforts before. It is not people's way with us. We had no notion Miss Nightingale would slave herself so on our account."

Indeed, she waits on us at dinner because no one else will, carries our parcels, brings us shawls and blankets against the cool ocean air, and sees to our every comfort insofar as she is able. She will be a wonderful "Lady-in-Chief" and I'm proud to serve beside her.

It is late and I must to bed. Tomorrow we arrive.

Your loving daughter,
Lucia
November 3, 1854

Chapter Three

Lucia was impressed with how warmly the nurses were greeted as they disembarked at Scutari. They were met at the dock by a crowd of sturdy fisherwomen who seized their bags and carried them to the hotel, refusing to accept the slightest gratuity.

The landlord of the hotel gave them dinner and told them to order what they liked, adding that they would not be allowed to pay for anything. The waiters and chambermaids were equally firm in refusing any acknowledgment for their attentions. Lucia had stayed in hotels fancier than this one, but never had the service been so generously given.

Once the nurses were settled in, Miss Nightingale and Mr. and Mrs. Bracebridge went on to the hospital to see to their accommodations for the remainder of their stay. When they returned later that evening, it was evident that the situation was not good. Mrs. Bracebridge held her lips pressed tightly together and stormed up to her room while Mr. Bracebridge followed, trying to be consoling.

Miss Nightingale waved off any questions and instructed the nurses to go to their beds and try to sleep. "We're going to need it," she added grimly.

The next morning at breakfast, Miss Nightingale tapped her water glass to get their attention. "Ladies," she began. "We shall be moving into our quarters in the hospital today. I will warn you, the conditions are not ideal. There is much work to do before we can begin treating patients as we'd like."

A small murmur rippled through the crowd of nurses. One had

the courage to speak what they all were thinking, "Oh, Miss Nightingale, when we arrive, don't let there be any red-tape delays, let us get straight to nursing the poor fellows!"

"The strongest will be wanted at the wash-tub. New occasions teach new duties," was the reply. The murmuring among them grew. "Now, now, ladies," Miss Nightingale continued. "I know how badly you want to get right to your nursing duties, but no amount of nursing will make up for the horrid conditions I witnessed last night. We will need to scrub everything from floor to ceiling, air out every room, wash what little linens are available and we must do something about the food. Mrs. Bracebridge and I will form you into work squads while Mr. Bracebridge confers with the surgeons about the rats and bugs."

The increased murmuring was clear indication that this was not what these women had signed up for, but Miss Nightingale was not finished.

"From this point on, you will wear your uniforms to indicate you are a member of the nursing team."

One nurse spoke up from the back of the room. "Miss Nightingale, must we wear the caps?"

"Of course," was her reply. "I require that you wear the full uniform at all times."

The young lady was adamant. "I came out, ma'am, prepared to submit to everything, to be put upon in every way. I can abide the grey tweed wrapper, the worsted jacket, the short woolen cloak, and even that frightful brown Holland scarf with 'Scutari Hospital' embroidered in red. However, there are some things, ma'am, to which one cannot submit. That is the way with me and the caps, ma'am. They suits one face, and but not another. And if I'd known, ma'am, about the caps, great as was my desire to come out to nurse at Scutari, I wouldn't have come, ma'am."

Miss Nightingale looked at her sternly, "If you can't see your way past the caps to the real work before us, then by all means, you may be dismissed to catch the boat back to London, where you will no doubt find a place that does not require the wearing of caps. If you choose to stay, however, you will submit to the rules in every detail. Do I make myself clear?" Her eyes scanned the room, looking for anyone else who might express their discontent. No one did.

Lucia looked at Jean, then at Amy, who raised an eyebrow. Lucia nodded slightly and returned her attention to Miss Nightingale and her instructions.

The rest of the day was spent moving the nurses into one tower of the Barracks Hospital. Lucia was lucky enough to have a cot under a south-facing window. That should afford a restful view of the clouds as well as a cool breeze if we should still be here when the weather turns warm, she thought. Once her few things were in place and she was properly clad in her uniform, she followed the other nurses down to the main floor where the scrubbing and cleaning began in earnest.

Every so often, Lucia would glance up from her scrub brush to see if her first impression was still a reality or if it was truly some nightmare her fevered brain had cooked up. Each time, she shuddered as she saw patients laying in their own excrement on stretchers strewn throughout the hallways, rodents and insects scurrying past them.

The stench from the cesspool under the hospital filled the air, forcing her to cover her nose with her handkerchief frequently to filter out the stench a little, but she kept at her work, hoping that this was not all she would be allowed to do during her stay here. It was apparent to her that the patients needed them even more than the filthy floors did.

She could see soldiers still dressed in the uniforms they'd been wearing when wounded. There were wounds that had barely been bandaged at all, and those were not with clean linen. She saw soldiers obviously sick and dying from disease, as well as the injuries incurred in battle. Some soldiers didn't even have a blanket, let alone a cot to lay on.

Yet here she was, scrubbing floors like a common chambermaid. It was infuriating! Still, Miss Nightingale knew her business. It was not up to Lucia to challenge her, so she continued scrubbing.

22

Ronald awoke to chaos erupting outside his hospital tent. He propped himself up on one elbow to peer out the open tent flap. He could see soldiers and pensioners scrambling through the mud to help the wounded move as quickly as their injuries would allow. His brows furrowed and he frowned. Something had changed, and it didn't look good.

The night before had been cold and wet, but the rain had stopped a bit before dawn. He could see dark clouds rolling across the sky as buckets, blankets, and other debris danced along the ground with the increasing wind. His scowl deepened as he began to suspect what was to come.

"What's going on, Sergeant?" the young man in the next cot asked.

"I don't know, lad, but I'm going to find out," he answered.

Before he could even stand up, a very large, very loud corporal darkened the opening. "All of you who can walk are to follow me. If you have the strength, help the fellow next to you who may not be able to walk on his own. Yer moving out."

"Why the rush?" the sergeant asked.

"Hurricane's comin'," was his curt reply.

Every man in that tent moved. The ones who could helped those who needed it. Those who couldn't help managed to get themselves outside between the rows of tents. The mud was slick, and as they slipped and slid their way to the dock, many stumbled and fell, but others helped them up as all felt the urgency of their departure. Five minutes later, it was raining more heavily than it had the night before. Still the soldiers trudged on.

What seemed like hours later, but what was truly only about ten more minutes of slogging through the mud, Sergeant Ferguson could see the masts of the ships in the harbor, the sound of the downpour had become swallowed up by the noise of the rushing wind and the flapping of the tents. The masts of the ships were swaying and he felt as if the ground were moving, rather than just the ships being tossed in the harbor.

As they boarded the *HMS Restitution*, the wind whipped at their coats and hats, the rain beat down on them, stinging where it bombarded bare skin.

"Is it safe to sail in this weather?" a frightened soldier asked the captain as he boarded.

"No choice, son," the captain answered, and then, noting the fear in the boy's face, he patted his shoulder. "She's a sturdy ship, lad. She's weathered storms worse than this. We'll be fine."

The men from Sergeant Ferguson's tent were the last to board. As soon as the last man set foot on the deck, the captain gave orders to heave to and set sail. Finding a place near the center of the deck, the sergeant sat down and found a rope, fastening it around his middle and hoping he was tied to something secure enough to keep him from sliding off the wet deck.

The ship rocked precariously as the sails were hoisted and positioned to catch the wind. The masts groaned under the pressure of the wind in the sails. Worried, the men looked up, and Ronald was certain they, like him, had a prayer in their hearts that they'd live to see the other shore.

Ronald looked towards the camp on the hillside they'd just left and the sight left him shaking. He could see tents leaping into the air and flying like bits of paper into the sky. He saw great barrels bounding along like cricket balls. Heavy wagons were thrown headlong through the camps, dragging bullocks after them as if they were mere kittens.

The wounded soldiers that had been left behind looked like ants trying to find shelter as their tents were blown away, but they found themselves being tossed across the ground like so many ragdolls. He saw men huddled next to walls on the beach, tied together as they tried to resist the force of the hurricane.

If the scene had not been so horrifying, the sergeant would have laughed aloud at Dr. Robinson, whom he knew was recovering from a recent severe attack of diarrhea. He was in his underwear and nightshirt, being carried on his servant's back up the hill to another tent, but before they could enter, that tent was blown away, as well. The servant stumbled backwards, dropping Dr. Robinson, who hurtled across the ground, his billowing blanket outspread around him like the wings of a giant bat.

It seemed after a time that they might make it out of the harbor without difficulty. The captain used the wind to his advantage and even though they were buffeted about, Ronald could see they were making progress.

Across the bay, other ships were not faring so well. The *Star of the South* and the *Medway* kept crashing into each other as the waves tossed them about. Smaller ships, driven against the rocks, broke up and sank in a few minutes.

On the other side, the little clipper *Wild Wave* rolled helplessly in the roaring breakers. Three cabin boys on the deck were trying to clutch at a rope, which someone had thrown down to them from the rocks above. Two of the boys were washed overboard. The third caught the rope and leapt ashore just as the ship disappeared in a scattered mass of splinters, broken masts, bales of cargo, hay, and boxes.

As they made their way to the harbor's mouth, he could see the *Prince*, which was a fine screw-ship with a crew of a hundred and fifty. She had lost two of her sails and was driven broadside on the rocks, smashing up in the moment of impact. The sergeant added a prayer for the men on those ships, as well.

His own ship was being rocked wildly on the roiling sea. He clung to the rope and anything else he could reach that seemed stable. He watched the captain at the helm barking orders and fighting furiously with the wheel. He ordered that the upper guns be pushed overboard, leaving the major portion of the weight they carried in the hold at the bottom of the ship.

The Duke of Cambridge, who was clinging to a mast near Ronald, was bewailing his fate, saying, "Oh! Is it come to this? Oh! Oh! We shall be lost." Other soldiers, tough and strong in the worst battles, broke down and cried, yelling as the waves crashed over them.

Through the skillful handling of the wheel, and by the gracious providence of God, the *Restitution* finally cleared the mouth of the harbor, but still the wind blew and the waves crashed. Three seamen were washed overboard as they tried to secure one of the sails that had been torn loose.

All morning, the torrent raged and the rain blew in sideways first from one direction, then another. The waves battered the ship and the men who clung for dear life to her masts, rails, and anything else that was fastened down.

By the time the wind slackened in the mid-afternoon, all aboard felt like drowned rats, weak and sick from being tossed about and from swallowing so much seawater. It was late afternoon before anyone felt comfortable enough to start to move about the ship.

As Sergeant Ferguson began to check on the men around him, he was grateful to see that all the men in his tent were accounted for. One had suffered another broken arm, his right arm having been slashed and broken by a Russian soldier's sword on the battlefield.

Another had dislocated his shoulder when a wave threatened to wash him overboard. He had clung so fiercely to the railing he was holding that his shoulder had given way, but he had stayed on board. He told the sergeant he was grateful for the strong hands that came from milking cows twice each day.

The captain ordered that an inventory be taken of the remaining supplies. All around the cold, wet men lay the remains of two sails that had partially broken away, broken lengths of rope, smashed boxes, and shattered barrels. Overall, they had come away with much more than any of them could have hoped for. They were alive, and it was a relatively short sail to Scutari.

Just as they were settling in, however, the air became much colder. It began to rain again, but that quickly turned to sleet, then hail. The captain suggested that they take shelter below decks, but no one took his suggestion. They were fearful that the wind would start again. They could imagine that the ship might capsize and they'd be trapped down below, unable to get out.

Finally, as the evening wore on, the rain and hail changed to heavy snow. The very wet, cold men huddled together, covering themselves with sail canvas and wet blankets. Soon, all the captain could see was snow-covered mounds where the men were huddled.

The next morning was bright and sunny. The snow melted quickly, and the men were in better spirits. The rest of the voyage was uneventful, save for the occasional seasick soldier who had to be steadied on the rails as he lost the last couple of meals he'd eaten.

Three days later, they finally sailed into the Scutari harbor. Orderlies from the hospital met them, as well as a contingent of female nurses, but there was no inappropriate behavior regarding the nurses. Indeed, the men were surprised, but honored that these angels of mercy would be attending them. They treated them with utmost respect.

Ronald was helping another soldier down the gangplank, his good arm around the man's waist. They stumbled a bit as the soldier's lame leg gave way. Then he felt someone slide under the man's other arm.

"I've got him," he growled.

"Here," she said softly, "let me help."

The melodic voice made him look up. He saw a particularly beautiful nurse reaching up to pull the soldier's other arm tightly around her own shoulders. Her black hair stood out in stark contrast to the white of her cap and the smooth olive complexion of her skin. Her brown eyes were soft with compassion, yet they held something else that he couldn't quite grasp. Instinctively, he knew that it would do no good to argue with her.

He nodded and they stepped out, carefully walking the short distance to the wagons, which would take them to the Barracks Hospital. The sergeant swore under his breath as he tried to pull himself up into the wagon. He couldn't use his right arm at all because of the shoulder wound, and he was still weak enough that he couldn't quite pull himself up with only his left. He felt a tap on his shin and looked down to see the same helpful nurse holding her hands for him to step into for a lift. He hesitated.

"Well?" her eyes sparkled with mischief. "Are you going to stay the night here on the dock or would you like a ride to the hospital?"

"Thank you," he said simply, placing one foot in her hands. She lifted as he pulled and he was into the wagon quickly. He looked back down at her and was surprised to see she was blushing.

"You're welcome," was her soft reply as the wagon rolled slowly away.

Chapter Four

Dear Mama,

Tonight, I am a happy nurse. We are finally able to do what we came to do. Until now, we have been scrubbing and scouring until our hands are raw from the effort, but Miss Nightingale insists that it will help our soldiers fight the infections that so often beset them if they can heal in a clean environment. I trust that she's right.

On Thursday last, we had 1,715 sick and wounded in this Hospital, among whom 120 Cholera patients, and 650 severely wounded in the other building called the General Hospital, of which we also have charge. Miss Nightingale received a message to prepare for 510 wounded on our side of the hospital who were arriving from the dreadful affair of November 5 from Balaclava, in which battle were 1,653 wounded and 442 killed, besides 96 officers wounded and 38 killed.

The doctors have been reluctant to allow us to do anything but the most menial tasks. However, Miss Nightingale told us to "Proceed until apprehended". Her hope is that once they see how useful we can be, they might be of a mind to allow us to help with actual nursing duties. There is so much to do, and even with the help of the orderlies, the doctors can't see to every need. I, for one, am glad to be working at nursing again, and hope the doctors will see reason.

We had but half an hour's notice before they began landing the *wounded. After collecting them from the dock, we commenced to create beds for them. Between one and nine o'clock we had the mattresses stuffed, sewn up, laid down – alas, only upon matting on the floor – the men washed and put to bed, and all their wounds dressed.*

Sadly, one amputated Stump died two hours after we received him and one Compound Fracture died just as we were getting him into bed. In all, 24 cases died on the day of landing. The dysentery cases have died at the rate of one in two. It's appalling how little care these men have received. I can only imagine what it must have been like in the tent hospitals they came from. Much like here. Too many wounded, not enough medical supplies, and not enough people to administer to their needs.

As I've described before, we have our quarters in one tower of the Barracks, and all this fresh influx has been laid down between us and the Main Guard, in two Corridors, with a line of beds down each side, just room for one person to pass between, and four wards. We are busier than I ever dreamed we'd be, yet Miss Nightingale won't allow any of us nurses into the wards after 9 pm. Only she and the orderlies are allowed to check on the patients at night.

A part of me is grateful we can get a partial night's sleep at least, yet it seems we could ease her burden considerably if she'd let us tend to them at night, too. We could set up a rotation so no one would have to miss sleep every night, but I trust her judgement and wouldn't think to challenge her decisions to her face, whatever I may think of them to myself.

Speaking of sleep, they have given the lights out warning, so I must close now.

Your loving daughter,
Lucia
November 14, 1854

"Nurse!" the orderly called. "Can you come look at this?"

Lucia looked up from the wound she was dressing. "Of course, I'll be right there."

She finished with a smile to the soldier she'd been treating. "Stay off that leg for another day or two. No dancing in the streets for you!"

The soldier laughed. "But I can't dance no-how!" he called after her.

She made her way to the orderly who'd called. "What's so urgent, Mr. Whitley?" she asked kindly.

"I be worried 'bout this guy's shoulder," he answered, his voice filled with concern. "It be hot, and seems like it's getting redder. He can't move it now, neither. He has some fever and must be in a lot of pain because he's getting surlier by the hour. He wasn't like that when he came in."

"I'll take a look," she said as she knelt beside the mattress on the floor.

Lucia lifted the bandage and carefully examined the shoulder, her thoughts filled with concern. Then she looked at the man's face and her heart skipped a beat. It was the same soldier she'd helped into the wagon. She hadn't been able to get his face out of her mind since that afternoon. Quickly, she regained control of herself and smiled at him.

"I'm going to need to look at the other side of that shoulder, Sergeant. We're going to roll you partway over now."

He let out a small groan, but then lay still while she looked at the exit wound. Nodding to the orderly, they rolled him back to lay flat on the mattress.

"I'm going to confer with a surgeon on this," she told the man. "You lay quiet and we'll be right back."

Lucia went to the end of the corridor where a surgeon and Miss Nightingale were talking.

"Excuse me," she interrupted, "I think we have a case that's developing gangrene. Would you please come look?"

Miss Nightingale opened her mouth, looking like she was going to reprimand Lucia for interrupting, but seeing the serious expression on her face, she closed it again. She and the surgeon followed Lucia back down the corridor.

After the surgeon examined the wound, he nodded at Miss

Nightingale, who rose and followed him a few steps down the corridor out of earshot.

"They're going to cut off my arm, aren't they?" the soldier growled with resignation.

"Not necessarily," Lucia tried to comfort him. "I think we've caught it early enough that it can be treated with success."

She looked at Miss Nightingale, who had become quite animated in her manner. The doctor's voice rose for a moment, his tone angry. "It can't be done."

"It must be done," was the reply. No argument. No excuses. No defending her position. She said simply, "It must be done," with such conviction that even that august surgeon decided not to argue.

"Fine. Have him prepped for surgery within the hour."

Miss Nightingale nodded. "He'll be ready." She looked back at Lucia, who nodded that she understood, then returned her attention to the soldier.

"We will be excising the wound in your shoulder," Lucia told him. "That means we'll be cleaning it out to get rid of the infection. Are you up for it?"

"Why don't you just let me die in peace?" he scowled. "What good's a horseman with only one arm?"

"You don't understand," she said patiently. "We're not going to amputate your arm. We're simply going to clean out the wound so it can heal properly."

"Do whatever you're going to do, but you'll be amputating it in the end," he grumbled. "You're just wasting your time on me."

Shaking her head, Lucia sighed. "I hope you can find a little hope in your heart, soldier, because with that attitude, you'll most surely die."

She stood and walked away, not seeing his eyes following her, a wishful desire beginning to glimmer in his eyes.

An hour and a half later, the surgeon was shaking his head. "I wouldn't have believed it if I didn't see it with my own eyes," he muttered.

Miss Nightingale and Lucia peered into the wound that he had just opened. It had yellow-green pus all through it and a foul odor, but that wasn't what caught their attention. Next to the scapula, lodged just in the head of the joint, lay another ball, which had created a star-shaped fracture and was preventing his shoulder from moving as it should.

The surgeon skillfully removed the ball, cleaned out the infected areas, and then sewed everything back together. The entire process took less than three hours, but Lucia was hopeful that he would regain full use of his arm in time. She couldn't understand why this soldier was so often on her mind, but she felt a need to be certain he was fit and whole again, insofar as she was able to facilitate that end.

When he woke several hours later with the headache that often follows anesthesia, he tentatively tried to move his arm, only to discover it was tied to his body and was quite immovable.

"Nurse?" he called out. "Nurse?"

Lucia was by his side almost instantly. "Are you in pain?" she asked, concerned.

"Not much," he answered, his voice hoarse. "Why is my arm tied down?"

"To keep you from ripping out the stitches," she replied. "The surgeon cleaned out your wound and removed this." She dropped the ball into his free hand.

He looked at it with a puzzled expression on his face. "I thought the ball went in the front and out the back. That's what the surgeon at the tent hospital said."

"Apparently, you had the unlucky fortune to have two balls rip into your shoulder and the balls go in where they like and pass through where they like, or not. In your case, one went through, the other lodged in deep," Lucia shook her head. "It's a wonder you could move at all!"

"So, I'm not going to lose my arm?" he asked, clearly still not quite believing.

"Not if we can keep the infection out," her voice was brusque with emotion she didn't understand and was trying to hide. She reached for the ball in his hand.

"I'd like to keep this, if you don't mind," he asked, looking up at her with wonder and amazement still in his expression.

"Suit yourself," she nodded. She checked his bandages, then smiled and moved away to tend to another soldier.

Sergeant Ronald Ferguson watched her, wondering why she intrigued him so. It's true that she's lovely, he thought, but I've met many lovely women and none has caught my attention as thoroughly as she has. Pondering that fact, he drifted off to sleep, not realizing that she was covertly watching him at every opportunity.

"This is the list of items I need from town," Miss Nightingale said, handing Lucia a small piece of paper. "I'd go myself or send Mrs. Bracebridge, but we're expecting more casualties any time now, and I need these as quickly as possible. Take Miss Wright, Miss Delaney, and Mrs. Lawfield with you, and please be quick."

"Yes, Miss Nightingale," Lucia replied.

She felt honored to be asked for such an important task. Usually, the lady chief preferred to procure the supplies herself. Sometimes, she'd send Mrs. Bracebridge, but never had Lucia seen her send anyone else.

After finding Amy Wright, Jean Delaney, and Martha Lawfield and informing them of the assignment, they hurried to the barracks tower to retrieve their jackets and capes. Amy lifted the universally hated brown scarf, wrinkled her nose, and announced, "I don't think I'll wear this. It's so frightfully ugly!"

Martha nodded. "Perhaps I'll leave my cap here, as well. It truly doesn't suit my face." She reached up and began removing the hairpins holding her cap in place.

Lucia chuckled. "I agree with both of you. However, we're required to wear the full uniform, including the scarf and cap. Miss Nightingale wants everyone to recognize us as part of the nursing team. The Scutari Hospital emblem lets everyone know why we're here."

Jean nodded. "Besides, Martha, when those little curls sneak out from under your cap, you look quite fetching."

Sighing, Amy wrapped the scarf around her neck. "I'll wear it, but I don't have to like it."

"Ridiculous," Martha agreed, glaring at the cap, and then

dutifully secured it to her hair again.

The four women trudged into town, reveling in the chance to be outside and breathe the fresh air. Lucia, for one, found the work satisfying, but also longed for a bit more leisure time to walk and breathe in air that wasn't filled with the smell of blood, sewage, and other not-to-be-mentioned odors.

As they passed the entrance to a pub, a young man stepped out and started to follow them. He whistled and grabbed Lucia's arm, turning her around to face him.

"You look like you could use a good time," he sneered with a leer.

Lucia tried to pull away, but he was too strong. "Please be so good as to let me go," she said, trying to keep her voice from shaking.

"Aw, come on, sweetie," he cajoled, pulling her close. "You know you want to."

As Lucia pushed against his chest, trying to free herself, Martha began hitting him with her bag while Jean pulled on Lucia's coat. "You let her go!" the two young women screamed. "Let her go!" Martha's hands flew to her mouth as she backed up against the wall in horror, unable to help or even scream.

The young man laughed and tried to force a kiss on the unwilling Lucia, who turned her head and continued trying to push away.

Suddenly, the man's arms were jerked away and she was free. It happened so quickly that she stumbled back, nearly falling, but other hands caught her, helped her to regain her balance, then respectfully let her go.

Lucia looked up into the angry face of Lieutenant General George Brown, who nodded, then turned his attention to the young man who'd assaulted her. He was being held by two soldiers who clearly had no intention of letting him go. Their faces were full of barely contained outrage.

The lieutenant general stepped toward the young man. "You must be new here." It was a statement, not a question.

Nodding, the man tried to explain himself, but was cut off by the officer's next statement.

"Because you're new, I'll take this opportunity to educate you on the proper way to treat a lady."

"Lady?" the young man snorted. "I don't see no lady here."

General Brown's face grew darker. "I want you to look closely at the way these ladies are dressed. Don't you see the emblem on her scarf? These are Miss Nightingale's women. These are the nurses that are helping our poor wounded lads at the hospital. This one might be the very nurse that may tend you if you're unlucky enough to be wounded. I recommend you leave her alone, or you'll live to regret it! Do you understand?"

His face growing pale at the implied threat and potential future consequence of his lascivious actions, the young man nodded. "I understand."

"Good. Now apologize to these ladies and we'll be on our way."

He turned to Lucia and mumbled an apology. The soldiers let him go and he fairly ran down the street, glancing back once to be sure they weren't following him.

The lieutenant general looked at Lucia and then at each of the women in turn. "I deeply regret any inconvenience to you ladies. I will be sure my officers keep an eye on that one. He won't bother you again."

Lucia smiled. "We thank you for your assistance, and will remember your kindness."

She took Jean's arm on one side and Martha's on the other. As they moved on to complete their assignment, all three women were grateful for the uniforms that had saved them.

"Now, aren't you glad we wore the scarves and caps?" she asked her companions when they were out of earshot.

Jean nodded, her breathing slowly returning to normal. Martha nodded, too, and vowed never to complain about the uniform caps again.

"How much longer do I have to wear this thing?" the sergeant growled.

"Until the surgeon says you can take it off," was Lucia's curt reply.

Her favorite patient wasn't her favorite because of his sunny disposition, that's for certain, she thought. Then why was he her favorite, she wondered as she adjusted the sling and tied it tightly around his chest so he couldn't move his arm.

"There," she said, trying to be more cheerful. "Is there anything else I can do for you?"

"Just leave me alone," he scowled, turning his face away from her.

With a small sigh, she cleared up the bandaging supplies and moved away from him. She wanted to help him, but she knew that until he made up his mind that he was going to get well, and was willing to work towards that end, there was very little she could do for him.

A half hour later, she was re-dressing the wounds of the soldier on the mattress next to him. The young man smiled gratefully, then asked, "Aren't you the nurse who sings? I've heard other soldiers talking about it."

Chuckling, she nodded. "I do sing from time to time. Would you like to hear a song?"

"Yes, please," he grinned broadly. "Do you know 'Blow the Candles Out'?"

"I do, indeed," she replied, chuckling to herself at the young man's bawdy song choice, and grateful she'd learned a few such tunes despite Mama's objections. Taking a deep breath, she started singing softly, then allowed her voice to grow as she noticed others in the ward listening.

She continued her work as she sang, moving from soldier to soldier, smiling, working, and singing. The men were enraptured, including the sergeant who tried to be so gruff. When the song ended and her voice faded, she smiled at the patients watching her.

"And now, my lads," she said cheerfully, "it's time for you to rest and time for me to move on to other brave soldiers who need their wounds dressed."

"Be sure to sing to them! That'll cure anything!" laughed a soldier from the far corner of the ward.

Laughing, Lucia nodded. "I'll do just that."

As she turned to leave, she caught a glimpse of her sergeant who was watching her with a bewildered look on his face. She smiled at him. He turned away, but she thought she caught a hint of a smile at the corner of his mouth. That's progress, she thought.

I hope.

Chapter Five

"First, you tell me I can't move it, now you want me to move it. Make up your bloody minds, would you?" Sergeant Ferguson was angry and decidedly uncooperative.

"Aye, I know ye be hurtin', Sergeant," the orderly said, "but if ye want to regain the use of yer arm, ye need to stretch it out several times a day."

"Go stretch out your own arm," he replied and turned his head away, hoping to prevent any further comments from the orderly.

"Is something wrong, Mr. Whitley?" Lucia asked as she approached. She knew very well what was wrong, but didn't want the sergeant to know she'd been listening from across the room.

"The sergeant be unwilling to move his arm, Miss Rix," he frowned.

"Sergeant, is this true?" she asked as she moved around the bed and sat on the floor facing him.

He just frowned and closed his eyes.

She sighed and looked up at the orderly. Smiling, she nodded indicating she would handle it.

"You're with the cavalry, aren't you, sergeant?" she asked sweetly. "Do they give you a horse or do you provide your own?"

His eyebrows furrowed as his eyes opened. He regarded her with suspicion on his face. "Depends. We can bring our own, but those who don't have their own are assigned one. Why do you ask?"

"Do you have your own, Sergeant?"

"No," his frown deepened. "Again, why do you ask?"

"So, your horse was assigned to you, is that right?"

His surliness was turning to anger now. "That's what I said. What's this got to do with anything?"

"Do you like the horse they assigned to you?" Lucia was relentless.

"He's a good horse. Get to the point."

"You didn't answer my question, Sergeant. Do you like the horse they assigned to you?"

"Yes. I like the horse! Why do you care?"

"I just wondered who was caring for your horse while you're here?" she asked, her voice calm.

The sergeant opened his mouth, then closed it again. Staring at her, he looked bewildered.

Lucia leaned closer and whispered. "Don't you think you'd better get to work so you can give him the care you know he deserves? You need to stop feeling sorry for yourself and start living again, Sergeant." She watched his face, then smiled, sensing from his expression she'd hit a soft spot.

Lucia sat forward and held out her hand, inviting him to do the stretches he needed to do. He looked at her hand, then turned his head away. She frowned and sighed, then moved on to dress the wounds of another soldier nearby, frustrated and worried about the man who refused to cooperate in his own healing.

As she stewed about it that morning, she recalled a cat she'd had as a girl. It was grey and white, with black paws and ears. Her father had given it to her for her eighth birthday. She promptly named it Clarabelle.

She loved her kitten and Clarabelle loved her. A year or so later, Clarabelle had a litter of kittens that died soon after birth.

Shortly after they died, Clarabelle stopped eating and drinking. It wasn't long after that she died, too. Her father had explained that perhaps Clarabelle didn't want to live without her kittens, and now she was with them in heaven. It had hurt, but Lucia had felt better knowing that God was taking care of them.

Glancing over at the troubled sergeant, Lucia didn't want to let this man succumb to the life of an invalid. She had to act or he would lose the use of his arm forever. If that happened, he might lose the will to live altogether. Lucia shuddered at the thought and vowed to do something about it. But what?

"Come in, Miss Rix," Miss Nightingale's voice was tired, but welcoming, nonetheless. "How can I help you?"

Lucia entered the little sitting room, which served as Miss Nightingale's office and reception room. She sat in the proffered chair, her heart pounding just a little. The proposition she had in mind was rather unorthodox and she wasn't certain how it would be received, but she was determined to try anyway.

"There is a certain patient who is not responding well to the treatment he's receiving and I'd like to propose a change in protocol, if you're inclined to hear me out," she'd rehearsed the opening sentence so often that it rolled off her tongue without conscious thought.

Miss Nightingale sat back and nodded. "Go on."

"There's a sergeant in the wards who had two bullets enter his shoulder. One exited out the back, the other lodged in deep."

Again, Miss Nightingale nodded. "I remember him. You say he's not responding well to treatment?"

"His physical body is healing nicely. It's his mental state that concerns me," Lucia stated. So far, the conversation was going just as she'd hoped.

"What seems to be the problem?"

"I'm not exactly certain. He fights the orderlies and even the nurses on the slightest treatment regimen. He will only do the stretches and allow dressing of his wounds under great protest. He doesn't talk to anyone. He won't get up for walks, even though he's been here nearly a month. I see his body wasting away, even though his wounds are healing." Her voice rose as she described the situation, reflecting the desperation she was feeling.

"That sounds serious. What would you like to propose?" Miss Nightingale was kind and her body language showed her interest.

"I'd like to ask that all nursing and care for this patient be stopped except for the necessary tending to his wounds. We can set up a small table at the end of the ward for his meals, but he'll have to find his own way to that table, whether that's walking, crawling, or creeping like a bug. I'd like to have the orderlies and other nurses not interact with him except, as I stated, to dress his wounds. I want him to ask for help, for conversation, for whatever he needs. My theory is that until he decides he wants to live, nothing we do will help him live. Does that make any sense at all?"

The lady chief pursed her lips and nodded. "That is a drastic prescription, Miss Rix, but I can see that in this case, it may be warranted. Let me confer with the surgeon and I'll get back with you by the end of the day."

Standing, Lucia said softly, "Thank you, Miss Nightingale. I appreciate your support and efforts on behalf of this soldier."

Miss Nightingale cocked her head. "Do I detect a special interest in this case, Miss Rix?"

Lucia blushed. "Perhaps a little."

Looking stern, she said, "Remember who you are, Miss Rix, and the rules you agreed to when you signed on to come here."

"I will, Miss Nightingale. I promise."

Lucia left with a bit more hope in her heart for the young sergeant lying in the ward, willing himself to die. At least, there was the hope that there might be hope.

The sun was just setting and the shadows were long in the ward where Ronald lay. He was puzzled. He'd seen orderlies and nurses bustling about in the ward all day. Yet no one had spoken to him. No one had tried to get him to stretch his arm, or take a walk. They hadn't even brought him food or water.

He'd noticed them placing a small table at the end of the ward farthest from him. He had seen them place food and water on it at regular mealtimes all day. He'd seen the other men have their food delivered to their beds, and some of them even had nurses or orderlies feeding them. Yet here he lay, all alone. No food, no water, and no conversation.

Once, he'd seen Miss Rix standing in the doorway to the ward watching him. She looked beautiful. Stern, but beautiful. One of the nurses had spoken to her and then looked his way. Miss Rix shook her head no, watched him for another moment, and then disappeared.

His stomach was beginning to rumble and he was thirsty. He tried to get an orderly's attention, but the man walked by as if he didn't hear him. Even Mr. Whitley, who'd always been attentive, was nowhere to be seen. What was this all about, he wondered. Do they want him to die of starvation? Or lack of water? Would they even leave his wounds to become infected and kill him off that way? Fine. If that's the plan, I welcome it, he thought.

Then his stomach churned again and he scowled. Not a very nice way to go though, I must say, he thought again.

He turned over and his mind wandered to another time he'd felt hungry. Only that time, he wasn't in a hospital.

He was fifteen years old. The farmer he'd been apprenticed to after his grandmother died was kind enough, and allowed him to spend time with the horses when his chores were completed, but he had no aptitude for farming.

After a year of trying to fit in, the farmer took him aside one day and told him he was to be apprenticed to a blacksmith. That was fine with him, as he'd be allowed to work with horses all the time, instead of just when he wasn't doing chores.

But the blacksmith was a brute who would beat Ronald for the slightest mistakes. After a year, Ronald decided being on his own was better than being beaten daily. He packed up his few belongings and snuck out one night, heading for nobody knew where.

The third night on the road found him huddled under a bush in a rainstorm, trying to stay dry. As he waited out the storm, he had nothing to do but listen to his stomach rumbling and think about the scraps of food the blacksmith would leave for him after his work was finished. He would have given almost anything for one of those scraps that night. Well, anything but go back to the torment of the whip.

A couple of days later, he'd resorted to stealing food off a recently abandoned table in a pub. He'd been caught by a large man in uniform. Deciding he had nothing to lose, he'd tried to bluster his way through.

"The gentlemen were finished, so I thought I might help myself to their leavings," he said, lifting his chin in a show of defiance.

"But 'twas theirs to leave since they paid fer it, ain't that right?"

Sighing, Ronald looked down at the food in his hand. "Yes," he muttered.

"You got coin to pay fer yer food?" the man's deep voice continued.

Ronald didn't say anything. He simply shook his head and reached to return the scraps to the table.

"You got an inkling to earn yer keep, or are ye set on stealing yer way through life?"

Surprised, the boy had looked up into a face that was stern but with eyes that sparkled with understanding.

"I'm meanin' to earn my way. It's just that I was so hungry..." his voice trailed off.

"Then let's sit and enjoy a meal together, boy, and let me explain how you never need be hungry again."

Thus, began Ronald Ferguson's recruitment into the cavalry, where he'd enjoyed decent food and was finally able to work with the horses he loved.

Yet here I find myself lying in a hospital in Crimea, starving once again, thanks to a high-handed nurse who thinks she can make me do what I have no intention of doing, he thought bitterly. Well, if she thinks she can force me to do her will, she's sorely mistaken.

Over the course of the next few hours, he alternated between listening to his growling stomach and resigning himself to this uncomfortable death. His dark thoughts were interrupted when Miss Rix approached his bed with the tray of dressing supplies on it.

"Finally," he groused.

She didn't say a word. She sat gracefully on the floor next to his mattress and began untying the sling.

"Aren't you going to ask how I am?" he growled.

She merely looked at him with an unreadable expression, then looked back down at her work.

He lay quietly under her ministrations for a long moment, then the questions he'd been asking himself all day came pouring out.

"Why is everyone ignoring me? Why hasn't anyone brought me food or water? Why haven't you insisted on stretching out my shoulder or making me walk in the corridor? What in bloody blazes is going on here?" his voice rose as his anger came to the surface.

Miss Rix watched his face as he ranted, finished her task, then stood up silently.

"Aren't you even going to answer my questions?" he raged.

She stood still for a moment, waiting, then turned on her heel and walked away, not looking back.

The sergeant was more frustrated and angry than ever. He didn't understand what was going on and it seemed he would get no answers tonight. He glared at the moonlit rectangle on the ceiling above his head. After what seemed like an eternity, he fell asleep despite his growling stomach.

The next morning, he was certain things would be back to normal. Everything on the ward seemed routine. Bandages were changed, sponge baths were given, breakfast was served... to everyone but him. He glared as each tray was delivered to another man on the ward. He saw a tray placed on the table, but no one said a word to him. Again, he tried to attract someone's attention to get some answers, but all studiously ignored him.

The morning dragged on, but finally it was dinnertime. Again, trays were delivered, patients fed, comforts seen to... everyone's but his, that is. The breakfast tray on the table was removed and replaced with a fresh tray of food.

He tried to turn away from it, but his wounded shoulder prevented him from laying on that side, so he had to try to be content with lying on his back. His now loudly growling stomach kept his mind on the food tray, however.

Sergeant Ferguson watched the shadows on the ceiling creep along as the minutes dragged by. His tongue seemed twice its size and dry as dirt in his mouth. He tried to lick his lips, but there was nothing to wet them. Even when he raised his voice, the staff ignored him. He received glares from his fellow patients for his loud protests, but no one talked to him directly. Was everyone in on this conspiracy to kill him slowly?

Supper was served right on time, to everyone else, and to the table that seemed so far away from him. He watched as the man next to him bit, chewed, and swallowed, obviously enjoying his meal. He wanted to drool as the man gulped the water from his cup, but there was no drool left in his mouth.

Finally, he could stand it no longer and rolled onto his good side, rolling himself up into a sitting position. He was breathing hard with the effort, but he was determined. He rested for a few minutes, then stood on wobbly legs, holding onto the wall for support.

Then, one step... two steps... three... then four. He was in the aisle between the beds, slowly making his way towards that bloody table and the food thereon. He stumbled a couple of times, but didn't see Miss Rix or Mr. Whitley standing in the doorway as they stopped each other from rushing to his aide.

Thirty-seven steps later, he was at the table. He reached out a hand to take the cup of water, and then heard the abrupt explosion of applause and cheers behind him. He turned and saw each and every man and woman clapping and whistling their approval and admiration for his effort.

Then he heard a soft voice behind him.

"Would you like a chair, Sergeant?" Lucia asked.

He turned his head and glared at her. "Now you want to help? All of you conspired against me, didn't you?"

She smiled and sat the chair behind him, pushing gently so he sat down without thinking. She pulled up another chair and joined him at the table.

"More like conspiring for you. We couldn't help you very well when you weren't willing to help yourself," she replied.

"Damned cruel way to prove your point," he muttered around a bite of beef.

"For that, I apologize," she said mildly. "I could see no other way to convince you that in the deep recesses of your mind, you truly want to live."

"What makes you think I want to live?" he asked, taking a bite of bread, and following it with a long swig of water.

She laughed. "For one thing, you're eating like a man who wants to live."

He looked at the nearly empty plate, then at the last crust of bread in his hand, then at her face, which in that moment had the glow of a woman who knows he has just proven her point for her. Nodding, he admitted, "I guess I do."

"Good!" she grinned. "Now the real work can begin. As soon as you're finished eating, we'll stretch that shoulder out and then see how far you can walk down the corridor. Then we'll start on some exercises to strengthen your legs and back. We'll have you back on your horse in no time."

He allowed himself to wonder for a moment if this handsome, willful woman was more beautiful because of her determination, or in spite of it.

When he'd finished his last bite, and swallowed the last drop of water, she offered him her hand. After a moment, he placed his hand in hers and allowed her to stretch out his shoulder, back, and arm.

A few stretches later, he realized she was humming. The tune was familiar, but he couldn't place it.

"What's that song?" he asked.

She smiled at him. "It's an old Scottish folk song I heard once. Do you know it?"

"I'm not sure. Could you sing the lyrics?"

"Of course."

"O where and O where does your highland laddie dwell;
O where and O where does your highland laddie dwell;
He dwells in merry Scotland where the blue bells sweetly smell,
And all in my heart I love my laddie well."

On the last chorus, Sergeant Ferguson found himself singing along under his breath. He remembered where he'd heard it now. His grandmother used to sing it to him as she rocked him to sleep when he was a boy. He hadn't recalled that memory for many years. It made him feel happy, but also sad at the same time.

Watching his face, Lucia guessed what was going through his mind. "Tell me about her," she requested.

"Hmm? Who?"

"The woman who sang that song to you," she clarified.

"She was my *seanmhair*. My mother's mother. When my mother died, she raised me. At least, until she died, herself," he said with a frown.

"How old were you?" Lucia asked, still stretching out his arm.

"I was eight when mum died, and thirteen when *Seanmhair* went."

"So young!" she exclaimed. "Where did you go after that?"

"There was a farmer on the other side of the county that was good friends with my grandparents. He took me in and put me to work caring for his livestock."

"That's where you learned how to handle horses?" she asked.

He nodded. "That's where I learned to love and respect them," he replied softly.

Lucia smiled. "I'm glad you had somewhere to go and someone to care for you. So many young men don't in that situation." She put the sling back on his arm and tied it securely. "Finished. That wasn't so bad now, was it?"

He looked surprised, his eyebrows raised as he stared at the reapplied sling, then back up at her. "No, it wasn't. Thank you."

Her eyes sparkled as she smiled back. "Maybe next time you won't give Mr. Whitley such a difficult time?"

He couldn't help but grin back. "I think I will continue to give him trouble, just so you'll come and sing to me again."

She laughed. "Sounds like I need to teach Mr. Whitley to sing."

"Oh please, no!" he laughed aloud.

Lucia patted his arm as she stood up. "You rest now and I'll check on you later."

Walking away, she felt almost euphoric. The past few minutes with him had been wonderful. No anger. No stress. He'd talked to her, opened up a little, and even laughed. Perhaps she was getting through to the man inside the anger. Perhaps… no, she couldn't think about that. It wasn't allowed. Taking firm hold of her thoughts, she put her entire mind on the next patient and his needs. Well, almost her entire mind.

Chapter Six

Dear Mama,

The weather is quite cold here, but our Barracks Tower is not as drafty as I'd feared it might be. Mrs. Nightingale has provided us each with warm blankets and we have rocks to warm and place at our feet at night. She continues to do the night rounds herself, although several have offered to spell her.

Sadly, she has had to send several nurses home for breaking the rules. She is very strict about them, which I think is just as it should be. She had to send one nurse back very shortly after our arrival. The woman simply refused to follow the rules.

A German sister from the Keiserwerth colony at Constantinople replaced her. Four of the six nurses supplied by St. John's House had to return, as well. Alas, they were not prepared for the discipline and privations here. Please don't fret about the word "privations", Mama. We have all we need; food, clothing, a roof over our heads and beds to sleep in. What I mean by privations is that they didn't have all they wanted, like gourmet food, elegant clothing, spacious living quarters and parties to attend. Indeed, we are well cared for, as Miss Nightingale provides all she can for us and the patients we treat.

We are very lucky in our Medical Heads. Two of them are brutes, and four are angels, for this is a work which makes either angels or devils *of men and of women, too. As for the assistants, they are all Cubs, and will, while a man is breathing his last breath under the knife, lament the "annoyance of being called up from their dinners by such a fresh influx of wounded". However, unlicked Cubs grow up into good old Bears, as Miss Nightingale says, tho' I don't know how. Yet certain it is that the old Bears are good.*

We have now four miles of beds, and not eighteen inches apart. The work is taxing, but has its own rewards. When a young soldier is able to walk again after the surgeon saves his leg from the ball that invaded it, all the ward sets up a cheer. When another soldier receives word that his injuries entitle him to return home, each of his comrades sends him on his way with well wishes and messages for their own loved ones at home.

It is true we have watched many perish from their wounds, or infections, or the dysentery, but those we grieve have gone on to their own rewards and are no longer suffering. That is my consolation.

One of our greatest challenges is the morale of those we treat. So many of them simply want to give up. Their wounds may not be life threatening, but in their minds, they are already dead. Those are the ones that break my heart.

One young man, a sergeant in the Scottish cavalry, has bounced back and forth between hope and despair so often, it's a wonder he's not dizzy! I wish I knew what I could do to help him realize how much he has to live for. However, he's alone in the world and can't see past his own pain and the current limitations placed on him by his injuries. Still, I will try, for he is a man who is certainly worthy to live.

You may be interested to hear about the new kitchens Miss Nightingale has set up. Each wing of the Barracks Hospital has one now. From them are distributed quantities of arrowroot, sago, rice puddings, jelly, beef tea, and lemonade upon requisitions made by the surgeons. This causes great comings to and fro. The orderlies wait at the door with requisitions. One of the nuns or a lady receive them, and see that they are signed and countersigned before serving.

We, among ourselves, call the main kitchen our own tower of Babel.

In the middle of the day, everything and everybody seems to be there; boxes, parcels, bundles of sheets, shirts, old linens and flannels, tubs of butter, sugar, bread, kettles, saucepans, heaps of books, and of all kinds of rubbish, besides the diets which are being dispensed.

Then there are the numbers of people; ladies, nuns, nurses, orderlies, Turks, Greeks, French and Sardinian servants, officers and others waiting to see Miss Nightingale; all passing to and fro, all intent upon their own business, and all speaking their own language. It's quite a sight to see.

All that being said, I feel a need ask for your help. We have had an influx of patients from the Russian attack on Eupatoria. It has increased our workload and our overcrowding problem. For many months, the space for each patient has been one-fourth of what it ought to have been, and there is no proper ventilation.

It is impossible to describe the state of the atmosphere of the hospital at night. I have seen some of the dwellings of the worst parts of most of the great cities in Europe in our travels, but have never been in any atmosphere that I could compare with this.

Hospital comforts, and even many hospital necessaries, are deficient. The supply of bedsteads is inadequate. The commonest utensils, for decency as well as for comfort, are lacking. The sheets are of canvas, and so coarse that the wounded men beg to be left in their blankets, even when they are riddled with holes from balls and rodents. It is indeed impossible to put men in such a state of emaciation into those sheets.

There is no bedroom furniture of any kind, and only empty beer or wine bottles for candlesticks. Necessary surgical and medical appliances are often either wanting or not forthcoming. The result of this state of things upon patients arriving after a painful voyage in an extreme state of weakness and emaciation, from wounds, from frostbite, from dysentery, may be imagined, and it is no wonder that cholera and typhus are rife. To date, the mortality of the cases treated for dysentery is forty-two percent. No words are necessary to emphasize so terrible a figure.

Miss Nightingale is generous with her personal funds for all she can procure, but her ability to provide for all the men, as well as the nurses, can only go so far. If you can see your way to implore your Ladies' Club for any kind of assistance, we would all be most appreciative, especially the poor wounded soldiers.

We are in need of sheets, blankets, socks, shirts, knives and forks, wooden spoons, tin baths, tables and forms, cabbage and carrots, operating tables, towels and soap, small tooth combs, precipitate for destroying lice, scissors, bedpans, and stump pillows. Anything you send will be gratefully put to good use. Thank you, Mama.

Please do not worry. I am healthy and happy in my work. It's nearly time for my shift on the wards, so I will close for now. I hope all is well with you.

Your Loving Daughter,
Lucia
December 12, 1854

That night, Lucia dreamed about her father again. This time, it was an incident just before he'd been lost at sea.

"What's wrong, *mia piccola luce?*" Roberto asked, his voice filled with love and concern.

Twelve-year-old Lucia couldn't stop her sobs long enough to answer. Her olive complexion was splotchy and her eyes were red and puffy from crying. Roberto took her in his arms and held her close, rocking back and forth just a little to soothe his daughter.

After a while, his ministrations finally had some effect as her sobs quieted to soft sniffles. He pulled back a little and reached into his pocket for his handkerchief. Dabbing her eyes with it, he smiled gently, then tucked his finger under her chin, lifting her face to look at him.

"Now, then," he said, "tell your papa what all this *tristezza* is about? Why is my Little Light so sad?"

Lucia gazed into her loving papa's eyes and wished more than anything that she could tell him what was troubling her.

"It's nothing, Papa," she said, her voice quavering. "I'm just being a little girl."

"*Sensa senso!* That is nonsense. My girl is growing into a *bella donna*. Such a beautiful woman. She makes me proud."

Lucia couldn't help but smile at her father's adoration of her. Even though her relationship with her mother was sometimes difficult, she never had to worry about what her father might think of her.

She sighed. "Mama says I must sing at the charity luncheon on Saturday and I have to wear a perfectly hideous grey dress with huge, puffed sleeves, a cinched-in waist, and a bustle the size of my pony's rump. I look like a giant snail carrying my shell on my backside!"

Looking thoughtful, her father nodded. "I think I see the problem. You hate to sing."

Puzzled, she looked sharply at him. "No, Papa. I love to sing. You know that."

"Ah yes. I remember now. Then it must be that you hate luncheons."

Shaking her head, Lucia smiled a little, recognizing the ploy her father often used to make her laugh. "No, Papa. I don't mind luncheons. There are usually lots of interesting people attending."

His eyebrows furrowed in mock concentration. "Then perhaps you hate charities?"

Lucia broke into laughter, in spite of herself. "No, Papa. I think charities are very worthwhile."

Looking truly confused, Roberto sighed. "Then I don't see what the problem is, Lucia."

Her laughter faded and she looked more serious, although not as distraught as she had a few moments before. "It's the dress, Papa. I hate the dress."

Realization apparently dawning, he laughed. "Ah, the dress. The dress *terribile*. How can that be helped?" He looked thoughtful, then mischievous. "Can you sabotage it?"

She matched his thoughtful look. "I don't think that would be wise. Mama might make me wear one of hers and that would be worse."

"Hmm. Can you become ill?"

"I could," her words were drawn out as she thought through this possibility, "but I really don't mind singing at these events. I just hate the dresses she picks out for me."

"Then perhaps it is time for *mia prima donna* to pick out her own dresses." He smiled tenderly down at her.

"She'd never allow that, papa." Lucia scowled.

"Then we shall not ask her," he announced decisively.

"What?"

"We shall not ask her permission. We shall simply go shopping ourselves. We shall pick out the perfect gown for you and sneak it into the house. On Saturday, you shall put on *l'abito perfetto* and descend the stairs like a princess. You will look so elegant; she must allow you to wear it." Roberto's enthusiasm was contagious. Lucia found herself getting excited.

"You mean it, Papa? I can pick out my own gown?"

"But of course, Lucia! If you are woman enough to know what you like, then you are woman enough to pick it out for yourself."

That very afternoon, Roberto and Lucia rode into town and saw a seamstress. When they were finished, Lucia was ecstatic. The dress would be perfect, made of watered silk, dyed in a vibrant pink that contrasted so nicely with her hair and skin. It would have short sleeves, a lace-flounced collar, and a long, pointed waist where tiny pleats would gather which would cause the skirt to spring out from the waist in the popular bell shape.

Lucia couldn't wait for it to be finished. She was both excited and scared for Mama to see her in it. It was so different than the one Mama had picked out that Lucia was sure there would be an argument over it, but Papa had said that if she appeared just as they were leaving, there would be no time to change, so Mama would have no choice but to let her wear it.

It was decided that Papa would pick it up on Friday and bring it into the house without Mama seeing. Then on Saturday, Lucia would put on her new gown and descend the stairs with her head held high, her bearing resembling a royal princess. Mama would have to see that this was so much better than *l'abito terribile* as Papa called it.

It was late morning on Saturday. Harriet Rix was standing at the bottom of the stairs tapping her foot. "Lucia! We are going to be late if you do not come down this instant."

"Coming, Mama."

Lucia brushed a piece of imaginary lint from her skirt, took a deep breath, and walked to the top of the stairs. As she descended the steps one by one, her heart raced in her chest. She kept a close watch on her mother's expression.

As Harriet turned around to see where Lucia was, her mouth dropped open like a fish out of water. Her eyes widened and her eyebrows raised. She closed her mouth and opened it again, presumably to say something, but nothing came out.

Lucia looked behind her mother at her father's expression. His was nothing short of proud and pleased. He grinned at her and nodded his approval.

When her mother recovered her ability to speak, her words were soft and not what Lucia expected to hear. "You are beautiful, Lucia. The gown is beautiful."

"Thank you, Mama!" she exclaimed. "I hope you are not too disappointed that I didn't wear the gray one."

"No, my dear, you obviously have better taste than I. Perhaps you should pick out your own clothes from now on."

Lucia awoke with tears soaking her pillow. She still missed her father. He had always seemed to understand her need for independence.

"I just don't understand, Mr. Whitley," Lucia's voice showed her frustration. "He was much more cooperative yesterday. What happened?"

"I don't know, Miss Rix," the orderly replied, "but he's been in a foul mood since I came on duty this morning."

Sighing, Lucia nodded. "Thank you. I'll check into it."

After completing the dressing she was working on, she made her way into the ward where her sergeant lay. She wasn't sure exactly when she began thinking of him as "her sergeant", but now she couldn't stop.

That wasn't a good sign, she knew. It showed a definite lack of professional distance. Still, when she thought of his eyes and the rusty red of his hair, and how he seemed so lost and alone, she couldn't help but think of him as hers.

Rather than go to him directly, she chose to check the bandages of a few other men in the ward, keeping a covert watch on him, trying to assess his mood. She watched as another nurse tried to check his bandages, but he growled and chased her off with a few choice words. She heard him fairly yell at an orderly who asked if he wanted to take a walk. Finally, he told the surgeon in no uncertain terms to take his "bloody bedside manner and stuff it into a dark hole".

Putting on her sternest face, Lucia made her move. She stepped deliberately over to his mattress, stood over him with her arms folded, and glared.

He looked up and glared right back.

"You're in a sorry mood today, Sergeant," she accused. "I've been watching you and you have certainly changed your attitude since last night."

"So?" his voice was gruff. "What's that to you?"

She raised an eyebrow, and answered, "You are my patient, and I thought we'd made some progress last night. When I left, I had the impression you had decided to work on getting well."

"So, I changed my mind. Just leave me alone," he ordered.

Lucia pursed her lips, considering her next move. "No, I don't believe I will. There is something chafing at you, and until we discover what it is, I don't think you'll get better."

"Who says I want to get better?"

"You did. Last night," was her retort.

"I lied," he stated flatly.

"I don't believe that. I think in that moment, you truly wanted to live. What's changed your mind?"

The sergeant didn't answer. He just turned his head away.

"Oh no," she said, her voice determined. "I won't let you evade the subject that way. I'm going to stay right here until you tell me what you're thinking."

"Then you'll be standing there for a very long time," he muttered.

Shaking her head, she gathered her skirts and sat on the floor facing him.

He turned his head and glared at her. "I said leave me alone."

"I will not leave you alone," Lucia replied calmly. "I intend to pull you through whatever this is, in spite of yourself."

His scowl deepened, but he didn't say anything.

"Shall I guess what has changed your mind?" she asked.

Still, he was silent.

"Someone offended you?" was her first guess.

He rolled his eyes.

"There's a lump in your mattress?"

Again, he rolled his eyes.

"You found a fly in your morning mush?"

His lips tightened, but she thought he might be trying to stifle a quirk of a smile.

"There's a rock in your shoe? Wait, you're not wearing shoes. Strike that."

This time, there was a definite quirk at the corner of his mouth.

"The sun is shining in your eyes?" she grinned. "No, that can't be, it's cloudy today."

He shook his head, but his smile peeked out again.

"Oh, oh, I've got it!" she exclaimed. "You want me to sing again."

She broke out in a raucous version of "Billie Boy". The men around them laughed and joined in. The sergeant tried to keep his gruff expression, but by the time they reached the chorus, he was smiling. By the second chorus, he was chuckling along with the rest of the ward. When the song was finished, he was wiping tears from his eyes from laughing so hard.

Lucia smiled at him. "There, that's better. You're much more handsome when you smile." She blushed as she realized that she'd said her innermost thoughts aloud without meaning to.

His eyebrows raised. "You think I'm handsome?"

She looked down to hide her embarrassment, then peeked at him through her eyelashes. "Yes," she whispered.

He leaned over and whispered back, "Well, I think you're beautiful."

Her blush deepened, and she reached out to brush his arm.

"I need to finish my rounds," she said softly, "but when I return, will you tell me what's had you so angry this morning?"

The smile on his face disappeared, but he nodded.

Satisfied, she stood up and moved away, glancing back once to see him watching her. She smiled at him and her heart skipped a beat when he smiled back.

After that, Lucia found herself looking for reasons to be in Ward B. At first, she didn't even recognize she was deliberately putting herself near the sergeant, but with each glance, each smile, her attraction for him grew. She kept her actions in check... mostly.

When changing his dressings, her fingers would linger just a bit longer than necessary. When working with another patient, her eyes would wander a little too frequently towards his side of the room. When doing mundane tasks like rolling bandages or cleaning bedpans, her mind was delightfully distracted by the image of his unruly red hair, or the twinkle in his eyes when he smiled.

Each time she caught herself in such a situation, she'd take herself firmly in hand and try to focus on her work, rather than the more pleasant distraction of her sergeant.

One afternoon, she was working hard to keep her mind on her work, when she glanced up and noticed her friend Jean talking rather intently with a patient in the corner of the ward. She saw Jean's hand flit gently up to brush the young man's hair from his eyes. She nodded, patted his arm, and moved quickly across the room to another patient.

Lucia cocked her head. Could it be Jean was suffering the same affliction as herself? Surreptitiously, she kept an eye on her friend. Sure enough, she recognized the glances, half-smiles, and distracted movements of a nurse falling in love with a patient. The familiar looks and actions disturbed her. Was she as obvious as Jean in her affection for Ronald? This was not good. She must stop this.

That evening, Lucia found a moment to speak to Jean alone.

"Are you glad you came?" she asked, not wanting to blatantly broach the subject.

Jean smiled, then looked up from her laundry. "Oh, yes, Lucia. More than glad."

"What makes you glad about it?" Lucia asked again, trying to sound casual.

Stifling a giggle, Jean answered quickly, "I just love taking care of the soldiers."

"Soldiers?" Lucia raised an eyebrow. "Or is there one particular soldier you love to care for?"

Astonishment crossed Jean's face for an instant before she recovered her composure. "I'm sure I don't know what you mean."

Lucia hesitated for only a moment before crossing to sit next to her friend. "I mean the corporal in the corner of Ward B."

Jean ducked her head and whispered. "How did you know?"

"You're not very subtle in your attentions to him, Jean," Lucia scolded. "It's plain for anyone to see who cares to watch you for more than five minutes."

Frowning, Jean looked up. "It is? Oh, dear. I suppose that's not good, is it?"

"No, it's not. You're not the first nurse to fall for a soldier, but Miss Nightingale has strict rules about that. If you want to continue nursing here, you'll need to be more careful."

"I will, Lucia," Jean's voice was fervent. "I promise."

Patting her hand, Lucia stood up and began dressing for bed. Her thoughts were in turmoil, however. The look on Jean's face echoed her own feelings for Sergeant Ferguson. As she climbed into bed, she made herself the same promise. "I will be more careful and professional in my duties. I promise."

Chapter Seven

"You never asked me why I have been so angry," Sergeant Ferguson commented as Lucia dressed his wounds later that week.

His hip was healing slowly, and the entrance and exit wounds in his shoulder were healing nicely, but the muscles and ligaments were still stiff and slow to move. His strength was slowly returning, but he still had days where his anger surged to the surface, touching everyone around him.

Lucia looked at him with compassion in her eyes. "You've managed to control it better these days, so I thought perhaps you'd prefer not to talk about it."

He sighed. "That has certainly been the case, but, after last night, I think perhaps it's time for me to tell someone."

Looking concerned, she asked, "What happened last night?"

"I…" he hesitated, "I've been having nightmares. Last night's was much like the others, except that I couldn't speak and I couldn't move. I could see and hear, but I was paralyzed and dumb with fear. Upon reflection, I think my mind is telling me that until I talk about these things, I won't be able to function normally again." He looked up at her with pleading in his eyes. "So, would you be willing to hear what I've been dreaming about… what I've been remembering?"

"Of course," she replied without hesitation. She continued dressing his wounds, grateful that he was finally willing to share what was upsetting him.

"I was dreaming about the Battle of Balaclava. No matter how my dreams begin, I always end up there."

"Is this dream more of a memory or more like an exaggeration of reality?" she asked, wanting to clarify what she was hearing.

"It happens in my dream the way I remember it happening," he replied.

Nodding, she said, "Go on."

"I was with the Scots Greys. We were under Lieutenant Colonel Henry Griffith, who answered to General James Scarlett. We'd heard that the Russians had stormed the Causeway Heights. General Scarlett assembled some of the Iniskillings and us Scots Greys at the foot of the heights, ordering us into formation. Then he sounded the charge.

"We started uphill from a standing start. The short distance between us and the Russians hardly allowed our horses to reach the trot. Moreover, the Russians were moving to meet us.

"I saw the Iniskillings hit the center of the Russian's Cavalry and we followed close behind on the left."

"Were you frightened?" Lucia interrupted to ask.

Ronald looked up at her with an amazed expression. "Frightened? There wasn't time to be frightened. We were fighting for our lives. In that moment, there is no thought, no feeling, just hacking and slashing anything that's not in a red uniform."

Lucia nodded. "More fear in remembering than at the time it happened."

"Right. The Russians started falling back, folding around our rear, but the Dragoon Guards crashed into them. I can still hear their cries of 'Faugh A Ballagh'."

"What does that mean?" Lucia asked.

"It's an Irish battle cry. It means 'clear the way'," Ronald answered, then continued. "We kept at them until they finally turned and fled. We pursued about three hundred yards, then Scarlett called us off as the gunners opened on them and gave them a fine peppering. The Russians retreated in the direction of the Causeway Heights.

Looking puzzled, Lucia asked, "Let me see if I understand. The Russians were retreating. Your commander called you off, but didn't re-engage when the gunners had them running? That doesn't seem right to me."

Impressed with her sense of battle tactics, Ronald nodded. "I didn't think so either. I expected we'd be ordered to follow when the gunners were through with them, but those orders didn't come, so we turned back. As I was trotting back in formation, I noticed a movement behind a bush to my right. Whoever he was, he wasn't wearing red, so I broke off to investigate. Coming around the bush, I saw a Russian Cossack. He was wounded in the leg. I looked up to get orders, but the squadron was already out of earshot. I dismounted, to see if he could walk. I'd thought to take him back as a prisoner. As I squatted down to assess the damage to his leg, he slashed at me with a knife."

"Oh, my!" her hand flew to her mouth.

Noticing the gesture, Ronald hesitated, then asked, "Are you all right? Shall I stop?"

Taking a deep, settling breath, Lucia shook her head. "I'm all right. Please continue."

"I felt it slice deep into my hip. I arched back, then twisted 'round to try and wrest the knife from him. He fought hard, I'll give him that. I had the advantage in that I was on top so it wasn't long before I had the knife in my hand with the point at his throat. The knee on my good leg was on his belly and his hair was in my fist. I told him to calm down and stop fighting, that I didn't want to kill him, but he kept struggling. I shook his head, still holding his hair, and told him to stop struggling. He seemed to relax for an instant, so I did, too. That was my mistake.

"He grabbed a handful of dirt and threw it in my face. It threw me off guard for only a moment, but he managed to roll away. I lunged at him, but he was trying to run in spite of his injured leg. I saw the guns mow him down before he got three steps. I collapsed on the ground, but it became apparent that the gunner's aim wasn't great, as I felt several balls hit the ground near me. I rolled back behind the bush, but not before what I thought was one ball found my shoulder and did all this! Turns out it was two."

Ronald nodded sideways at his bandaged shoulder. "Damned short-sighted gunners!"

"What happened after that?" Lucia was beginning to understand Ronald's anger now.

"From my vantage point, I could see nearly the whole valley. I watched as Scarlett and his men pulled back. That's when I noticed that the Light Brigade was standing at the other end of the valley, just watching. Why hadn't they joined us in the charge? I couldn't figure it out. Just as I couldn't figure out why Scarlett wasn't pursuing the Russians. He just let them go! It didn't make any sense to me. It still doesn't."

"What happened next?" she asked, enthralled with his tale.

"I laid back and waited. I thought sure someone would miss me and come back for me. I didn't dare poke my head up or try to get anyone's attention. That gunner might still be on the ridge just waiting for just such a move. I heard horses after a few minutes and peeked out to see what was happening. I saw the Lights coming towards the valley the Russians had just entered. I remember thinking, 'Finally'. I rolled my head to see what I could see ahead of them and was shocked. The Russians had stopped retreating and had formed a trap with soldiers and cavalry on each side of the valley. I couldn't see to the end, but was certain they had that way blocked off, and I saw Russian gunners on the heights. It was obvious to me that the Lights were heading into an ambush. I looked back and started to try and stand to warn them, but the first weight on my hip and I collapsed again. They rode past without even seeing me.

"I watched them ride by and saw one man, Nolan I think his name was, ride out in front of Cardigan."

"In front of his commander?" Lucia was incredulous.

"That's what he did." Ronald affirmed. "He hadn't gone twenty yards when that blurry-eyed gunman killed him.

"I watched as the Lights stormed into that valley, hacking and slashing their way. They were ferocious! Then the Russian guns opened up on them. I saw men and horses falling left and right. I expected to hear Cardigan sound retreat, but I was shocked to hear him sound the gallop instead. He was taking them deeper into the valley! After a few long minutes of carnage, it got worse. I heard the bugle sound the charge. I couldn't believe it! I looked to see what Scarlett and his Heavies were doing. They were just standing there! They weren't moving to support; they were just standing there. I don't know who these generals are, but they aren't worth their weight in powder or wadding!

"I was certain the Lights were lost. I closed my eyes and tried to block out the sound of the slaughter. Then I heard the sound of hooves coming from the direction of the valley. I looked over and saw two groups of survivors breaking through the Russian trap. They were still too far away for safety, though. They came under fire of those damn guns again. A few still managed to get away, riding by me as though I wasn't there. They made it to the camp, and only then did the Heavies move forward. I saw a French cavalry form on their left. The Frenchmen charged the flank of the Russian battery, forcing them to drag away their guns.

"Then, not five yards away from me, I heard General Lucan's voice. I don't know who he was talking to, but he said, 'They have sacrificed the Light Brigade; they shall not have the Heavy, if I can help it.' Then he told his bugler to sound a retreat. The entire cavalry turned and galloped back to the encampment."

Puzzled, Lucia asked, "But who rescued you? Obviously, someone found you."

Ronald nodded. "It was a Frenchman. As the French brigade came down from the Heights, one horseman saw my red coat behind the bush and came 'round. He pulled me up to lay belly down in front of him on his horse, then brought me back to camp. That's how I ended up here.

"All because of stupid generals who don't support each other, and nearsighted gunmen who can't tell the difference between red coats and black ones."

"Well, I am glad you are here." Lucia's voice was soft and soothing, as she stood to go. "You may be wounded, but you'll heal. I'm certain the nightmares will subside in time, but if they don't, if you need to talk again, I'm here and willing to listen. You are safe, Sergeant. Keep reminding yourself of that."

She smoothed the blanket around his wounded hip and pulled it up a bit at his chest, careful to hide the tenderness that was growing in her heart for him. "Thank you for sharing that with me. It took great courage and I hope it helps."

"I hope so, too," he mumbled as she moved away. "I hope so, too."

He couldn't have explained the lump in his throat to anyone. He didn't want her to go. He longed to feel her gentle touch and hear the happy lilt in her voice as she sang. Yet she came and went to him as she did to all the men. It was obvious she was as much above him in station as he was to a cockroach. Sighing, he turned over and tried to sleep, hoping the nightmare wouldn't follow him into dreamland this time.

Dear Mama,

Happy Christmas! I know you won't receive this until well after the holiday, but I'm thinking of you, especially today. Have you attended many parties and events this holiday season? Here, it is pretty much business as usual. We tend to the patients during the day, prepare their diets, change their bandages, visit with them when we have a minute to spare, which isn't as frequent as they would like.

We had a happy surprise the other day. Queen Victoria sent a package filled with comforts and useful articles for the soldiers, and some warm scarves for the nurses. The men were quite touched that their Queen would remember them at holiday time. I think it was a wonderful gesture on her part.

We've made some progress with the sergeant I wrote you about. He still has moments when he wants to give up, but mostly he's cooperative now. He's part of the Scottish cavalry unit and has such a delightful accent. I never tire of hearing him speak. Although, he says he never tires of hearing me sing, so I suppose that's fair.

I had an extraordinary experience last evening. Miss Nightingale invited me to attend her on her nightly tour of the hospital. We went 'round the whole of the second story, into many of the wards and into one of the upper corridors. It seemed an endless walk, and it was not one easily forgotten. As we slowly passed along, the silence was profound; very seldom did a moan or cry from those deeply suffering ones fall on our ears. A dim light burned here and there.

Miss Nightingale carried her lantern, which she would set down before she bent over any of the patients. I much admired her manner to the men. It was so tender and kind. I only hope I can be as tender and kind in my ministrations to the men under my care. The men adore her.

One fellow told me that before she came, there was cussin' and swearin' from every man, but since she arrived, not one has felt the need to use such language. Indeed, the corridors and wards are silent as churches, especially at night, each man handling his own pain in a dignified manner, with great regard for his fellows and for the staff that attend to them, especially Miss Nightingale.

We are having an impromptu concert this evening to celebrate Christmas. One fellow has his harmonica and another his tin whistle. One of the orderlies has a guitar, as well. Our plan is to sing as many carols as we can remember.

Two of the nurses have made paper lanterns to decorate the wards and Miss Nightingale managed to obtain the ingredients for a lovely Christmas pudding. Of course, I'll sing whatever the lads request, and we plan to end with Silent Night. It seems to cheer them, and brings me pleasure as well.

I hope your Christmas is lovely. I miss you and am ever grateful for your love and support in this endeavor.

Your loving daughter,
Lucia
December 24, 1854

Chapter Eight

The lamps were burning brighter than usual after dinner. The orderlies had turned them up in anticipation of the Christmas party to come. When it began, the staff split themselves between the four wards and wandered up and down the corridors, singing carols, telling stories, and relating Christmas poems. It wasn't long before everyone was feeling festive, smiles were plentiful, and laughter punctuated the singing frequently.

Miss Nightingale floated between the wards and corridors wishing everyone a Happy Christmas. No one questioned her sincerity, although a few remarked that she looked especially tired that evening.

Sergeant Ferguson watched it all, hoping for a glimpse, or rather more than a glimpse, of his favorite nurse. He joined in the singing when he knew the song, and laughed at the stories and funny poems shared by staff and patient alike. Finally, his wish was granted and she entered his ward with a broad smile and cheery greeting for all.

After singing a couple of familiar carols, she asked for requests. One boy, two beds down from the sergeant asked for "Great Plum Pudding". Laughing, she complied, moving to his bed and seeming to sing just to him. He blushed and thanked her. Another lad asked for another song and received the same treatment.

So, that's how to get her attention, the sergeant thought. He racked his brain trying to think of a song she might know, but, alas, his brain turned to mush every time he looked at her. After half an hour of taking requests, she asked that each man join her and the men in the other wards and corridors in singing Silent Night.

She moved to the doorway and nodded to another nurse who waved down the corridor. In a moment, Lucia began. Her voice was soft and throaty, as if she were trying to hold back tears. She nodded and smiled at the men in beds next to her and they joined with her. It wasn't long before the entire ward was singing and the sergeant heard the walls resound with the hundreds of voices singing throughout the hospital. Lucia was crying openly now, as were many of the men, lending a depth of meaning to the familiar words.

"Sleep in heavenly peace,
Sleep in heavenly peace."

As the last words faded away, there was reverent silence as each man contemplated and knew that this was a Christmas they would never forget. They also realized that for many, it would be their last.

When they had wiped their tears away, the nurses and orderlies began serving the Christmas pudding. The laughter and chatter resumed as the men dug into the rare treat.

Sergeant Ferguson was thrilled when he saw Lucia approaching him with a small bowl. As she bent to hand it to him, he caught her arm.

"Please." His voice was quiet but insistent. "Please won't you come back and stay with me for a while later?"

She frowned a little. "It's after nine, Sergeant. I'm not allowed to…"

"Please," he begged. "Just for a moment. I have something for you."

Hesitating, she finally nodded. "I'll try."

He smiled as he let go of her arm. "Thank you."

Two hours later, the sergeant was trying to resign himself to the idea that she wasn't coming. He sighed. It was too much to hope for. She obviously had too much integrity to ignore the rules. Or perhaps she hadn't been able to get past Miss Nightingale or the orderlies. Or perhaps she was celebrating with the other nurses and had forgotten all about his invitation. Or perhaps…

Just then, he saw a shadow in the doorway. She slipped in

noiselessly and seemed to glide towards him like a wraith. When she reached his mattress, she melted onto the floor with no sound at all.

"What can I do for you, Sergeant?" she whispered.

"Thank you for coming," he whispered back. "I wanted to give you something for Christmas, so I asked Mr. Whitley to buy this for me. I hope you like it."

He handed her a small box tied with a string. She took it in her hand and shook her head. "I don't think I can accept this," she began. "I'm sure there's a regulation somewhere that…"

"Please," his eyes were pleading, "I don't care about regulations. I just want you to have this… as a remembrance."

She hesitated, then untied the string and opened the box. Inside was a tiny, carved horse.

"It's beautiful," she exclaimed quietly. "What is it made from?"

"The shopkeeper told Mr. Whitley it was carved from a whalebone and is supposed to bring good luck."

Lucia smiled. "It's exquisite. Thank you. I will cherish this both for the gift itself and as a remembrance of you."

She started to stand, slipping the gift into her apron pocket, but he touched her hand. "Will you stay for a few minutes please? I am hoping that talking with you just before I sleep will keep the nightmares at bay."

Glancing at the door, she nodded. "Only for a minute," she warned. "If Miss Nightingale catches me, I'll be sent home so fast both our heads will be spinning for a week."

"I understand," he whispered.

"What would you like to talk about?" she asked. "Something to give you happy dreams?"

He chuckled. "Yes. Tell me about you. Where did you grow up?"

"I grew up in London," she replied, her eyes getting that faraway look that happened when she was remembering. "My father owned a fleet of merchant ships that ran cargo from Neápolis, Sardinia to London."

"He's Sardinian?" he asked, surprised. "But isn't your name Rix? That's not a Sardinian surname."

She smiled. "My father was Sardinian. His name was Roberto Rizzi, but he used the English name Rix when doing business in

England. He said it made him more accessible to his British customers. He was very successful, so he must have been right about that. Mama says I get my dark looks from him. She's blonde and blue-eyed, whereas I have black hair with brown eyes, like my father. She says I have his temper, too, although I've seen her angry enough times to doubt that he's the only donor to my passionate approach to life."

Looking amused, he queried sweetly, "You're passionate?"

She blushed, realizing her somewhat dubious choice of words in this instance. Choosing to ignore the question, she went on, "Papa met Mama at the Adelphi Theatre. She and Uncle Edward had gone to see the play 'The Young Widow', and Papa had brought a young lady of his acquaintance. Mama tells the story that the young lady left in a huff halfway through the play because he was staring at Mama instead of paying attention to her," Lucia laughed. "That was Papa. He was in love with Mama from the first time he saw her. He used to tell me that once he saw her, no one else in the world existed. Until I came along, however."

"I can imagine he was as much in love with you as he was your mother."

"Very much so," she smiled. "Which has caused a few hurt feelings along the way, I'm afraid. Mama is a good woman, but she's also a bit selfish, possessive, and quite over-protective... and very much enthralled with High Society and all it has to offer."

Raising an eyebrow, the sergeant cocked his head. "With that kind of perspective, I'm surprised she allowed you to come here. This isn't exactly a society function."

Lucia shook her head. "No, it isn't, and I worked hard to get her to agree, but I think deep down, she's proud of me and of the work we're doing here."

"Your father's probably popping his buttons over it."

"He would be," her voice was sad, "if he were still with us."

"Oh, I'm sorry," he said, realizing he'd missed her use of the word 'was' earlier.

"It's all right. He passed away when I was twelve. He was sailing through the Strait of Gibraltar, on his way back to England after picking up cargo in Sicily. An unexpected storm rose. They say his ship crashed on the rocks and all hands were lost. I used to lay awake at night and imagine that he'd survived somehow, and that he'd come walking up the path unexpectedly someday and surprise us all."

"That's a hard dream to give up," the sergeant remarked.

"Yes, it is," she agreed, "but once I did, I moved ahead with my life with the idea that I want to make him proud of me, even if he's not here to say it."

"I'm sure he's very proud of you," the sergeant stated matter-of-factly.

Nodding, Lucia smiled. "Thank you, Sergeant."

"Please, call me Ronald... or Ron, if you prefer," his voice held a tenderness that made her heart skip several beats.

"I... I'm not certain that's appropriate," she stammered, blushing.

"Well, then," he mused, "what if you call me Sergeant during the day and Ronald at night when no one's around?"

Looking shocked, she pulled back a little. "I don't plan to be here at night after this. Once might be forgiven, but more than that and I could be in serious trouble."

He sighed. "I understand, but I'd love to see you again outside of your nursing duties."

"I don't think that's a good idea," she whispered, suddenly aware that her heart had just dropped down into her boots. "Miss Nightingale frowns on fraternizing between nurses and soldiers. I don't think she'd approve."

"Well, if you change your mind, you know where I am."

Suddenly, he grasped her hand, turned it over, and kissed her palm. His lips were soft and sweet against her skin. She began to tremble as she fought the urge to run her fingers through his rust-colored hair, curling just a little at the ears. Tears welled in her eyes as she gently pulled her hand away.

"I must go." Even her whisper was hoarse with emotion.

He didn't say anything, just smiled a wistful smile and nodded.

She stood and turned away, trying hard to calm her breathing and her racing heart.

"Good night..." he started to say, then stopped. "I don't even know your name. I can't call you simply Nurse now. That puts you in the realm of all the other nurses and you are far too beautiful and precious for that. Pray tell, what's your name, Nurse?"

Looking back, she whispered, "It's Lucia."

"Good night, Nurse Lucia," he smiled.

"Good night... Ronald," she smiled back at him for an instant, and then was gone.

The next morning, Lucia reported to Mrs. Bracebridge for her assignment.

"If you have time, Miss Rix," the older woman looked up from the papers on her little desk, "would you check the wards for stray books? We have several that have gone missing from the reading room and Miss Nightingale would like them rounded up. Don't take the ones that are being read, but if you see any lying around..."

"I understand," Lucia smiled.

It was generally understood that the reading room was available to any patient who wanted something to pass the time, but sometimes they neglected to return them when they were finished with them, or when they were discharged.

Her morning was busy, but uneventful, as she was assigned to Ward A where there were no distractions for her. As she prepared to take her mid-day break, she gathered several books she'd found and made her way to the reading room.

She opened the door and caught her breath as she interrupted a passionate kiss between a nurse and a patient. Stepping back, she took one more glance into the room before closing the door, confirming her fears. The patient was the corporal from Ward B, and the nurse was Jean. This was not good at all.

Forgetting the books in her hand, she strode quickly down the hall towards the kitchen. She had no idea what she was going to do. It was tantamount to mutiny in Miss Nightingale's opinion for a nurse to fraternize with a patient, but, knowing how Jean feels, she thought, how could I report her?

Lucia reached the kitchen and absentmindedly laid the books on a table and filled a bowl with soup. Without conscious thought, she took a spoon from the utensil bin and made her way to a semi-quiet corner. She couldn't have told anyone what kind of soup it was, or even what it tasted like. Her mind was too occupied with the dilemma she faced.

On the one hand, Lucia believed in the importance of obeying rules, especially rules that were for the best good of all. On the other hand, Jean was simply acting on emotions that Lucia herself was feeling, but was that a good enough reason to flout the rules? To disobey express orders? But what was the harm? Was it harming the corporal to have a beautiful nurse love him? Was it harming Jean to finally find a man who was obviously as in love with her as she was with him?

Shaking her head in confusion, Lucia deposited her bowl and spoon in hot, soapy water, then started to return to her duties, no closer to an answer than she had been before her abbreviated meal.

"Miss Rix," a voice called as she reached the kitchen doorway.

She turned to find Amy holding the books she'd left behind.

"Are these yours?" the older woman chuckled.

"Oh, no," Lucia replied, a bit embarrassed. "I found them lying around in Ward A and was planning to return them to the reading room."

"I suggest you return them before you return to duty or someone might accuse you of stealing them," Amy laughed.

Lucia tried to laugh, but only succeeded in an awkward-sounding snort. "Right," she managed as she took the books and made her escape.

Approaching the reading room door, she hesitated, then knocked softly before entering. Relieved to find the room empty, she placed the books on a shelf and left quickly, still unsure what she should do about what she'd seen and determined that she would never be caught in such a compromising position.

Dear Mama,

What a mess we have here! Day before yesterday, six nurses approached Miss Nightingale and asked to be released from their contract because they want to get married. They were followed by six soldiers, sergeants, and corporals, who asked for their hands in marriage.

My dear friend, Jean, has fallen for one of these soldiers. His name is Dell Lassiter. He's a corporal with the Fifth Dragoon Guards. I know she loves him, but I do wish she had shown more restraint. Ah, well. It is done now. She will be making her way home to London in the next few days. As soon as the corporal is released from the hospital, I'm sure he'll be joining her there.

Needless to say, Miss Nightingale was not happy with either the nurses or the soldiers. She told them all plainly that she was disappointed in their lack of professionalism and their blatant disregard of the regulations, but after all was said and done, she honored their request. Her face looks so determined, yet sad these days, Mama.

It doesn't help that we have a new influx of wounded with Cholera and Typhus. Miss Nightingale tends to the worst of them herself. We have lost three nurses and seven doctors who took ill only last week. Miss Nightingale and Mrs. Bracebridge tended the nurses through it. Miss Nightingale took on two of the doctors herself, but even they have succumbed to the sickness. We are doubling our efforts at sanitation, trying our best to keep the illnesses contained so as not to lose the entire hospital to them.

Through it all, Miss Nightingale is ever present. There were five soldiers who came in a few days ago that the surgeons determined were too weak for surgery. Miss Nightingale took them in hand and nursed them day and night. This morning, every one of them was declared strong enough to withstand the surgeries they need. She is an angel and tyrant, all rolled into one.

With the exodus of the six nurses and the departure of those doctors and nurses who died, you can imagine we are very short of hands, so I must keep this brief. I pray all is well with you.

Your loving daughter,
Lucia
January 6, 1855

Mr. Whitley pulled and stretched the young sergeant's arm, working out as much of the stiffness as possible. Ronald was unaware of any discomfort the stretching usually caused. His mind was elsewhere.

That is, until Miss Rix walked into the room. Then, the orderly's job was significantly more difficult as his patient turned and strained his head to keep his eyes on the pretty nurse.

"Sergeant," he chided, gently, "'twould make me job much easier if ye'd pick a spot to look at and not continually turn yer head from side to side."

Ronald chuckled. "I have picked a spot, Mr. Whitley. Is it my fault if the spot is a certain nurse's face and it keeps moving?"

Returning the chuckle, the older man replied, "There are few more beautiful spots to choose from, I'll warrant, but it's hard to know which direction to stretch yer shoulder if yer head and body keep twisting to see her. Besides, ye need to remember that Miss Nightingale has strict rules 'bout fraternizing."

"Is it fraternizing to gaze on beauty like that?" the sergeant asked, trying to sound innocent.

The orderly shook his head. "Not if ye stick to lookin' and don't get any other ideas in yer head."

He finished the stretches and helped Ronald lay back on the mattress. As he stood up, he glanced up to see Miss Rix approaching them.

"How's our patient, Mr. Whitley?" she asked, smiling.

"He's doin' fine, Miss Rix. All stretched out and seems to be healin' right proper."

"Good. I'll check his bandages. Would you check on the private over there? He says his leg is cramping up."

"Of course." Mr. Whitley moved to do as he'd been asked.

Lucia kept her eyes carefully on her task, but Ronald didn't even try to hide his emotions. He was fully and completely in love with her. That revelation disturbed her and thrilled her at the same time, because she was falling in love with him, too.

She fussed a bit with his bandages, then smoothed his blanket, then handed him water, all the while keeping her eyes averted from his face.

I suppose when love strikes, she thought, it doesn't much care for rank or rules. Still, she must not let their emotions rule the day. There are rules about such things, she told herself sternly.

"That should feel more comfortable," she said, trying to regain some semblance of professional demeanor.

"Thank you," Ronald said simply. He started to reach for her hand, but she stood abruptly and turned to go.

"Won't you stay a bit?" he asked.

She smiled down at him. "Not this time, Sergeant. There are others who need nursing."

Chapter Nine

"What's that man's story, Mr. Whitley?" Ronald asked.

"I heard he be on picket when the rest of his picket be killed," the orderly answered.

"Is he going to live?"

"Looks that way. The surgeon trepanned him and he seems to be doin' better."

"What's that mean?"

Mr. Whitley looked up. "Trepanning is where they burr a hole into his skull to relieve the pressure. Usually, that's all it takes to start healin' from a blow to the head."

"Unbelievable." Ronald was amazed. "I can't wait to hear his story."

"Me, too."

A few hours later, another soldier was brought in. As he was laid on the mattress, he looked around. Seeing the soldier with the battered head, the soldier asked, "Is he going to be all right?"

"So they tell me," Ronald answered.

"I'm glad. He's a real hero!"

"Oh?"

"He stumbled into camp last night carrying a man on his shoulders, and then fell down insensible. They say his entire picket was killed except him."

"I heard that, too. I think there's more to this story than we know," Ronald mused.

That evening, the soldier began to come around. Lucia was

instantly by his side. "Take it easy, soldier. You're going to be fine, but you need to lie quiet for a while and let your head heal."

"Is he alive?" the man mumbled.

"Your comrade? Yes, indeed! He's alive. It's Lieutenant General Brown," she answered, smiling.

At that moment, the lieutenant general, though badly wounded, appeared at the man's bedside.

Looking up, the soldier tried to smile. "Oh, General Brown, sir, it's you I brought in, is it? I'm so glad. I didn't know, sir, but if I'd known it was you, I'd have saved you all the same."

Chuckling, the general nodded. "That is the true soldier's spirit, my boy. Thank you for saving my life!"

Ronald shook his head. That's a story for my grandchildren, he thought. That thought made him start to wonder if his children would have his red hair or the jet-black hair of their mother. Then, realizing where his mind and heart were taking him, he shook his head and tried hard to focus on something else… anything else.

Later that night, after lights out had been sounded, Lucia was staring up at the few stars she could see through the small window above her cot. The night was cold, but she didn't feel the chill. Thoughts of a certain sergeant in Ward B kept her mind occupied enough that the winter air didn't affect her. She sighed softly.

"What's wrong, Lucia?" Amy asked from the next cot.

Turning to look at her friend, Lucia smiled. "Nothing, Amy. Go back to sleep."

"I wasn't sleeping," her friend admitted. "I'm too cold. Aren't you cold?"

"No, I'm just thinking."

"About what?"

Looking back at the stars, Lucia answered, "About love."

"What about it?"

"About what it feels like, how does it happen, when it happens, that sort of thing."

"I suppose it happens when the right person comes along," Amy said, irritably.

With a small sigh, Lucia answered, "You're probably right."

After a few moments, Amy looked at her friend suspiciously, "Do you think you're in love, Lucia?"

There was silence for a few moments before Lucia answered. "Maybe. Perhaps not. I don't know."

Frowning, Amy sat up, wrapping the blanket around her shoulders. "This sounds serious. Start talking, friend."

Realizing her mistake, Lucia backpedaled. "It's nothing, really. I'm just being a silly woman who's alone and far from home."

"And?"

"And nothing. I'm just lonely. That's all."

"What's his name?" Amy was relentless, and Lucia knew she wouldn't be able to keep it from her much longer.

"Ronald Ferguson," she finally admitted.

"The red-haired sergeant in Ward B?"

"The very same."

"He's not bad looking, so far as Scots go," Amy agreed. "Tell me what's happened so far?"

"Nothing, really. He gave me a Christmas gift. That's all."

Amy cocked her head to one side. "Sounds like more than that, to me."

Lucia sighed. "Nothing else has happened. I just can't get him out of my mind. When I eat, I think of him. When I work, I think of him. When I try to sleep, I think of him. I just can't stop."

"Well, maybe you'd better try harder," Amy warned. "You know how Miss Nightingale feels about nurses fraternizing with the patients."

"I know. I'll try harder," Lucia promised.

She turned onto her side, closed her eyes, and tried to think of home, Mama, bread pudding, lamb stew, potatoes, carrots, horses, Ronald. Her muscles relaxed and she drifted to sleep dreaming of being carried off by a certain red-haired sergeant on his white steed.

Lucia pressed her lips tightly together, trying to control her emotions. The dressings she was folding took the brunt of her frustration. She hadn't been assigned to Ward B for several days and it was driving her crazy. She had been assigned there every day last week, and this week, nothing.

Lucia had grown quite fond of seeing Ronald every day, and was annoyed that she'd had no excuses to see him since last Sunday. What could she do? What reason might she invent that would take her into his presence again without arousing suspicion?

Finishing the dressings, she placed them in the cupboard, then went on to her next task. It was nearly lunchtime and she needed to check the diets for the men on Ward C. Most of them were well enough to eat whatever the cooks served, but two needed special diets, as they were recovering from belly wounds.

On the way, she met Amy heading to Ward B struggling with two trays of food. That gave Lucia an idea.

"Mrs. Wright, may I help you with those trays? They look heavy," she offered, hoping she sounded innocent.

"Yes, thank you." Amy relinquished one tray gratefully. "I don't know why the cooks insist on loading these trays so heavily. We make at least three trips per ward, anyway. One more won't make that much difference."

"I agree. Maybe we should suggest it?"

Laughing, Amy adjusted the tray in her hands. "Wouldn't do any good. The cooks are all men and they load them as if they were carrying them themselves. They don't think about us poor women who are actually doing the carrying."

"Perhaps you're right. We do the best we can, right?"

"Right. Can you manage that door, Miss Rix?"

"I think so," Lucia replied, attempting to push the door open with her elbow. At first, it didn't budge, then it opened so suddenly she nearly fell over backward. After a moment of awkward juggling, she managed to right herself and the tray, only spilling a little broth from one bowl.

"Nice recovery, Miss Rix," Mr. Whitley commented as he approached and took the tray from her. "I'll take it from here."

Not wanting to leave just yet, she grasped at one last straw. "May

I help you serve, Mr. Whitley?"

"No, thank you," he replied. "Mrs. Wright and I ha'e it well under control."

Fighting to hide her disappointment, Lucia turned to leave, but managed to catch a glimpse of Ronald. He was watching her, and smiled as their eyes met. She returned his smile and reached for the door. As she did, her eyes met Amy's.

"Careful, Miss Rix," she warned. "Don't get too close."

Lucia was unsure how to answer. Did her friend mean it as a warning not to run into her loaded tray, or a warning to stay away from Ronald? She opted for a nod and a non-committal, "I'll be careful. Thank you, Mrs. Wright."

Returning to her own duties, Lucia's mind relived that brief eye contact and smile over and over. Each time, her heart beat a little faster, and the smile on her face grew a little broader. She was extra cheerful to her patients that afternoon, a favor that none of them suspected stemmed from a single look and smile.

Mr. Whitley shook his head. "I can't, Sergeant," he said, his voice wistful. "I wish I could, but it would mean me job and hers if we was caught."

"Then don't get caught," Sergeant Ferguson stated flatly. "Please, Mr. Whitley, I have to see her. She hasn't been on the ward all day and I'm going crazy to catch just a glimpse of her. Besides, it's Valentine's Day and I have a little something for her."

"Perhaps she be avoiding you?" the orderly suggested. "Perhaps she be smarter than both of us and is stayin' away on purpose?"

Ronald sighed. "Perhaps, but if so, don't I have a right to know that?"

The orderly looked down at his shoes. The big toe peeked out a bit at the end, showing the threadbare socks that barely kept his feet from freezing.

Ronald didn't think he wasn't seeing shoes or socks, though. He looked like he was remembering something.

"Have you ever been in love, Mr. Whitley?" he asked, feigning innocence.

The orderly nodded. "I was just remembering when me and my sweetheart were courting, so many years ago. I remembered what it was like when I didn't see her. Minutes seemed like hours and hours seemed like days. It nearly drove me crazy, too.

"In fact, even now, even after she's been dead for nigh onto twenty years, I still feel a little crazy that I can't see her smiling face, feel her soft skin, smell the sweetness of her hair, hear the laughter in her voice as she scolds me."

Ronald tried to be patient as the orderly wrestled with his request. Finally, he looked up and nodded. "All right," he agreed. "I'll give her your note and bring one back if she sends it. But don't ask me to do no more."

Smiling his relief, Ronald agreed. "Thank you, Mr. Whitley. I'm forever in your debt."

The orderly nodded and left the ward. It didn't take him long to find Nurse Rix. She was tending to a soldier in the corridor nearby. He knelt beside her, looking intently at the wounded man on the floor.

"How's he doin'?" he asked.

"He's doing well, Mr. Whitley. Thank you for asking. Is there something I can do for you?"

"Yes, Miss Rix. When you have a moment, I need to confer with you about a certain patient," he avoided looking at her directly, but noticed she tensed just a bit.

"Of course. I'll meet you at the end of the corridor in just a moment."

He nodded and rose, moving between the mattresses on the floor, stopping twice to check bandages on the way. In a few minutes, he saw Nurse Rix moving toward him. She, too, was checking on patients as she went. He nearly chuckled as he thought of how it must have looked if anyone had been paying close attention. Rather suspicious, he thought.

When she reached him, he turned away from the patients in the corridor and leaned in just a little. "There's a man in Ward B that is in pain. He asked me to give you this."

Her face went white as she glanced over her shoulder to be certain no one was listening. She took the paper and put it in her apron pocket without looking at it.

"Thank you, Mr. Whitley. I'll look into as soon as I have a minute," she said, her voice quavering just a little, but her words sounding very professional.

"I'll be here for a few more minutes, if you need me, Miss Rix," he said, looking at her directly for the first time.

She nodded and turned back to her work. He watched her for a moment, and saw her kneel next to a sleeping corporal. Pretending to look under his bandage, he saw her pull the note from her pocket and read it quickly, then stash it back in her apron.

Walking over to a small table, she turned the paper over and scribbled on the back. Folding it carefully, she wandered to a table where Mr. Whitley was stacking bandages. Taking a stack he'd just finished, she slipped him the folded paper. He nodded at her and made his way back to Ward B. Hopefully, the note said what Sergeant Ferguson wanted it to say. The man needed something to smile about.

Long after lights out, Ronald propped himself up on his elbow and looked around. All was quiet. He struggled a bit to stand up, but finally managed. To anyone else, it would look like he was going to the water closet, he hoped. However, instead of stopping at the water closet, he moved a few steps down the corridor to a small door, which led to another closet where the clean linens were kept. Opening the door, he stepped inside.

Nearly half an hour later, the closet door opened and he slipped out, closing it behind him. He nearly stumbled, but finally made his way back to his ward and bed. He did not see the shadow that ducked behind the door at the end of the hall.

However, a few minutes later, two eyes narrowed in anger as they observed the closet door open again as they recognized the blushing, dark-haired nurse exiting, then moving in the opposite direction towards the nurses' quarters as she tucked something into her apron pocket. Ducking quickly into the corner, the blushing nurse was as oblivious as the sergeant had been to the fact that they had been caught.

Chapter Ten

Dear Mama,

Happy Valentine's Day! I know you won't get this until long after, but I want to celebrate this year. The reason this year is different is that a sweet sergeant gave me a hand-drawn valentine. He did the artwork himself and it is delightful. He even created a word play with my name. He's sketched a soldier smiling at a nurse. The caption reads, "Hey Luscious! Want to be my Valentine?" It made me laugh.

Try not to worry, Mama. I know the rules about fraternizing with the patients and have no intention of letting things get out of hand with this sergeant or any of the other men I treat. It's just nice to be remembered on the day set aside for lovers, isn't it?

Thank you for the supplies you and the Ladies' Club have sent to us. They arrived yesterday in good order, and will be put to good use immediately.

Everything here is much the same. More wounded arrive each week and we do what we can for them. It is difficult with so many patients and so few medical staff. Miss Nightingale is working herself into an early grave, I fear. I overheard Mr. Bracebridge telling his wife, "We cannot prevent her self-sacrifice for the dying. She cannot delegate as we could wish; but the cases are so interesting and painful; who could leave them once taken up? Boys and brave men dying who can be saved by nursing and proper diet."

He's right, of course. We all work hard and try to do our best for them, but none of us can equal the care and attention of Miss Nightingale.

You mentioned in your last letter that you've suffered storms and extraordinary winds in London. The weather here is cool, but not too cold, for which we are eternally grateful. Our poor patients have enough to suffer without suffering from the cold, as well.

Miss Nightingale visited the hospital at Balaclava last month. Upon her return, she praised the medical staff here at Scutari. She said it was a pleasure to work with professionals who keep petty bickering out of the hospital. Rumour has it that she's written a letter to Lord Raglan on the subject. As for myself, I'm grateful for the nurses and orderlies I work with here. Each one has put forth their best efforts to care for the poor soldiers who need us so badly.

I understand that there is much debate among the High Society folk in London regarding the coming Season. I hope that this year they keep it simple, out of respect for the men fighting here, and the women waiting for them at home.

I, for one, am glad to be here, doing what I can for them.

I hope all is well with you.

Your loving daughter,
Lucia
February 14, 1855

"Mr. Whitley," Ronald motioned for him to come closer.

"Yes, Sergeant. What can I do for you?"

"I haven't see Miss Rix for several days. Is she all right?" he asked.

The old pensioner hesitated. "She's been feeling a bit ill, and rather than expose the patients, Miss Nightingale has ordered her to bed until she's feeling better."

Ronald frowned. "What's wrong with her? Can I help?"

"I couldn't say," the orderly hedged. "I don't think there's anything you can do, but I'll be happy to ask, if you like."

"Please do." Ronald was frustrated. He had freely admitted to himself that he was in love with this dark-haired angel and it pained him that she was suffering while he lay here, helpless on his mattress.

Mr. Whitley nodded and moved on to the next patient.

Later that afternoon, Ronald found himself sitting in the small reading room, staring out of a window, not really seeing what was on the other side of the frosty glass. Instead, he was seeing a scene from long ago.

There were trees, flowers, and green fields beyond the stone wall that surrounded the front yard of his grandmother's small house. That scene usually brought him peace and contentment, but not today.

The doctor had just left after examining his grandmother. He hadn't said a word, just looked with pity at the thirteen-year-old boy and with a slight shake of his head, he'd departed. Ronald watched him go, then looked down at his hands.

What would become of him now? He'd seen enough death in his life to know that it always meant change.

It changed when his father had died during the plague. He and his mother had moved in with her parents.

It changed when her parents had been killed in an accident during the awful fog of 1833. His mother had never quite recovered. The bank had taken the farm and they'd moved in with his father's parents.

It changed when his mother died two years later. He was convinced it was from a broken heart. Some days, he wished he could die of a broken heart. His heart was certainly broken enough, he thought.

His father's parents were kind, and his grandfather had tried to teach him how to farm, but Ronald wasn't patient enough for farming. He wanted adventure and excitement, as most boys do in their preteen years.

Then, it changed again when his grandfather died. It was just he and *Seanmhair*. They were happy, mostly.

Young Ronald's desire for adventure had caused him to get into a few scraps, which in turn caused her a few tears, he knew. Now, he wished he could take them all back. She was dying and he didn't want her to go.

With a heavy sigh, he stood up and went into her room. She was lying on the bed, looking so small and frail under the hand-woven blankets. He could feel the tears welling up in his eyes and he fought hard to blink them back. After a couple of gulps and several deep, shaky breaths, he finally felt he was under control.

He stepped to the bed and knelt beside it, taking the tiny hands in his. He marveled that his hands were larger than hers, even at thirteen. Lifting her hand to his lips, he brushed it softly with a tender kiss. She squeezed his fingers and he looked up to see her watching him with those ever-kind blue eyes.

Her eyes were always filled with affection for him, no matter what trouble he'd just caused. Yet now, the depth of her love was brimming over and touched him deeply. He could no longer hold back his own tears. Putting his head down next to hers, they cried softly together for what seemed like an eternity.

When his tears were spent, he lifted his head and saw her eyes were closed. Not wanting to disturb her, he started to place her hand back on the blanket. Her grip tightened. He looked back at her face and was surprised at her expression.

"*Seanmhair*, why are you smiling?" he asked, incredulous.

"Because you are a fine boy growing into a fine young man," she whispered.

He dropped to his knees again and whispered back, "You never told me that before."

Her smile broadened. "Because I didn't want your head filled with overly grand ideas about yourself. You needed to learn to think of others first. And you have." Suddenly, she looked serious. He leaned in to hear her whisper. "Go find Mr. MacConaill. He has a farm on the other side of the county. He is a good man and has been a good friend to your *seanair* and me. He's already agreed to hire you as an apprentice. That will earn your room and board and teach you what you need to know to survive in this world."

Her face reddened as she fought to keep back the coughing that threatened to consume her. Ronald waited for the spell to pass, hoping it wouldn't take her last breath. It didn't. As she lay weakly, recovering, he stroked her white hair.

"I'll do as you ask, *Seanmhair*," he promised. "I'll make you proud of me!"

"I am already proud of you, Ronald," her voice was barely audible.

She raised her hand to caress his cheek, took a slow, deep breath, and let it out with a smile. Her eyes closed. He watched her, waiting for her next breath, but it didn't come. Ronald was amazed at how peaceful she looked lying there, as if she was simply asleep. He imagined she would wake up any moment and ask why he wasn't milking the cow or feeding the chickens, but she didn't. She just lay there, looking peaceful, unmoving.

Ronald sat beside her, not noticing the shadows growing long in the room. It wasn't until the room was so dark he couldn't see her face anymore that he finally moved. He took two coppers from the box on the table and placed them on her eyes. He leaned down and kissed her forehead, barely noticing that it was already cold to his touch. He knew he would always remember the chill of that final kiss, and the chill that filled his heart in that moment. Love was too painful. Loved ones always died, so perhaps, love needed to die, too.

That moment changed Ronald Ferguson. He had kept his heart locked tightly away ever since so he didn't have to feel the pain of loss again. That is, until now. Nurse Rix had found the key to the lock and had opened his heart wide, letting love flow in and fill him once again.

Blinking rapidly to force the tears back, the sergeant took a deep breath. Grief was no stranger, but he couldn't bear the thought that the sweet nurse lying upstairs might be another victim to that enemy called Death. He looked around and saw an orderly leaning against the doorway.

"Orderly?" he called.

"Yes, Sergeant?"

"Would you find Mr. Whitley for me?"

"Of course."

A short time later, Mr. Whitley entered the reading room. He looked around, spotted Ronald, and made his way between the soldiers lounging on the chairs and floor reading.

"How can I help ye, Sergeant?" he asked.

Ronald motioned for him to come close. Then he whispered, "I need to see Miss Rix." His voice was adamant and full of emotion.

Mr. Whitley pulled back and examined Ronald's face. He shook his head slowly. "I dinna ken how we can do that," he said softly.

"Please," Ronald begged, still whispering. "I can't lose her, too! I need to see that she's going to be all right."

After a long moment, the orderly shook his head. "I'm sorry, Sergeant. It dinna be possible. Just try to be patient."

Nodding, the sergeant sighed. He would try to be patient, but patience wasn't his strength.

In the Nurses' Quarters, Lucia Rix was tossing and turning. Her skin was alternately hot and sweaty or cold and clammy. It felt like tiny bugs were crawling all over her skin. Her stomach hurt and her head felt as if it were going to explode.

She had to ask for help to go to the water closet, and when she was there, it seemed the diarrhea would never stop. She had no appetite, even for the easy-to-digest delicacies that came from the now well-organized kitchen. When she did force herself to take a few bites, it generally did not stay long in her stomach.

Amy and the other nurses took turns taking care of her, making sure they followed Miss Nightingale's instructions about washing their hands and keeping things as sanitary as possible. Amy was worried. It seemed she could see Lucia growing thinner by the day. She was very dehydrated already and there didn't seem to be an end in sight.

"How is Miss Rix?" Amy jumped as Miss Nightingale seemed to appear out of nowhere.

"Frankly, I'm worried," the young nurse answered, looking back at her friend. "She hasn't been fully conscious for several hours. She tosses about as though she can't get comfortable, and doesn't respond when spoken to. She's losing fluids rapidly and her weight is dropping dramatically. I'm afraid she's not going to make it."

Miss Nightingale stepped up and took Lucia's pulse. She lifted her eyelids and looked into each eye, then felt the back of her neck. Pursing her lips, she nodded.

"You may be right, Mrs. Wright, unless we intervene."

"Intervene? How?"

"It's a new method I've just heart about. A doctor in Finland has tried it with some success. It's called subcutaneous hydration."

"Subcutaneous... that's under the skin, isn't it?" Amy asked.

"Yes. In most cases, fluid is injected under the skin to be absorbed by the body more rapidly than more conventional methods. However, Miss Rix is going to die unless we do something more aggressive."

With that enigmatic statement, she turned on her heel and left the room. She returned a short time later with a surgeon in tow.

"I tell you, it can't be done!" the surgeon insisted.

"I tell you, it must be done or this nurse will die," the lady chief's voice was calm but firm. Amy recognized that tone. It meant that no matter what anyone said, Miss Nightingale would not be swayed.

The surgeon examined Lucia and clucked his tongue thoughtfully. When he spoke, it was with reluctant agreement. "I'm afraid you are right, Miss Nightingale. This nurse is dying, and she's dying rapidly. Prepare her for surgery."

As the surgeon was leaving, Amy looked up and asked, "May I observe?"

"Yes. It may save more lives if more people know about this technique."

Half an hour later, the surgeon returned. Lucia was lying on her stomach, eyes closed, her back laid bare, several layers of towels under her and surrounding her, with a pile of clean towels nearby. There were several pans of water that had been boiled and cooled on the floor. Next to the cot lay a tray with a scalpel, some soft, clean cloths, and a bowl with a syrupy substance in it.

The surgeon knelt on the floor with Miss Nightingale beside him. He took the scalpel she handed him and cautiously cut the skin across her shoulders from blade to blade.

Amy swallowed hard and forced herself to watch. She noted that he cut only the skin layers, and a bit into the fatty layer, carefully avoiding the muscle underneath. Once the long cut was made, he began pulling the skin back slowly, severing the fibers where it was stubbornly refusing to peel away. The moment he'd pulled back enough to make a sizable pocket between her shoulder blades, he nodded to Miss Nightingale.

She took the first pan of water and slowly poured it into the pocket of skin he'd just made. They watched as the fat and muscle gradually absorbed the water like a dried-out sponge, pouring more in as the water level dropped. When the water level was stable, with a thin layer of fluid lying on top of the fatty tissue, the surgeon carefully lay the skin back in place. Miss Nightingale held it in place while the surgeon applied the syrup to the incision with a cloth.

"The next couple of hours will tell the tale," he commented. "Continue the intestinal hydration treatments, and when she wakes up, try to get her to drink sips of water. As much as her stomach can tolerate."

"Understood," the lady chief replied as she stood up.

"Miss Nightingale," Amy asked when the surgeon had gone. "What was that syrup the surgeon applied?"

"Collodion. It's made from gun cotton soaked in ether. We've found it adheres more firmly than adhesive plasters on large wounds. It dries almost instantly forming a 'second skin' which keeps the water where we want it and keeps dirt out of the incision."

"Amazing," the nurse shook her head. "Simply amazing."

Turning to Amy, Miss Nightingale spoke softly, "Stay by her, Mrs. Wright. Don't let her try to turn over until all the water has been absorbed. Watch her closely and apprise me of any change."

Amy nodded as the lady chief left. She cleaned up the area, disposing of the wet and bloody towels, praying that this extreme measure would save her friend.

Chapter Eleven

"Mr. Whitley, it's been more than a week. Why can't you get me in to just see her?" Ronald was feeling desperate. "Even a quick peek from the doorway would help."

With a heavy sigh, the orderly tried to explain once again. "She is recovering in the nurse's quarters. Men are not allowed anywhere near there. There is simply no way to get you there without being seen."

"Doesn't she come out for walks? You've made me walk the halls often enough," his voice showed his frustration.

Mr. Whitley smiled patiently. "I know it's frustrating, but she will be returning to duty soon enough. You'll just have to be patient until then."

Ronald scowled and let out a little harrumph. "Patience has never been one of my virtues, Mr. Whitley."

"Then this is a perfect time to cultivate it, don't you think?"

Resisting the urge to throw something at the retreating back of the orderly, Ronald lay back and stared at the shadows dancing on the ceiling. He had to see her somehow. His imagination was running wild with him. He had to see for himself that she was healing as Mr. Whitley insisted she was.

As he lay there, an idea began to form. It was hazy at first, then began to take shape. Of course! Even sick nurses had to use the water closet sometimes. Perhaps, if he could sneak up to the corridor where their toilet was, he could hide and catch a glimpse of her if she got up in the night. It just might work.

Ronald waited until after Miss Nightingale finished her nightly rounds before implementing his plan. When he saw her little lamp disappear into the corridor, he slowly sat up, watching closely for any movement from his fellow patients, or from the corridor he was planning to enter. Every inch was painstaking and as silent as he could make it.

After sitting up, he reached for his boots. Looking down at the heavy footwear, he decided stocking feet would be quieter. He stood and was grateful that his hip was healed enough to hold his weight without too much discomfort. Stepping softly, he made his way to the doorway and peered around it into the corridor.

He had a good idea of which direction the nurse's quarters were. Just past the reading room at the end of the corridor was a door that was always shut, except when a nurse was coming in or out. That had to be it.

Each step was torture as it both brought him closer to his desire and at the same time held him back, as he felt the need to walk carefully so as not to trip over the mattresses and wounded soldiers that littered the floor. It wouldn't do to wake one of these sleeping heroes and give himself away.

He was at the reading room door when he heard voices from the other end of the corridor. He tried to disappear into the little alcove created by the doorway, holding his breath as long as he could. The voices came closer and he recognized Mr. Whitley and one of the other orderlies as they checked on each soldier along the corridor. Thank goodness there were no soldiers lying close to the reading room door, Ronald thought.

Step by step, soldier by soldier, the two drew closer and the sergeant grew more nervous. What if they discovered him? He could say he was feeling restless and wanted a book to read. No, that wouldn't work. Miss Nightingale's rules about that were very specific and followed to the letter. No reading after the lights were out. "These brave men need their rest," she'd say.

"I'm going to check on the corporal in Ward C," the second orderly said.

"Fine. I'll finish here and meet you there in a few moments," Mr. Whitley replied.

Taking a slow, deep breath to calm himself, Ronald waited, hoping Mr. Whitley would leave soon. The corridor grew silent and Ronald dared to peek out. He was startled to see the orderly standing two feet away, staring right at him. He gulped, licked his lips, and waited.

After a long, uncomfortable moment, Mr. Whitley stepped close and whispered. "Yer determined to see her?"

Ronald nodded.

Shaking his head at the lunacy of the idea, Mr. Whitley moved toward the closed door and motioned for Ronald to follow. He reached out and pushed the door open a crack, peering into the darkness on the other side before stepping back.

"There's no one in the corridor. If you step inside and feel along the right-hand wall, you'll find an alcove where you can hide and wait. The door to the nurse's toilet is on the opposite wall. Stay quiet enough and you might catch a glimpse of her. But if you get caught, I had nothing to do with this."

Nodding again, Ronald slipped inside the door and felt along the right-hand wall as per his instructions. He found the alcove easily enough and slipped inside it to wait.

It wasn't long before he heard the rustling of someone entering the short corridor. He saw a white-clad figure enter the doorway opposite his hiding place, but he couldn't tell in the dark who it was. He frowned. How would he know if it was her? There wasn't enough light to see specific features. Was this all to be a lesson in futility?

The door opposite opened again and he froze in position, but squinted his eyes, hoping to see who it was. While he couldn't recognize the woman, he saw enough to know it wasn't his sweet Lucia. Lucia had dark hair while this woman's hair was decidedly lighter, yellow or gray, he guessed.

What's more, she moved back towards the large room at the end of the corridor and he realized she'd had no idea he was there. That was perfect. He felt a twinge of guilt as he settled in to wait once again. He wasn't really hurting anyone. Just hoping for a glimpse of his Nurse Lucia so he would know that she was all right.

The next two visitors were disappointing, as well. One was too tall, the other too fat. He stifled a sigh. Would this night end without his goal being realized? If it did, how was he going to get out without being seen? He knew the nurses arose early, but he wasn't certain exactly what time. Maybe he should give up and return to his mattress before he was caught.

Just as he was about to slip out of his alcove, he heard another rustle, but this time, he heard a voice.

"One step at a time, Lucia. You can make it."

Ronald's heart skipped several beats as he realized she was up and walking and he was about to see her. The rustling came closer and closer. He willed himself to melt into the door at his back, to be invisible.

Then, he saw her. Well, he saw two women in white gowns entering the doorway across from him. One had gray hair braided down her back. The other's hair was long and dark. Then they were gone, disappearing into the depths of the water closet.

He held his breath waiting for them to emerge. When they did, his breath caught for a different reason. The dark hair around Lucia's face framed her pale skin so that even in the darkness he could see she was thinner, but she was alive. She was walking.

Ronald smiled and had to fight to resist the urge to race to her and take her in his arms, hold her and promise never to leave her again. He wanted to caress her dark hair and soft cheek. He wanted to pull her close and smell her fragrance. He wanted to…

Suddenly the door from the corridor opened, nearly flattening him as he pulled his stomach in and prayed his feet wouldn't stop the door and give him away.

"How is she?" It was Miss Nightingale's voice.

"Much improved," the other nurse said. "She's visiting the toilet regularly, has started taking in beef broth and soft pudding, and this morning complained that she was hungry."

Both ladies laughed softly.

"Some friends you are," it was his beloved Lucia's voice, "laughing at my discomfort."

"It's just that we are filled with joy at your rapid recovery, Miss Rix," Miss Nightingale reassured her. "Yet the night is not over and you are not cleared to return to your duties, so back to bed with you."

All three ladies moved slowly into the large room. Ronald stayed quiet until he could hear nothing but soft snoring coming from that mysterious chamber. Then he moved slowly towards the door and pulled it gently. It didn't move. Frowning, he pulled harder. It still didn't move. Biting his lip, his eyebrows furrowed, he tried not to panic. Had Miss Nightingale locked the door when she came in? Was he locked in? Was he going to be caught after all?

Stepping away from the door a little, he again took a couple of deep breaths to calm himself. He reached out and tried once more. This time the door moved slightly. That's when he realized his foot had been holding the door closed. He grinned at his own foolishness, moved back a few more inches, and opened the door enough to let himself through. Closing it behind him, he quietly made his way back to his mattress and slipped under the blanket.

He couldn't sleep, though. He kept seeing her face before him, smiling, her eyes dancing, her lips so inviting.

"May I assume you accomplished your mission?" Mr. Whitley asked softly as he knelt beside the sergeant.

Ronald smiled a contented smile and nodded.

"I'm glad. It's a terrible thing to be separated from the one you love." The orderly made a visible show of checking the wrapping on Ronald's shoulder and nodded. "Try to get some rest, Sergeant."

For the first time in two weeks, Ronald Ferguson did just that, dreaming of a dark-haired nurse, who sang like an angel.

Dear Mama,

My friend, Mrs. Wright, told me she'd written to you describing my recent illness. I don't know what she wrote, but let me assure you that I am recovering nicely. Miss Nightingale and the surgeons here are professionals, through and through. They gave me the best of care and I'm sure I'll be ready for light duty in a week or so.

I understand that Tsar Nicholas I has died. Someone said he caught a chill while visiting his troops here in Crimea. While I'm sure the

Russian people are mourning his loss, perhaps it will mean this war will end soon. His successor, Alexander II hasn't been in favor of Prince Menshikov since they lost the battles at Alma and Inkerman. I hope that the new tsar will decide to pull his troops back home to Russia.

Either way, I'll be happy to be back on my feet and helping the poor soldiers who've been wounded in those battles. It will feel wonderful to be of use again.

I hope all is well with you.

Your loving daughter,
Lucia
April 7, 1855

The first time Lucia returned to duty, she was overjoyed to be assigned to Ward B. She would see her sergeant again! It had been nearly two months since she'd contracted the dysentery, and almost seven weeks since her miraculous surgery. She was grateful for the skillful surgeon, and especially for Miss Nightingale's insistence that he try the new procedure on her. The long, red scar along her shoulders would be a constant reminder of God's goodness and mercy.

As she entered the ward, her eyes darted to his bed and her lips turned up of their own accord as he looked up to see her. He smiled back, but didn't immediately look down as he usually did. She broke their gaze as Amy pushed her gently from behind.

"Yer in my way, Miss Rix," she complained playfully. "If you can't stomach the work, then it's back to bed with you."

Laughing, Lucia moved further into the room, turning to examine a nearby patient. She did her work conscientiously, but her eyes kept wandering to a certain sergeant's bed only to find he hadn't taken his eyes off her the entire time she'd been in the room.

She made her way around the room and finally, logically, it was his turn.

"How are you, Sergeant?" she asked, avoiding looking him in the eyes. She began unwrapping his shoulder bandages, but he caught her wrist.

"I'm much better now that I see you," he answered quietly.

Her eyes met his then, and she felt as though the entire world melted away and no one existed except the two of them. She smiled. "I'm glad to see you, too."

"I nearly went crazy when they wouldn't tell me how you were or what was wrong."

She ducked her head. "I was a pretty sick nurse," she whispered.

"So I hear. I don't ever want to be separated from you again, Lucia. I love you! I didn't realize it until you got sick, but I love you."

Lucia's smile faded and her eyes took on a troubled look. "You can't, Ronald. We can't."

"Why not?" he demanded.

"Nurses are not allowed to fraternize with patients," she recited sadly. "It's against the rules."

"Sometimes you have to bend the rules, just a bit. Love doesn't care about rules. It just is. I love you."

Lucia sighed. "Maybe when this war is over…" her voice faded.

Shaking his head, Ronald pulled her close, his breath was sweet on her face. "I can't wait that long. Meet me tonight in the linen closet. Doesn't Miss Nightingale say, 'Proceed until apprehended'? Let's proceed, Lucia."

Lucia pulled back, brushed a stray lock of hair from her face, and looked at him with longing in her eyes. "I'll try," she whispered. She finished wrapping his shoulder efficiently, and then started to stand.

He touched her hand bringing her gaze back to his. "Please, Lucia. Don't just try. I'll be waiting."

Her other hand brushed his as she gathered her things. She smiled at him, then moved on to the corporal in the next bed.

Across the room, another nurse was not fully attending to the soldier in front of her. She had one ear open and one eye watching the scene unfolding at the bedside of a certain red-haired sergeant. Her breath was fast and shallow. Her lips compressed into a thin line. This must not continue, but as of now, it was her word against that of Miss Rix and the sergeant. She'd need proof if she was going to stop this immoral behavior, so she simply listened, watched, and made her plans.

The moon was just peeking over the windowsills when Sergeant Ferguson let himself into the linen closet. He didn't have to wait long before the door opened again and a sweet, familiar scent wafted in. His arms opened to envelope her before she was fully inside.

"Ronald!" she exclaimed, trying to keep her voice low. "Such enthusiasm could get us into trouble."

"Trouble be damned," he chuckled. "Nothing matters when you're in my arms."

She nearly giggled aloud, but pressed her lips together to silence her own exuberance. "I've missed you," she said.

"I've missed you, too."

He pulled her into a long embrace, breathing in the scent of her hair, feeling the soft curves of her body melt into his. Looking down, he bent his head as her face lifted to his. Their kiss was sweet as honey, fanning the flames in their hearts.

Lucia pulled back first, gasping for breath a little as she reached up to stroke his face. "You make me want to forget the world, Ronald."

"Good," he grinned. "Forget it. Nothing exists but you and I, and this moment in time."

He pulled her in for another kiss. She relaxed into him for a moment, then pulled back again.

"That's not realistic," she chided him gently. "We can't keep meeting like this. If we are caught, I'll be sent back to England and we'll never see each other again."

"Then let's get married," he proposed, suddenly serious.

She cocked her head, and shook it slowly back and forth. "Married? I couldn't do that to Miss Nightingale. She's already lost so many nurses to marriage, not to mention those who've died from dysentery and typhus. I made a commitment to serve with her and I intend to honor that commitment."

Ronald frowned. "I'm all for honoring commitments, but where does that leave us?"

With a long sigh, Lucia leaned back and took his hand in hers. She turned it palm down, stroking the back, then down the length of each finger. He closed his eyes, taking in each sensation with deep desire building inside him. Finally, she turned it palm up and brought it to her lips. When her kiss deepened into his palm, his body shuddered as he groaned and reached for her.

She allowed him to pull her in and enjoyed a long, sweet kiss, savoring the taste of his mouth against hers, the safe feeling of his arms around her. Then, once again, she pulled back.

"Thank you for showing me what love is, Ronald," she whispered. "I'll never forget you."

Before he could respond, she had opened the door and taken a step into the corridor. Then he saw her freeze in mid-step and heard her gasp.

"I warned you, Lucia," the unseen voice was harsh. "I warned you not to pursue him. But you didn't listen and now I have no choice."

"Amy, please," Lucia's voice was fading as she followed the older nurse down the corridor. "You don't understand..."

Ronald stood dumbfounded for a few moments, wondering what had just happened. They had shared a beautiful moment. She obviously felt the same way he did, he was sure of it, but she'd said, "I'll never forget you," like they were never going to see each other again. Then that other nurse had showed up and threatened... what? Whatever it was, Ronald was certain it wouldn't be good for either of them.

He stepped out of the closet and saw one of the orderlies waiting for him. He had a smirk on his face that told the whole story. He'd been sent to be a witness and he was going to enjoy telling every sordid detail he could remember or create. Ronald sighed. This was going to be worse than he thought.

Chapter Twelve

The small room was heavy with the silence that precedes difficult conversation. Lucia dreaded what was to come and just wanted it to be finished, but Miss Nightingale continued with her paperwork as if nothing was amiss.

Several long moments later, she looked up. Her grey eyes were deep and sad. Her face reflected her disappointment and concern. She searched Lucia's eyes, seemingly trying to decipher her very soul. Finally, she spoke.

"You know why I've called you here, Miss Rix?"

Lucia nodded.

The lady chief sat back in her chair, toying with the pen in her hands, still watching Lucia's face.

"Our vocation is a difficult one as you, I am sure, know; and though there are many consolations, and very high ones, the disappointments are so numerous that we require all our faith and trust, but that is enough. I have never repented nor looked back, not for one moment. We have rules to keep us safe, regulations to keep the hospital running in an orderly fashion, protocols to help keep the patients comfortable and as happy as we can make them in their terrible afflictions. This vocation requires sacrifice; some sacrifices are easy, others are quite difficult, and some... some feel impossible."

She looked at the pen in her hands absently. "We cannot dictate the whims of the heart. Of that, I am keenly aware. However," she looked up and her gaze was so intense that Lucia wanted to sink through the floor, "we can dictate our own behaviors. The actions whereof you have been accused, should they be true, show willful disobedience and indicate a deliberate lack of respect for this hospital, the patients we serve, your fellow medical staff, and myself. I will ask this only once. Whatever you tell me, I will believe because I know you to be an honest woman. Have you been fraternizing against regulations with," she looked down at the paper on her desk, "Sergeant Ronald Ferguson?"

There was no hesitation on Lucia's part. "Yes, Miss Nightingale, I have."

Miss Nightingale sighed and placed the pen on the paper, then sat back and folded her hands in front of her. "What would you have me do, Miss Rix? I understand that your heart has overtaken your senses. Women... and men... often make foolish decisions in times like these. While your actions are not directly harming anyone here, they do set a terrible example for the younger nurses. They disrupt the patients who can overhear your whispered conversations. They have, I am sure, distracted you from your own work. How can you keep your mind on the task at hand if you are mooning over the patient across the room, however handsome and wonderful he may seem to you in this moment?"

She paused a moment before continuing. "You are an excellent nurse, Miss Rix, one of my best. I have come to value and trust your instincts and your work ethic. You have a calming demeanor and an efficient way of handling the patients. However, as much as I would like to look the other way, I cannot. Sergeant Ferguson is not yet ready for discharge, so I have no alternative but to discharge you and send you back to London. I want you to know I hold no animosity toward you, and wish only the best for your future."

She looked at an open ledger by her right arm. "The HMS Amphion is sailing on Tuesday afternoon. Pack your personal belongings tonight. I will arrange for you to stay at the hotel until your boat sails. As of this moment, you are no longer part of the nursing staff here at Scutari."

The lady chief stood, indicating that the interview was over. She held out her hand and Lucia took it. "It's been a pleasure working with you, Miss Rix."

Lucia was in shock. She'd suspected this would be the result when Amy told her she was going to inform Miss Nightingale of their clandestine meetings, but to have it so sudden, and so final, was still a shock to her mind and heart. Tears filled her eyes as she turned to leave. Stopping at the door, she looked back and asked timidly, "May I tell him goodbye?"

Miss Nightingale looked up. Her face softened. "Yes. You may have ten minutes, supervised, in the morning after breakfast has been cleared away."

"Thank you," Lucia could barely choke out the words before her emotions overtook her.

She stepped out and closed the door softly behind her, then leaned against it, fighting to regain control. She didn't want anyone to see her fall apart. She needed to find a quiet place to mourn in solitude. There was a storage room on the upper floor above the kitchen. The noise from the kitchen would mask her sobs, and the items there were seasonal, so it was unlikely anyone would disturb her.

Keeping her teeth clenched and her head high, she walked with deliberate swiftness, hoping others would see her haste, assume she was on an important task, and not try to delay her. It nearly worked.

She passed the traitor in the corridor just outside the kitchen. Amy looked at her coldly and asked, "Have you seen Miss Nightingale, then?"

Lucia nodded and clenched her fists, willing them to stay at her sides even though she knew scratching this woman's eyes out would do much to alleviate the volcano welling inside her.

"And...?" Amy prodded.

Lucia swallowed hard, opened her mouth, then closed it again as the tears that were so close threatened to overtake her. She shook her head and turned away.

"Did she dismiss you?" Amy was relentless. "Or is she going to ignore your behavior because you're her favorite?" Her voice dripped with disdain.

Incredulous, Lucia turned slowly back to look at her former friend. "What?"

"Everyone knows it," Amy tossed her head. "Miss Nightingale likes you best."

"Why do you think that?"

"She always confers with you about the patients' well-being. She gives you the best shifts. You got the cot under the window. She tended you more than any of the other nurses when you were sick. You were the one who got the special surgery. None of the others did. She never asks the rest of us what we think about a patient's protocol or emotional state. She never asks the rest of us about scheduling shifts or patient's special diets. You are the favorite. Admit it."

Shaking her head in disbelief, Lucia started to deny the allegations, but Amy wouldn't let up.

"You, the one she hand-picked from the Institute for Gentlewomen where you worked together for... how many years? You, the pampered, favored daughter of a wealthy merchant. You, who know nothing about real poverty or want. You, who can't begin to imagine how hard the rest of us have worked to get where we are. You, who think you can flout all the rules just because you want a little playtime with a handsome sergeant. Well, no more, Miss Rix." Her voice rose and became shrill with the jealousy she'd suppressed for so long.

Tears ran unheeded down Lucia's face. She'd had no idea that Amy felt that way. She thought they'd become friends, good friends, during their service here. Yet all along, this seemingly sweet older woman felt such deep jealousy for Lucia and what she perceived she had. It was more than Lucia could bear.

"I'm sorry, Amy," she whispered. "I had no idea..."

"Save it!" Amy screamed. "I don't want to hear your simpering mock apology. I don't..."

"Ladies!" Mrs. Bracebridge's voice was sharp, cutting Amy's tirade short. She stepped toward them and took each by an elbow, steering them into the kitchen and through it to the back door. After closing the door behind them, she turned and faced the two women.

Amy started to open her mouth but Mrs. Bracebridge raised a warning finger, silencing her. She looked at Lucia, who had no intention of saying anything.

"I have only two things to say to the two of you," she began sternly. "One, you will never raise your voices in this hospital again.

We have patients trying to heal, nurses trying to attend them, and doctors trying their best to save them. None of these people need to listen to two childish women wailing at each other like cats in heat. Second, you each have someplace to be, don't you?" She waited until each woman nodded.

"Then be on your way there now."

Amy stepped inside first, her face flushed with rage, her fists clenched. She stormed through the kitchen, bumping into several cooks, and knocking over two trays as she went. She didn't slow down, but steamrolled her way back into the corridor.

Lucia followed more slowly, trying to keep her expression passive, but her very posture telling of the deep sorrow and humiliation she felt. She stopped and helped the cooks gather the trays, plates, and utensils. She reached for a fork that was lying a little behind her and brushed a hand that was reaching for it at the same time.

She looked up into the deep blue eyes of Mrs. Bracebridge. She pulled back and looked away. She felt the woman's hand under her chin, lifting her face. When their eyes met again, Lucia could no longer keep control. Tears flowed freely again as she tried to pull away, but the older woman wouldn't have it.

She pulled Lucia into her ample bosom and held her close while she sobbed, taking no heed of the hustle-bustle of the kitchen that had resumed all around them.

At the first sign that the sobs were ebbing a little, Mrs. Bracebridge pulled her handkerchief from her pocket, handing it to Lucia. "Dry your eyes for now, child. I can see there will be many tears to come, but for now, let's find somewhere a bit more private."

Lucia allowed herself to be led to the little alcove that Mrs. Bracebridge used for an office. Sitting on the stool she was offered, she kept her eyes lowered, trying to maintain what little control she had recovered.

"Would you like to tell me what this is all about?" Mrs. Bracebridge asked kindly.

Shaking her head, Lucia mumbled, "It wouldn't help. I've made a mess of things and nothing can fix it."

"Why don't you tell me and let me see if I can find a way."

Lucia took a deep breath, looked up and the entire story tumbled out, as if the words had such a desire to be told that nothing could hold them back. When she reached the part about Amy's fit of rage, Mrs. Bracebridge held up a hand.

"I was there for that part. No need to rehash it."

"So, you see, there's nothing anyone can do. Miss Nightingale has made up her mind and I don't blame her at all. I'd make the same decision in her place. As for Amy... Mrs. Wright... I had no idea she felt that way. I'm not sure what I could have done if I'd known, but it makes me so sad to know she's harbored such ill-will and I was clueless."

"People can hide their true feelings quite successfully when it suits them," Mrs. Bracebridge observed. "I'll keep an eye on her. As for the other matter, I'll speak with Miss Nightingale and see if we can temper your sentence, or perhaps even commute it for a time. We need you here, and I hope we can find a way to keep you."

"Thank you, but please, don't. That would only prove Mrs. Wright's point, wouldn't it? If you manage to keep me on, she will assume that it's because I'm favored above her. She'll be even more jealous and perhaps cause more trouble than one little yelling match." Lucia looked down at her trembling hands. "Besides, I don't think I can work here anymore. My feelings for Sergeant Ferguson are so strong; it would be too great a temptation for me. I'm certain I'd not have the strength to keep the rules, no matter how sincerely I promised."

The tears that fell this time were ones of resignation. They were slow and deeply sad, but not the torrents of desperate sobs that had racked her body before.

Mrs. Bracebridge watched her for a long moment, then nodded. "As you wish, my dear. If you'd like, I can send a letter of recommendation to whatever hospital you wish to apply to. You will get the highest recommendation from me, and from Miss Nightingale, too, I'm certain."

Nodding, Lucia stood to go. "Thank you. If you don't mind, I need some time to pack and think."

"Of course."

She'd only gone a couple of steps when Mrs. Bracebridge called to her. "Miss Rix?"

Turning, she answered quietly, "Yes?"

"May I offer to supervise your farewells tomorrow morning?"

Lucia smiled through her tears. "Thank you, Mrs. Bracebridge. I can't think of anyone I'd rather have."

Chapter Thirteen

Dear Mama,

I am coming home. I'm sorry to be so blunt, but I didn't know how else to tell you. I have fallen in love with a soldier here and the regulations forbid fraternizing. I know what you must be thinking. "How could you, Lucia?" or "I told you it was a dangerous place, Lucia!" or "What will the neighbors think, Lucia?"

Well, Mama, I could because he's wonderful; kind to animals and people who love them, adamantly against cruelty to them, his touch is gentle, his green eyes express the feelings of his very soul, his hair is rust-red, and best of all, he loves me, too.

Scutari has not been as dangerous as you might have thought. The dysentery was bad, but otherwise, I have been as safe as I would have been at home. The soldiers have all been perfect gentlemen, and my sergeant has not forced his attentions on me. He's been a gentleman through and through.

As for the neighbors, you know how I feel about that. It's none of their business and if they choose to gossip about it, let them. I don't care, and I'm sorry if you do.

I'll be sailing on the HMS Amphion, which is scheduled to arrive in London on May 8. No need to meet me at the dock. I can find my own way home.

Your loving daughter,
Lucia
April 15, 1855

"What am I going to do without you, Lucia?" Ronald's voice shook with emotion. "You have become my world, my everything!"

Lucia raised her chin a bit, took a deep breath and answered, "You will continue to get well, my brave sergeant. You will breathe in and out. You will do your stretches and take your walks. You will eat every nourishing thing they place before you. You will work at healing until you are well enough to leave here. Then you will come to me in London and we will work out the rest of our lives together. That's what you're going to do."

Ronald smiled at her spunky attitude and reached for her hand. "And what are you going to do?"

Looking away to stare out the window for a moment, Lucia looked thoughtful. He knew she'd been avoiding that question, but he also knew she'd have to face it eventually.

"First, I'm going to face my mother and tell her what's happened. Then, I'm going to look for a position at a hospital in London. Then, I'm going to work and sing and wait for my sergeant to come and rescue me."

She looked back at him and smiled through her tears. "And I hope he comes very soon."

He started to pull her to him, then looked over at Mrs. Bracebridge who was standing out of earshot near the reading room door, but he knew she could see everything they did. He appreciated that she'd cleared the reading room for their final farewells, but wished she had cleared herself out, too.

"Does she have to be here?" he asked, irritated.

Nodding, Lucia answered, "Yes. Otherwise we couldn't say goodbye at all." She looked down. "Not that I want to say goodbye."

With a deep sigh, he agreed. "I don't either. I wish you could stay, or I could come with you. I'm afraid I'll never see you again."

Her eyes snapped up to meet his. "Of course, you will. You're going to rescue me from my mother, remember?"

Laughing in spite of himself, he nodded. "That's right. I must save the damsel in distress."

She visibly relaxed and took his hand, touched her finger to her lips and then into the center of his palm, never taking her eyes off his.

He bit his lower lip and repeated her actions. The meaning of that gesture was clear, and his heart longed to take her in his arms and give her a proper farewell kiss.

Mrs. Bracebridge cleared her throat. Lucia looked over at her and nodded. They both knew it was time to go. She turned back to Ronald and tried to smile. "I will see you soon, my sergeant, won't I?"

"As soon as I can arrange it, Lucia *mia*."

The use of her father's language broke down Lucia's final defenses. Tears flowed freely down her cheeks. Without thinking, Ronald pulled his handkerchief from his pocket and handed it to her. She wiped her eyes and gave it back to him. He took it, kissed it, and handed it back. "To remember me," he whispered.

She touched it to her lips and before either of them knew what she intended, she leaned forward, wrapped her arms around his neck, and kissed him fervently. His arms enveloped her of their own accord and he returned her kiss.

Surprisingly, Mrs. Bracebridge waited for a moment before calling. "Miss Rix, it's time to go."

Reluctantly, the two let go of each other and stepped apart. No further words were spoken. They didn't need them. Stepping backwards to keep him in sight as long as she could, Lucia nearly tripped on a chair behind her. Flushed with emotion and embarrassment, she kissed his handkerchief and waved it before disappearing through the doorway a moment later.

Ronald stood motionless for a few moments, unwilling to believe she was truly gone. Then sinking into a chair, he allowed the full impact of his emotions to take over. The tears came unbidden and sobs racked his entire frame. How could one woman have taken his heart so completely in such a short time? He didn't know, but vowed he would work even harder to heal and become strong. He would find his way to London and rescue his damsel, his Nurse Lucia, and marry her.

Meanwhile, in the carriage, Mrs. Bracebridge tried to comfort a sobbing Lucia. "There, there, child. You will see him again, of that I'm sure. He obviously adores you and that kind of love cannot be separated forever. He'll find a way."

Lucia tried to calm herself. Taking several shaky breaths, she held his handkerchief to her nose and sniffed. It had his scent. That threatened to undo her once again, so she placed it in her lap and swallowed hard.

"I want to thank you," she whispered, her voice hoarse. "For allowing us to…"

Mrs. Bracebridge waved her hand dismissively. "Nonsense, Miss Rix. I know what it means to love someone and be required to leave them. That kiss will keep your memories and love strong until you are reunited."

Smiling, Lucia threw her arms around the older woman and hugged her tightly. "Thank you for understanding. I shall miss you."

Returning the hug, the veteran nurse whispered, "I shall miss you, too, Miss Rix."

The voyage home was uneventful. Lucia remained in her cabin for most of the voyage, eating only sparingly, and coming out for brief walks on the deck in the evening. A few of the other passengers tried to engage her in conversation, but her answers were short, followed by a polite request to be excused. It didn't take them long to stop trying.

Once they docked in London, Lucia gathered her belongings, and with her head held erect, her chin high, her jaw set firmly to keep her emotions in check, she started down the gangplank, hoping her mother had listened to her request to stay home. She hadn't.

Near the bottom of the gangplank sat her mother's carriage, complete with her mother standing beside it, handkerchief in hand, and a distraught expression on her face.

Lucia sighed. It was to begin already, then? So be it. She stepped carefully onto the dock and braced herself for her mother's tearful greeting.

Harriet wrapped her arms around her poor, exiled daughter and wept openly on her shoulder. Lucia awkwardly tried to return the hug, but it was nearly impossible with her bags in her hands. Thankfully, the carriage driver rescued her... from the bags, anyway.

After what seemed like an eternity, Harriet eased her hold on her daughter and leaned back to look into her eyes.

"I'm not going to ask what you were thinking, Lucia," she began.

"Good," Lucia stated, "because I don't want to talk about it."

"But," Harriet continued as if she hadn't heard, "we will need to discuss how we want to handle this with the neighbors. They will talk, you know, and we can't have them ruining your reputation with the Season already begun."

Lucia frowned. Was that all her mother thought about? How this would affect her reputation with the elite in Society?

"Mama," she began, but Harriet was turning, linking her elbow with Lucia's, already planning and scheming how to minimize the damage done by Lucia's unwise choices in that wild, dangerous place. Young ladies simply shouldn't be permitted to go to such uncivilized areas of the world, especially when there were unscrupulous soldiers loitering about just waiting for a chance to have their way with them. The very idea!

Harriet chattered all the way home, alternating between mourning her daughter's loss of innocence and plotting how to convince the neighbors that she was perfectly pure and ready to find a suitable husband.

Lucia sat silent, unable to fathom how her mother could so callously disregard the truth, not to mention her daughter's feelings. It was all about Harriet Rix in her mind, wasn't it? Lucia sighed. Her sergeant truly was going to have to rescue her from her mother.

When they arrived home, Harriet had apparently worked it all out and decided they would simply have to host a welcome home party for Lucia. That would dissuade the neighbors from thinking Lucia had been sent home in disgrace, even though she really had.

"Mama, I don't feel like a party," Lucia started to protest.

"Nonsense, Lucia," Harriet would not be dissuaded. "It's the perfect thing to put that ugly business out of your mind and prepare your mind for the gaiety of the Season. Perhaps this year you'll finally find a husband."

"Mama…" Lucia looked into her mother's eyes and saw a dangerous glint she recognized from her childhood. Her mother had set her mind to this and arguing would only cause more trouble for Lucia. She stifled a sigh and tried to smile. "All right, Mama. But can we wait a week so I can recover from my voyage?"

"A week? Certainly not!" Harriet exclaimed. "Each day that passes gives others more opportunity to spread lies about you. Two days. Friday evening will be perfect for your welcome home party. There's much to do but you needn't worry about any of the preparations. I'll handle everything. Take your things up and unpack. Then check your wardrobe for a suitable gown. We must present our best selves now, mustn't we?"

With that, she turned and strode down the hall, calling for the chef, obviously in full hostess preparation mode now. Lucia shook her head and reached for her bags that had been deposited on the floor of the entryway. Before her hand could close around the handle of the largest one, a rather calloused male hand beat her to it. Involuntarily, she gasped and looked up, unreasonably expecting to see a certain red-haired sergeant. Her face fell as she recognized the much older face of the gardener. She recovered quickly.

"Thank you, George," she said sincerely.

"These are much too heavy for the likes o' ye, Miss Rix," his voice was soft and gravelly, and his manner was one of great respect and deference. He nodded and smiled as he lifted her bags and waited for her to start up the stairs.

She smiled back and led the way to her room. There are some things that are nice to come home to, she thought.

Dearest Ronald,

I have arrived safely in London and not quite as safely at home. Not to worry, though. Mama is being her usual self and I haven't forgotten how to stay out of trouble with her; namely, go along with most everything she says. As an example, she's planned a rather elaborate welcome home party for me for this evening.

Her idea is that if we present ourselves (meaning if I present myself) to the public as quickly as possible, that should hamper any efforts at gossip that could affect my (her) reputation for the rest of the Season's events. We all know that the London Social Season is just an excuse for the aristocracy to parade their eligible young ladies in front of the equally eligible young men at so-called charity luncheons, formal dinners, fancy balls, and other equally pretentious social gatherings. If the woman is lucky, she'll be singled out for possible marital bliss. It's a farmer's market for potential wives and I really want no part of it.

I'd rather just slip back into my old routine and let the neighbors say what they will. However, in Mama's home, we obey Mama's rules, so we're having a party. Mama insists I sing at least three songs for our guests during the event. Thankfully, I am in fair voice, and am looking forward to that portion of the party, anyway. I have only been home four days, and already Mama has me scheduled to perform at four other events.

I hope you won't misunderstand. I don't mind performing. It makes me happy to sing. I just hate that Mama has set her hopes on finding me a husband at one of these events. I've tried to explain about us a hundred times, but I don't think she understands... or maybe she doesn't want to, but don't worry. It's a tough job, but I can handle Mama.

I'm almost afraid for you to come to London, though, especially during the Season. There are so many pretty young women that are coming out this year. I'm afraid one of them will turn your head and I'll be left a lonely spinster, singing for my supper until I can no longer carry a tune. Perhaps you had better wait until the Season is over. Then I won't have to worry so much about the competition.

I will say the gowns they are wearing this Season are something to behold! Those skirts must have at least twenty yards of fabric in them. I don't know how they can even dance in them. Again, I hope you won't misunderstand. I do enjoy dancing, although not as much as I enjoy singing, but with a skilled partner, dancing can make the world and its troubles disappear for a few fleeting moments.

I never thought to ask before, but do you dance, darling? I mean, did you dance before your leg was injured? If you did, I'm sure it would come back to you very quickly, especially if I was the one in your arms. And if it didn't, who would care? Being in your arms with music in the background would be enough for me.

You told me when I left that I was to take good care of myself. You'll be happy to know that Mama has made that a bit easier. She's hired a personal maid to help take care of me. She says it's so I'll have someone to help me dress and style my hair for all the events this Season.

Personally, I think it's so she'll have someone to spy on me. Not that there's anything to report, except that I'm forever mooning over a certain handsome sergeant. It's not so bad, though. Susan is a sweet young girl who is very attentive, but seems to understand my need for privacy, too.

I've decided to find something to keep myself busy. I plan to seek a position at a hospital here in London. I can't see myself waiting around, playing to Mama's vanity by focusing solely on Society's opinion of me.

I hope this finds you in good spirits and well on your way to recovery. I look forward to the day when you will grace my doorway with your presence.

Ever yours,
Lucia
May 11, 1855

"Mama, I don't understand why we have to host a luncheon. My lovely welcome home party was a great success and the Season is already well underway."

"Lucia, you know as well as I that Mrs. Potter has been spreading rumours about you already. Mrs. Smythe told me that she heard Mrs. Billings say that you are no longer pure and thus unfit to be considered an eligible maiden this Season. With those kinds of rumours going around, we can't take any chances. We must nip this in the bud, Lucia. Therefore, a luncheon to quell any suspicions is just the thing. You will sing, of course, and I will mingle, spreading my own version of the truth, even though we both know what the truth really is." She gave Lucia a stern frown. "Mind you don't ruin everything by even thinking about that awful soldier in Scutari. He is good and well out of your life."

During her mother's tirade, Lucia caught her breath and tried to control her temper, but at the word "awful" being ascribed to her dear Ronald, she lost control.

"His name is Ronald," she growled through gritted teeth, "and he is not awful. He is a wonderful man, a sergeant with the Scots Greys cavalry, and I intend to marry him." Her voice rose with each sentence, but she avoided yelling, even though she wanted to yell, scratch, hit, bite, and kick her mother in the shins.

Harriet's face darkened. Her voice became shrill and grating. "Lucia Grace Rix! You will never, ever entertain such a thought again. That man will never come close to you again, let alone marry you. You will join the eligible ladies this Season, and you will find a suitable husband this year. Enough of this. I want you to be sure you are dressed appropriately for the luncheon, and practice at least four songs for the event. Now run along. I have much to prepare."

With that, her mother turned on her heel and marched purposefully away, avoiding any more argument with her daughter. Lucia sighed, shook her head, and dutifully went to her room to decide what might be "suitable."

Chapter Fourteen

The next event of the Season was an afternoon tea, a coming out party for the Bakers' daughter. Harriet insisted that Lucia be invited to sing, although this neighbor wasn't elite enough for her daughter to be "a real debutante" and so she wouldn't be presented to the Queen. This was an unofficial coming out by Mama's standards, but Elle would have a better chance at raising her station in life by enduring this ordeal and those that would follow in the coming months.

"It's good practice," Harriet said. "Besides, there will be several eligible young men attending and we must take advantage of every opportunity, mustn't we?"

Lucia chose not to reply. She just nodded her head as if she agreed. She enjoyed singing, but had no interest in any "eligible young men" who might attend. Susan helped her dutifully don a blue brocade gown with its delicate lace and ribbon trim. Truthfully, she didn't mind this gown.

The full bell skirt accentuated her naturally tiny waist and she felt pretty wearing it. She didn't have to bother with a corset, but the fullness of the skirt troubled her. It seemed such a waste of material for one dress. In fact, she wouldn't be surprised if two decently sized dresses could be made with not much loss of volume.

The day of the tea was warm, but not hot, thankfully. As they walked the short distance to the Bakers' home. Lucia raised her face to the sun and imagined Ronald walking beside her instead of her mother, who rambled on about proper deportment and wondered which young man would be interested in Lucia.

Elizabeth Baker was a petite young woman, with a sallow complexion and limp hair that refused to remain in the elaborately coiffed style of the day. As she descended the stairs, looking like a scared rabbit ready to bolt, Lucia felt sorry for her. She remembered well how it felt to come out to the grand Society crowd and to be presented to the Queen.

She smiled as Elizabeth, or Elle, as she preferred to be called, passed her, hoping it would give the young lady a bit of courage. At least she wouldn't have to go through the ordeal of being presented to the Queen, Lucia thought, recalling her own presentation and coming out.

On the day of her own court presentation, Lucia wore a white evening dress with short sleeves and a train that she had to hold on her arm until she was ready to be presented. Her arms and hands were covered by long, white gloves. She had a veil attached to her hair with three white ostrich feathers and soft, white slippers on her feet. She'd carefully carried her slippers until they were safely inside the palace, so as not to soil them.

Her mother's pearls around her neck felt strange, since she'd not worn jewelry other than the simple cross her father had given her on her eleventh birthday. She was still upset that Mama had insisted on the pearls instead of the cherished cross.

They'd waited with the other debutantes and their sponsors. The young girls whispered to each other as their mothers gossiped together. Mama soon found someone to pass the time with, but Lucia felt awkward and out of place. Finally, it was Lucia's turn. She and her mother entered the Queen's drawing room and Lucia handed her card to the Lord Chamberlain.

He announced her name while a gentleman-in-waiting spread out her train. She didn't start out across the great room at first. She hesitated, awed by the high ceilings with their huge chandeliers, heavy velvet draperies framing the windows, the enormous painted murals on the walls and the lush floral rugs covering the floors.

When her mother gave her little shove, Lucia carefully glided forth toward a group of royal personages, all dressed in richly colored, glittering gowns and uniforms. As she measured each step, she prayed that her steps would be steady, that she would not trip or otherwise disgrace herself or her mother, that she would not fall as she curtsied, that her feathers would stay in place, and then she saw her.

If she was in awe before, it was nothing to what she felt as she approached the Queen, who looked so regal in her green silk gown with all its flounces and lace, and Lucia had never seen so much jewelry on one woman in her life.

The huge brooch at the Sovereign's neck looked like it would tip her over, if she stood up without help. The crown on her head seemed much too heavy for her slender neck. She wore several rings and bracelets, including the one Lucia had heard so much about, the one set with Prince Albert's miniature.

Feeling awed over the Queen's appearance and the regal setting, she had an overwhelming desire to either drop her jaw and openly gape at the sight, or turn tail and bolt. She kept her feet moving forward and her mouth politely closed, however. She made her full curtsy until she was nearly kneeling, then bowed, and kissed the Queen's hand.

As she touched her lips to the hand of the Queen, she wasn't thinking about the power represented by this hand, or the historic decrees it had signed, or the times it had been raised in a gesture heeded around the world. Lucia was wondering how in the world she was going to stand up without falling over. She was hoping she wouldn't run into the doorway or some odd piece of furniture since she couldn't see where she was going. She couldn't look around, because the proper exit was to leave without turning her back to the ruling monarch.

Then, the sign of fealty was over and it was time to rise. Thankfully, Lucia rose without incident, curtsied again to the other royalty present, finishing with one last brief curtsy to the Queen. She reached for her nine-foot train to drape it over her arm and get it out of the way, but she bungled it a little. She was saved by an attentive lord-in-waiting who retrieved it for her and draped it over her arm. Then, step-by-careful step, she backed out of the room.

Lucia noticed the liveried servants posted strategically to help her should she stumble. Although grateful for their presence, she managed to negotiate her exit beautifully with no embarrassing misfortune.

She remembered how relieved she'd been when she successfully backed into the long picture gallery without an incident. She didn't recall the huge, ornate portraits that hung in that hall. All she could remember was feeling weak knees and a pounding heart that she'd pulled it off without incident. She did remember her mother squeezing her arm and smiling proudly at her. That was enough.

After being presented to the Queen in the morning, her mother had insisted they host a tea that afternoon to celebrate. She'd worn the same white gown for her presentation to Society, but this time she held a tiny bouquet sent by her mother's brother, since her father couldn't send it himself.

The bouquet was as big around as an ordinary saucer, and just as flat on top as a saucer placed upside down. The flowers were rosebuds, massed tightly together and arranged in a precise pattern; three pink rosebuds were in the center, around them a row of white violets, around these a single row of the pink roses, surrounded again by violets, and so on for five rows. The bouquet was set in stiff, white lace paper, the stems wrapped in white satin ribbon, with streamers of white and pink ribbons about a quarter of an inch wide and tied to hang twenty inches or so long.

Lucia recalled that her hands were shaking so much, the streamers seemed to dance before her as she descended the stairs to the awaiting guests.

She remembered she'd been more nervous about tripping on her gown and falling down the stairs than she'd been about her exit from the Queen's presence. However, her fears were unfounded as she was so graceful in her descent that Mama had complimented her on it later.

As Elle's guests gathered in the salon after tea, Lucia moved inconspicuously to the front of the room and waited until Mrs. Baker announced her. As she looked at the faces of the guests who were chatting quietly, she couldn't help but wish that Ronald was among them.

When she'd been announced and the guests were quiet, Lucia began by singing "The Old Arm Chair", which always reminded her of him. Her voice was low and throaty, reflecting her emotions as she thought of him. It reminded her of the stories he'd told her of his mother in Scotland.

"I love it, I love it, and who shall dare,
To chide me for loving that old arm chair,
I've treasur'd it long as a holy prize,
I've bedew'd it with tears, and embalm'd it with sighs;
'Tis bound by a thousand bands to my heart.
Not a tie will break, not a link will start;
Would ye learn the spell, a mother sat there,
And a sacred thing is that old arm chair."

When she finished, the guests hesitated for just an instant, then applauded politely.

Harriet stepped up to her daughter and whispered in her ear, "Something a bit more exciting, if you please, Lucia. No more laments."

Sighing softly, Lucia looked up, pasted a bright smile on her face, and started again with "Merry Bells of England". The guests were soon smiling back and seemed to enjoy the lively tune, clapping enthusiastically when the final note faded.

The rest of the afternoon went quickly, with two other performers and a short visiting time after. On the way home, Harriet chided her for her choice of music for the first piece.

"You must be more careful what you choose to sing, Lucia," she scolded. "You want to draw the audience in, not put them to sleep. We're trying to catch the attention of an eligible husband, not chase him away with laments."

Lucia opened her mouth to argue, and then thought better of it. It would do no good, anyway. Instead, she only half listened to Mama. The other half of her brain was focused on her Ronald, wishing he wasn't so far away.

My sweet Lucia,

Words cannot express my sorrow at your departure! It seems nothing holds any pleasure for me now. Food tastes like sawdust, the sun is no longer bright, the moon hides her face, even the birds have refused to sing for missing you.

To make matters worse, I received word that they are shipping me out to a rehabilitation hospital. If we'd known that sooner, perhaps you could have stayed on at Scutari and we would at least have been in the same country with maybe a slim hope of seeing each other from time to time.

Still, it will be good to leave this place. It no longer holds any appeal to me whatsoever. Additionally, I will be good and rid of the smug face of a certain older nurse who shall remain ever nameless to me. She seems to delight in tormenting me with sly questions about my newfound availability, as if I would look her way twice even if I weren't madly in love with you.

You are not to worry about her, though, my love. I am scheduled to leave on Wednesday for the Castle Hospital on the Genoese Heights and will no longer have to endure her insufferable advances. I must admit, however, to entertaining thoughts of leading her on just so she could be "caught" the way she "caught" us. In my opinion, this hospital could do without her "services".

Enough of that. I am anxious to hear how your welcome home party turned out. Has your mother continued to be as difficult as you thought she might be? I hope not. I hope it has been a smooth transition for you and that you will find a position quickly, for I know you are never so content as when you are nursing or singing.

As I read your letter describing your performances this Season, I wish more than ever I could be there to hear you sing, to dance with you, to watch your eyes sparkle in the moonlight. I have done some dancing in my time, but not very much. I enjoy it with someone I like. I'm sure I would thoroughly enjoy it with you.

By the way, who do you think I am? Casanova? I don't even know any other dark-haired nurses, except my sweet Lucia. I'm strictly a one-woman man... one in each town. I'm not serious, darling. I only have eyes for one woman. She has dark hair, brown eyes, and olive skin. She wears a nurse's uniform. Now do you worry about competition? Please don't.

I know we are too far apart to make what I am about to write appropriate, but I must write it or my heart will burst in my chest. Sweet Lucia, I asked you once if you would consent to marry me. The situation then would not allow you to accept my proposal, but now we have no such restrictions, so I will ask again. Miss Lucia Rix, will you do me the honor of becoming my wife?

Meanwhile, I will continue to do my exercises, take my walks, and eat my dinner like a good little soldier, so I can soon be well enough to rush to London to the side of my favorite nurse.

I think of you constantly and have wondered if you are thinking of me. The short time that we spent together was the last time for me in a good many things. You have the honor of being my last kiss since that time by the way. In fact, I expect I shall never kiss another woman again. I can't imagine kissing anyone else but you.

I'll write you again soon, dearest.
Ronald
June 1, 1855

With a deep sigh, Lucia entered the hansom cab behind her mother. As much as she detested many of the Season's events, the Royal Ascot was the worst. She was certain that most the Society ladies had no interest in the horse race at all, but were there to show off their finest attire and their most pompous manners.

It was simply ridiculous, and why Harriet insisted they attend was beyond Lucia's comprehension.

It wasn't that she minded staying with her uncle and his family. They had a lovely estate near Windsor Castle, which would allow easy access to all the festivities. It was four days with a constant parade of events, each of which requiring a different ensemble and had different societal rules and expectations. It was all too tiring, and Lucia would much rather have stayed at home in London.

Harriet was simply thrilled that this year they would be seen in the most influential circles. Because Lucia had performed so beautifully at the Reynolds' garden party last month, Mrs. Reynolds had seen that they were invited to watch the races from the Royal Enclosure. This was such a wonderful opportunity, wasn't it? There would be the most eligible highborn gentlemen in attendance. It was simply too much, wasn't it?

Lucia listened with only half an ear. The rest of her was wishing she could be anywhere but on her way to such torment. The dresses alone were torture enough, not to mention that she would have to wear a hat at all times. She would be required to carry her fan and her reticule and her shawl, and take care that the voluminous folds of her dress didn't get caught on a chair or table or nail sticking out from some board somewhere.

She almost giggled at that. Imagine! The Queen would never allow anything so sloppy as a nail to stick out from anywhere that she might be. That image would take her far that weekend, she decided. When she found herself tiring of the pomp and circumstance of the event, she'd find something ridiculous to laugh about. That's the ticket.

As a result of her determination, Lucia relaxed and did enjoy herself. When she started to become bored, she'd look for something out of place, or overblown, or exaggerated to the point of lunacy. That would take her mind off the insane need some of these people had for showing off their wealth or standing, or whatever they felt brought them power or prestige.

Several times, she caught her mother looking at her with a bemused, almost confused expression. That made her laugh to herself even more. If her mother only knew what she was really thinking.

What Lucia didn't notice was a certain tall, dark-haired man watching her from a distance, but Harriet noticed and was quite pleased.

"Mother!" Lucia was livid. "I've already told you, I'm not interested in having gentlemen callers. I have no intention of making myself available, as you put it. I am in love with Ronald and will be faithful to that love no matter how long it takes."

"I'm sure he's…" Harriet hesitated. "How shall I put this? I'm sure he's a fine man in his own circles, but you and I both know he wouldn't fit in with our Society friends. Besides, you're here and he's so far away. Finally, you don't know that he's ever coming to London and you're certainly not going back to Crimea."

Gritting her teeth to keep from screaming, Lucia growled, "He most certainly is coming to London as soon as he's released from the hospital. We have promised our love to each other and you're not going to dissuade me from that promise. I will sing and attend as many events as you like this Season, providing it does not interfere with my work at the hospital, but I will not entertain gentlemen callers, and that's final."

With that pronouncement, Lucia grabbed her summer cape from its hook, slammed her hat down on her head, and if the front door hadn't been so heavy, she would have slammed that, too.

The sky was blue, with a few fluffy clouds meandering their way from west to east. A pair of turtledoves watched her from a nearby tree, hoping she wouldn't look up and see their nest, while a woodpecker hammered at a tree on the other side of the street. The air was fragrant with summer blooms, which attracted fat honeybees that buzzed incessantly.

Lucia neither saw nor heard the beauty around her. Her world was dark and gloomy. Her sweetheart was far away in who knew what kind of danger, and her mother was determined to pair her with some high society dandy, refusing to allow Lucia to choose her own husband. Her work and her music were all that kept her sane, these days.

With a deep sigh, she rounded the corner and nearly collided with her friend, Jean.

"Oh, Jean!" she gasped, catching her breath and Jean's arm at the same time.

"Lucia!" Jean's greeting sounded surprised and happy at the same time. She pulled Lucia into a firm hug, then pulled back and looked at her critically. "You look terrible," she observed.

"Thank you," Lucia frowned. "Just what I needed to hear."

Shaking her head, Jean's face showed concern. "I don't mean you look sick or anything. You just look... well, angry. No, angry isn't strong enough. You look like you're ready to go to war and run the Russians clear back to Russia all by your little self. Is that an accurate description?"

Lucia chuckled in spite of herself. "Yes, except it's not the Russians I'm currently wanting to run off."

Jean nodded. "Your mother?" she guessed.

"Who else?"

"What's she done this time?"

"The same as always." Lucia fell into step with her friend. "She's determined to marry me off to the richest society fop she can find."

"So, things are over between you and your sergeant?" Jean frowned. "You seemed so perfect for each other."

"We are not over!" Lucia exploded, turning on her friend. "That's the problem. She won't accept that I'm spoken for. I have no intention of allowing her to arrange courtships for me. I am going to marry Ronald and that's that."

Jean backed up a step, raising her hands in surrender. "Slow down, Lucia. I'm not the enemy here. I've been out of touch for a bit and wasn't sure of the situation. Now I know, so let's figure out what to do about your mother."

Sighing, Lucia reached out, taking Jean's arm gently. "I'm sorry, Jean. I don't mean to yell at you. I know you're not the enemy. I just wish my mother wasn't either. I don't know what to do with her."

"Maybe she's the one who needs a husband," Jean offered hopefully.

"It would never work. She's still madly in love with my father and vows she'll never remarry."

"So, if she can vow to not marry, why can't you?"

"I'd have to become a nun for that to work."

Jean raised an eyebrow and looked at her friend pointedly.

"You're not suggesting…" Lucia couldn't believe her ears.

"No, not really, but if your mother thought you would turn to that rather than marry a man she picked, maybe she'd stop trying to arrange a marriage for you."

Lucia chuckled. "Are you forgetting that I'm not Catholic?"

"Oh, right," Jean laughed. "I sometimes forget that not everyone believes the way I do."

"It's all right. I love you anyway."

With that, the two women walked side-by-side for the better part of an hour, discussing this plot and that, dismissing as many as they brought up. In the end, it was decided that Lucia would just have to stand her ground and discourage as many suitors as her mother paraded before her and each would pray in her own way for Ronald's swift release, so he could come to London and rescue her.

Chapter Fifteen

Dearest Ronald,

You will be happy to know that I survived the welcome home party, and even managed to enjoy myself, at least while I was singing. It brings me such pleasure to let my voice ring out and feel the approval of the small audience in attendance. However, let it be known that it will never be as pleasing as your approval when I sang for you in Scutari.

Speaking of singing, I must tell you that your question sent my heart singing the most beautiful song. You asked me again to marry you. How can I answer anything but YES! I know Mama will want an official proposal when you arrive in London, but for now, rest assured that I have eyes only for you, my dear. However much Mama may protest and try to convince me to consider other prospects, I have no desire to spend the rest of my life with anyone but Ronald Ferguson. Mrs. Ronald Ferguson has a nice ring to it, don't you think?

I hope you are settled into Castle Hospital and they are speeding you on your way to recovery, for that is one step closer to our reunion and the lives we will share. I would count the days, but as we do not know how many there will be, it would be a fruitless effort on my part and fraught with disappointment when my imagined number of days proves to be in error.

So, I will instead count the stars in the sky with the idea that you will be looking at some of the same stars. That thought makes the distance a little less intimidating, don't you think?

I do have good news to share. I have a new job. I am working at the Great Ormand Street Hospital in Bloomsberry. It's a relatively new hospital and I already feel I'm fitting in well there. I'm quite relieved to have work again to keep my mind occupied and my hands busy. The days and nights become quite long when I'm missing a certain sergeant so much.

I received a letter from Mrs. Bracebridge and she shared with me some of the comments you made to her about me before you left. I feel quite complimented, darling! You are a very nice person to say such kind things about me. I'm going to have to think of something equally nice to say on your behalf. There are times when I wish I could relive those days in Scutari. Not every day, mind you, just the ones where we were able to share precious private moments, but nice things are seldom repeated, so I'll have to be content with the memories.

Better yet, I'd love to have you here sharing precious private moments with me. For example, right now, I'm sitting comfortably in the garden next to our hawthorn hedge, which has a few lingering blooms. The scent is still heavenly. There is a light breeze blowing, which makes the leaves rustle. It's a very pleasant sound and makes me smile. I'm looking at the Valentine you drew for me. It brings me great comfort. The only thing that would make me feel more comfortable is if you were by my side.

I must say I enjoyed the little drawing of us dancing in your last letter. It made me smile and imagine the day when we can make that little sketch come true.

Jean just came down and we are going for a walk. It's a beautiful evening with almost a full moon. That is quite romantic, I think. Doesn't it sound nice to you, too? The only thing that would make it better is if I were walking with you instead of Jean. I wish you were here to join me for dinner. Maybe we could pack up a picnic and eat in the park? In the summer, we frequently eat outdoors in the garden. It's a nice break from the formal dining room.

I heard a song at a party last Saturday. One of the other guests sang it, "My Bonnie Lies Over the Ocean". I think I'll take a walk to the ocean and throw a kiss in there and pray it reaches you ever so quickly. I would much rather deliver it myself though.

However, I must be content to leave you with all my love and kisses in this letter. I hope that is not too bold of me!

Lucia

June 22, 1855

Lucia held the last note longer than perhaps was necessary, but it felt so good to hear the high note clearly ringing through the room. Besides nursing, singing was her favorite activity, so she didn't really mind when her mother volunteered her to sing at so many events this Season. Those attending seemed to enjoy her music, which was nice, but that wasn't why she enjoyed it. There was something about letting her voice ring out, expressing all her pent-up emotions, both happy and sad, that made her heart swell with joy.

As the last echo faded, everyone stood and applauded loudly, obviously wanting more. Lucia would have gladly accommodated them, but her mother knew the value of leaving an audience wanting. She stood and insisted that her daughter needed to rest her voice.

Almost immediately, Lucia found herself surrounded by admirers, both male and female. After a few moments, her head was swimming with all the compliments and thanks and "Won't you come and sing at my event next week" invitations. This was the part she hated. She always felt closed in, bombarded, almost like a prisoner. It was quite a contrast to the elation she'd felt moments before.

Just when she thought she might lose all control and scream at everyone to just leave her alone, she felt a strong, gentle hand touch her elbow and heard a deep voice, quiet in her ear, "Shall I help you escape, dear lady?"

Her breath caught in her throat and her heart skipped a beat as she imagined her sergeant appearing out of nowhere to rescue her. However, when she looked up, her rescuer was a thin, dark-haired man she didn't recognize. She simply nodded and allowed herself to be led away to a quiet corner where a chair was provided for her.

Closing her eyes, she took a few deep breaths, and then opened them again to thank her benefactor. Her eyebrows shot up when she saw him holding out a beautiful cup of sweet punch. She took it gratefully, and without thinking, drained it in one swallow.

He laughed and she realized she'd just broken several rules of etiquette. Looking around, she was grateful her mother wasn't anywhere to be seen. She smiled up at the amused gentleman before her.

"Feeling better?" he queried.

"Much better," she replied honestly. "I'm afraid we haven't been introduced, however, and I shouldn't be speaking to you."

The young man laughed and motioned to an older woman nearby. "Mrs. Lundlow, would you please introduce me to this beautiful and talented young lady."

Mrs. Lundlow looked from him to Lucia and smiled. "Of course," she agreed. "Miss Lucia Grace Rix, may I present Mr. Gerald Michael Asher?"

Gerald bowed deeply, then turned to the older lady. "I thank you, Mrs. Ludlow. You have done me a great service."

She smiled up at him and replied, "It was my pleasure, Mr. Asher."

Turning back to Lucia, Gerald grinned. "Mrs. Ludlow is our neighbor on the north," he offered by way of explanation as the woman moved away to offer them a bit of privacy.

"I see. She seems delightful." Lucia smiled back at him.

"She is, Miss Rix. Would you care to take a breath of fresh air?" His smile was genuine, and she found herself smiling back.

Nodding her assent, she arose, and they made their way through the crowd to the large double doors leading to the gardens. There were several couples enjoying the lovely trees and flowers, so Lucia felt safe even though she was walking with a total stranger.

They were silent for a few moments, just breathing in the fresh floral scents of early summer. Then Gerald broke the silence.

"Your mother tells me you've been singing all your life?" It was more of a question than a statement, intended to start a pleasant conversation, but at the mention of her mother, Lucia stiffened.

"You've spoken with my mother?" She was careful to keep her voice even and calm.

"Yes, she and my mother were talking in the foyer before you began singing. Mother introduced us and your mother couldn't stop talking about you. She's very proud of you, you know."

Shocked and dismayed at being the subject of conversation, Lucia fought to regain her composure. "Proud of me?" her voice quavered just a bit.

"Oh, yes," Gerald didn't seem to notice her discomfiture. "She spoke very highly of you, how hard you practice, and how generous you are with your talent. Preparing for and singing at so many events must be exhausting for you."

Singing? Her mother was proud of her singing. Not her nursing. Not the time she'd spent caring for soldiers in Crimea, but her voice.

"It's not as difficult as she made it sound, I'm sure," Lucia replied. "I'm more tired after a shift at the hospital than after singing at an event like this."

"Hospital?" Gerald was genuinely confused.

"Yes." Consciously making her voice bright and cheerful, Lucia continued, "I'm a nurse at Great Ormund Street Hospital in Bloomsberry."

"That's amazing. What made you decide to become a nurse?"

Lucia was pleasantly surprised that Gerald didn't seem phased by her chosen occupation. So many of her mother's friends were shocked and dismayed by her choice. Nurses weren't held in the best regard in High Society circles. She answered his questions and told him stories, both of her work in London and in Crimea.

Those stories seemed to fascinate him the most. He listened intently as she described the conditions they'd found, and the efforts Miss Nightingale and her team of nurses took to create more sanitary conditions for the soldiers they treated. Before they knew it, the afternoon sun was sending long shadows into the gardens.

A voice from the house called Lucia's name.

"That's Mama," she smiled. "She'll be wondering where I've

been."

"Oh, she knows." Gerald grinned broadly. "She's been watching us from the doorway for quite some time."

Sighing, Lucia shook her head. "I might have known."

"May I call on you this week?" the young man asked.

"I think not," she answered. "Remember the sergeant I was telling you about?"

He nodded.

"I'm..." she hesitated, not sure how to label their relationship.

"You're in love with him?" Gerald asked helpfully.

Smiling, she nodded back. "Yes. I don't think it would be fair to him if you were to call on me while he's not here to defend his rights."

Gerald laughed. "That sounds fair, but may we speak when I see you at future events?"

"Of course," was her reply. "You are a delightful conversationalist."

"Thank you," he bowed, then took her arm to lead her inside.

July turned out to be hotter than usual. Lucia wanted nothing more than to jump in the water and race the sculls to the finish line, but that would be unseemly and entirely inappropriate, especially during the famous Henley Royal Regatta. It would create quite the scandal, she was sure. Still, it was tempting. She settled for fanning herself to get a little breeze going.

"Stop that!" Harriet hissed.

"Stop what?" Lucia asked absently, watching the sculls glide through the inviting water.

"Your fan." Her mother looked around with pursed lips. That meant she was afraid someone was watching.

Lucia looked at her fan curiously. "My fan?" she asked puzzled.

"You're fanning yourself much too quickly. Have you forgotten that means you're engaged? You'll chase off any eligible suitors with that gesture."

Frowning, Lucia deliberately resumed fanning herself and raised an eyebrow at her mother. "I am engaged, Mama. If my fan tells the world, then I'm thrilled to have another way to announce it."

"Mrs. Rix, Miss Rix, how wonderful to see you again," a deep voice spoke from behind them. "It's a beautiful day for a regatta, don't you think?"

Turning her head, Lucia smiled at Gerald. "It certainly is, although a bit hot for my liking," she replied.

"Why, Mr. Asher, how lovely to see you here!" Harriet gushed.

"Whom do you favor in the Grand Challenge?" he asked conversationally.

"That's the next race, isn't it?" her mother asked.

Nodding, Gerald gestured to the line-up of racers getting ready to start.

"Do you see the blue scull with the men in yellow shirts?

"Yes," Harriet answered, seeming to be enthralled with this conversation.

"That's Josias Nottidge and Albert Casamajor. They are favored in this final race. The red scull to their right is oared by William Short and Edward Cadogan. They are also popular this year."

"How interesting. Whom do you favor, Mr. Asher?" her mother continued.

"Well, to be fair, Josias and I have known each other for years, so I'm partial to his team."

Harriet laughed. "That's understandable."

Lucia watched the interchange with an amused expression. If she didn't know better, she would assume her mother had designs on young Mr. Asher. She was almost flirting with him.

"…think, Lucia?" her mother was asking.

"What do I think about what?" she asked, a bit embarrassed that she'd not been listening.

Frowning, Harriet clarified, "About who might win this race. Whom do you think will win?"

"Oh," Lucia looked out at the racers who were beginning to glide through the water. "I really don't have any idea."

Her mother shook her head, her frown deepening. Her eyes narrowed and she tipped her head deliberately at Gerald, her meaning clear. "Talk to him," her gesture said.

Stifling a sigh, Lucia returned her mother's frown, then looked back at the racers.

"I don't know who will win, but it has to be cooler down on the water than it is up here," she commented.

Gerald looked at her and smiled. "Then perhaps we should find some refreshment? If I may be so bold, I have found that wilted women are something to be avoided at all costs."

Lucia's eyebrows shot up and she almost giggled at the unexpected phrasing.

He returned her smile with a twinkle in his eye.

The racers were just passing them, catching Lucia's attention. "Let's watch the finish of this one, then we'd love to join you in some refreshment," she offered.

"Excellent," he seemed genuinely pleased, and her mother nodded in approval.

When the race was over, he escorted them to the tent that housed the victuals generously provided by the Queen. It seemed everyone had the same idea, however, and the tent and area leading up to it were quickly becoming over-crowded.

"Oh, dear," Harriet moaned. "I'm afraid we've waited too long and must fight the masses if we want anything to eat."

"No matter," Gerald laughed. "My aunt has a summer home near here. I invite you to join us for tea. Aunt Flo serves the most sumptuous sweetmeats with tea, and she's always prepared for unexpected guests."

"Aunt Flo? You don't mean Florence Nightingale?" Lucia blurted out.

Gerald looked puzzled. "No, Florence Asher," he replied.

Disappointed, Lucia nodded, "I'm sorry. When I hear the name Flo, I automatically think of Miss Nightingale."

"You worked with her in Crimea, didn't you?" he asked as they made their way to the carriages.

"Yes," she replied simply. "She's a grand lady and I could see her providing sumptuous teas for unexpected guests. Although, now that I think of it, she's still in Crimea. It was silly of me to assume your aunt would be her. I truly wasn't thinking."

"Don't fret about it," Gerald assured her. "I heard Miss Nightingale has been ill. Are you sure she's still there?"

Lucia thought for a moment. "If I know Miss Nightingale, she'll stay until her last breath, or until the last soldier is discharged for home."

"She sounds like a grand lady. I'm sure you miss working with her."

"She is and I do." Feeling suddenly very sad, Lucia decided she didn't feel like being social. "I'm sorry, Mr. Asher. May we beg off your kind invitation? Perhaps another time?"

Harriet's eyes widened in shock at her rudeness.

"Of course, Miss Rix. Another time, then. I believe this is your hansom?" He acknowledged each woman with a short, gracious bow, then disappeared into the crowd.

Harriet glared at Lucia when they were settled into the cab. "What was that all about?" she demanded.

Looking out the window, Lucia sighed. "I'm hot and tired, Mama. I just want to go home."

"Mr. Asher is a perfectly eligible gentleman and you treated him quite rudely," she seethed.

"I'm sorry, Mama. I'm just not feeling very social today."

"You'll never catch a husband if you allow your little discomforts to get in the way of a perfectly good opportunity," her mother warned.

Suddenly angry, Lucia turned on her mother. "Mama, I am an engaged woman and I don't appreciate you parading me in front of so-called eligible bachelors. Ronald Ferguson is my fiancé, and I wish you would remember that."

"Well!" her mother huffed and turned her face away.

They rode in silence for several miles, each woman staring out of her respective window. Then Lucia heard her mother sniffle. She shook her head with a small sigh. She hadn't meant to hurt her, but it was very frustrating that Mama didn't seem to accept her engagement. Still, Lucia knew she'd have to apologize sooner or later. Better sooner, she thought.

"I'm sorry, Mama," she sounded sincerely contrite. "It must be the heat causing me to be irritable."

Harriet didn't say anything, but reached her hand over and patted Lucia's, nodding.

Well, it was something. Lucia wasn't naïve enough to think this was over, but maybe in time, her mother would accept Ronald as her intended. Maybe.

Chapter Sixteen

My Dearest Lucia,

Happy days are here again! I just got a nice, long letter from that sweet nurse in London who said yes to my proposal. Miracle of miracles! Your answer made me so happy! I've been walking around with a smirk on my face ever since. Hardly anyone believes me, until I show them the letter. Most of the men thought I'd never even hear from you again, but I knew better. Our love is too strong to let mountains or oceans come between us. I like the idea that we may be seeing the same stars. It does make the distance between us seem smaller somehow.

Your letter was indeed the nicest I have ever received. The ending "all my love and kisses" was exceptionally pleasant. To imagine once again being in your arms as we share our love and kisses brought a smile to these lips! Don't worry about shocking me with your letter endings. I loved it.

You know, I'm sure, just how I feel about you. If I don't write very often is no sign that I don't think of you. If I wrote every time I thought of you, I would be writing every minute of my life, and you would spend all your time reading my letters. You can't get any work done that way.

So, you wish our days together in Scutari could be lived over again? Darling, I'd willingly give up almost anything to be there with you again. Just to be near you would make me so happy, I'd probably be speechless. *Perhaps our day will come when we can be together again and really enjoy ourselves, openly and without feeling as if we need to look over our shoulders.*

Until then, perhaps I can grace more letters with my artwork. I would enjoy the thought of making you smile. I just had a brilliant idea. When is your birthday? I'd love to create a birthday card for you.

I'm glad Mrs. Bracebridge shared my compliments with you. You deserve every one of them and more. She is indeed a woman of honor, so I felt comfortable telling her exactly how I feel about you. I hope you don't mind.

You said something about the nice things seldom being repeated. If ever it is within my power, I shall do my damnedest to repeat our best moments. When I am finally released, London is my first stop. That's a promise! I know I'll be on my way as soon as I've healed enough to travel, and if I'm extra lucky, I'll be back before then.

To say that I enjoyed our brief time together is a rank understatement. It's practically all I ever think about. Many times, I have wondered what might have happened if Amy hadn't caught us in the closet and reported us to Miss Nightingale. Do you think you could have stood for having me around for another month or more?

Congratulations on your job. Just think, if they draft enough men, you may become Head Nurse of the entire hospital. Keep plugging away, Luscious! That's a phrase one of the navy boys taught me the other day. He came here from the bombardment of Sevastopol on June 17. He said it means to keep plugging up the holes in the boat until the battle is won.

In your case, I mean for you to keep working hard and you'll advance faster than you ever thought possible. Not that you crave advancement, I know, but your talent and abilities are sure to be recognized at some point in your career.

Since my last letter to you, I have been taking instructions on a new job myself. I am going to be one of the orderlies here in the rehabilitation hospital. That will help me fill my time, and I am looking forward to being of use again. This will leave me less time for writing you, however. That part makes me sad.

Your description of being so comfortable in the garden makes me smile. Please save a comfortable spot for a very tired, very lonely soldier. I only hope that our dreams will someday come true. Won't it be wonderful? I hope it won't be too long.

One of the boys just started singing the song you mentioned, "My Bonnie Lies Over the Ocean". So, I took your suggestion and threw a kiss in the bay near here. I hope it reaches you quickly.

All my love goes with this, darling. Pleasant dreams.

Love and kisses,
Ronald
July 13, 1855

With the summer so hot and dry, both Lucia and her mother spent most afternoons either in the drawing room or on the bench in the garden where occasional breezes cooled them somewhat. The Season had slowed with the summer heat, but there continued to be a few charity luncheons and dances arranged by Society parents who still had debutantes that were not yet spoken for. Each passing event was pure torment for Lucia. Even the ones where she'd agreed to sing were barely tolerable.

One such luncheon on a particularly hot July afternoon, Lucia was preparing to perform, when she spotted Gerald near the back of the room. She hadn't seen him in several weeks, and wondered where he'd been off to.

Her performance went well, and she slipped out to a side balcony before too many people managed to hem her in. As she stepped to the railing and looked out over the garden, she smiled. The Wetherfords had a beautiful garden this year, despite the lack of rain. "I wonder how they manage that," she thought.

"The flowers look as beautiful as you," spoke a deep voice

behind her.

Startled, she turned around to see Gerald's laughing eyes gazing at her.

"Oh," she laughed. "I'm afraid I'm much more wilted than they. What do you think the Wetherfords are doing to keep them blooming so beautifully?"

"I dare say, they have gnomes out there all night, watering them," he joked.

"And where are they obtaining such precious water?" she joined in with his tale.

"From the secret underground spring, of course," he laughed.

"Oh, of course. How could I have forgotten the source of their secret wealth? Water is more precious than gold these days, isn't it?"

Nodding, he agreed, "Indeed it is. Since you've admitted to being a bit wilted, may I interest you in some refreshment?"

"I'd adore something to drink," she smiled.

Gratefully, she followed as he led the way to the refreshment table. Handing her a cup of punch, he took one for himself, then led her to a quiet corner where they could talk.

As they settled into their chairs, Lucia looked at him through lowered eyelashes. He's quite handsome, she thought, but not as handsome as Ronald. He speaks well, but I miss my sergeant's voice and the intensity of his moods. Still, Gerald is fun to talk with, and since he knows there is no future between us, I suppose he's safe enough.

Across the room, Harriet sipped her punch and smiled.

My dearest Ronald,

I'm glad the ending of my last letter didn't shock you. It seems words are inadequate for expressing my feelings for you. I hope you have some sense of just how much I miss you. I, too, long for the day when we can be together again.

I rather like that you called me Luscious. I had to pull out the lovely Valentine you drew where you first addressed me as Luscious. I treasure it, along with all your letters. It conjures delightful images in my mind, but those would definitely be too forward to describe in a letter. Perhaps I will share them when you come to London.

My birthday was April 10. Don't worry about missing it, though. I deliberately didn't tell anyone. There were far more important things to think about than celebrating the day of my birth. In a way, I'm sorry you didn't know, though, because one of those drawings for a birthday card would have been highly treasured.

That brings up a question in my mind. When is your birthday? It seems I should have asked that question months ago, but better late than never, I suppose. I wouldn't want to miss celebrating it with you.

While I was reading your last letter, Mama made the remark that she would certainly like to know how you could find so much to say to a girl you barely know. She doesn't understand our connection, does she? We can say nothing that the outside world thinks is relevant and still find words to express our love. Maybe someday she'll open her mind and heart to what we mean to each other.

I hope that you aren't working too hard in your new orderly duties, but I'm sure it feels good to be of use again. That's exactly how I felt when I started work at the hospital. The work is very satisfying, but sometimes sad, too.

Last night, while I was working at the hospital, a Major who had been admitted a few days ago called me over and asked if I could help him write a letter to his wife and children. He was wounded two months ago, and still doesn't have good use of his hands. I was quite busy with other patients, but told him I'd come as soon as I had a few minutes free. It was nearly midnight before I got to him, but he was still awake and so grateful for my help.

I can imagine how his wife must be feeling not hearing from him for so long. I go a little crazy when I don't hear from you as soon as I'd like. I feel badly for her and for him, which doesn't make much sense, because

I've never seen him before and no doubt will never see him again, but the idea that he has been out of touch for that long just makes me so sad.

Oh my! My black cat just fell in a bucket of white paint and is it ever a mess. Don't laugh, because it really isn't funny. Well, maybe a little funny, so you can snicker if you want to. I'd like to write more, but my cat is meowing and crying and I'm afraid she will start to paw at the door with her painted paws, and I can't let that happen, even though I'd much rather write to you than try to clean her up.

All my love and kisses,

Lucia

July 31, 1855

My dearest Lucia,

I know that in one sense, I shouldn't write tonight. I'm so mad I can hardly see or think straight. After being recommended last week for release, I was quite ready to pack my bag and be on my way to you. For no damn good reason at all, the powers that be, the men that are supposed to run this hospital, namely one Dr. Edmund Alexander Parkes, thinks that I'm not fit to leave yet. I'm so mad at this whole mess, I could scream.

And yet, no matter how loud you scream, it doesn't make a particle of difference to them. I realize you don't understand much about military politics, but I've got to have a vent for my anger somewhere, so I hope you don't mind. I think this is about the most idiotic thing I ever ran into. Am I forgiven for this anti-social and rather unbecoming outburst? I'll try to contain my anger and focus on more pleasant things.

I'm sorry about missing your birthday. You didn't say anything, so I'm sure no one at Scutari knew it was your birthday. You had no celebration and no recognition. That's not acceptable to me. I'll not make the same mistake again.

Since I missed it this year, perhaps this little sketch will do. Next year, I'll draw an especially nice card for you, complete with a personal poem. Better yet, perhaps I'll be able to deliver it in person. We'll hope for an end to this war so that will be possible.

My birthday is August 13th. I have no plans to tell anyone. I wish I could celebrate it with my Angel from Scutari Hospital, but since that's not possible, there's no point in mentioning it.

I'm so sorry about the cat, but I just couldn't help laughing as I read about it. Might I suggest you keep a bucket of black paint on hand, just in case it happens again?

Thank you for all the letters you keep sending. They excite me, and I can't wait to read the next one. You see what you do to me? When they arrive, my mind stops, the efficiency of the hospital is disrupted because everything must wait until I've read your latest arrival. No matter that the nurses "must change the bandages immediately" or the head orderly insist that "now is the time to take that patient for a walk." Your letter is much more important than any of that.

Darling, I must close now, as it is getting late. I'm hoping and praying that we'll soon be seeing each other.

All my love to a very sweet girl,
Ronald
August 1, 1855

The carriage pulled up in front of the palace and Lucia tugged nervously at her gown and hair. She knew the flounces of white lace and pink ruffles were fashionable, but the petticoats underneath felt uncomfortably hot and cumbersome. Her lace shawl was necessary for propriety's sake, but even that additional layer of fabric was too warm for this hot night. The pink ribbons holding the dainty frill in her hair kept tickling her neck. She wished they weren't so long.

"Stop that at once," her mother scolded. "It's not like this is the first time you've been to a court ball."

"I don't see why I have to attend this one, then," Lucia frowned. "I was presented to the Queen more than eight years ago."

"Don't be silly," Harriet reprimanded her again. "You're going because you're still single, and this is the best place to find an eligible young man for you. It's the last court ball of the Season and could be your last chance to find a husband."

"Mama," Lucia started, but her mother cut her off.

"No more. We have arrived. You will make yourself available to any who wish to dance with you. You will converse pleasantly and comport yourself with dignity and proper decorum. Do you have your fan?"

Sighing, Lucia relented. "Yes, Mama. I have my fan." Then under her breath she muttered, "I'm a grown woman and know how to behave properly."

The footman opened the door of the carriage and helped the ladies alight. After a few moments in the ladies' dressing room, where they deposited their wraps and made sure their hair was not mussed and their gowns not soiled, they emerged into the Marble Hall to join the crowd preparing to climb the Grand Stairs. Lucia was surprised as her heart began to beat faster.

In the Green Drawing Room, they joined the queue of people making their way through the Picture Gallery, waiting to be announced before entering the ballroom. She noticed others marveling at the array of portraits on the high walls, a bevy of royal visages seemed to look down at the assembled crowd parading before them. Approaching the door to the ballroom, Harriet dropped two calling cards into the silver tray the Lord Chamberlain offered.

As they were announced and entered the ballroom, Lucia couldn't help but be awed again by the sight. She craned her neck to see the ceiling that seemed to reach the sky, with chandeliers graced by blue, red, and gold filigree work, which theme was carried down to the huge paintings of angels hung high on the walls.

Her attention was drawn to the enormous alcove at the other end of the room where the Queen sat with her Prince Albert and other royal guests. The archway over her alcove was graced with awe-inspiring statues of angels, soldiers, and pegasi.

Harriet urged her forward, and they moved toward the red velvet chairs lining the room, greeting other guests as they went. Mingling with other guests, Lucia struggled to find the polite words to say. As much as this place awed her, she also wished to be anywhere but here. Her mother's plan to find her a husband irked her to no end. Why couldn't her mother simply accept that she was betrothed to Ronald? Lucia had no interest in anyone else, especially anyone who might attend this lavish function.

"Frowns do not become you, Miss Rix."

Turning, Lucia was a bit surprised to see Gerald standing beside her. "I'm sorry," she forced a light laugh. "I didn't realize I was frowning."

"Well, frowning doesn't quite do your expression justice," he admitted, continuing to grin down at her. "If I were to hazard a guess, I'd say someone has angered you and you were contemplating the best way to do away with them. Perhaps murderous would be a better description of your expression."

"Oh my! I never thought of myself as a murderess. Perhaps I'd best watch what I'm thinking when in polite company."

"You don't need to concern yourself on my account, but someone else might get the wrong impression and call a constable."

Lucia's laugh was genuine this time. "We can't have that, now, can we? Especially in such an elegant setting. It would certainly cause all sorts of gossip and rumours."

"Something to be studiously avoided, I'm sure. Will you grant me the honor of the next dance?" he asked politely.

"With pleasure, sir," she answered, allowing him to lead her to the floor. The music began, a beautiful new waltz by Johann Straus Jr. Although it had been more than a year since Lucia had danced, she found Gerald to be an excellent partner, and relaxed easily into his arms, gliding almost effortlessly around the floor.

As they danced, he continued their light banter, which aided in her ability to relax. When the dance was over, he escorted her back to her mother, who was looking very pleased with herself.

"May I impose myself for another dance a bit later?" he asked.

"Yes, of course," Lucia answered, pleased.

The evening passed quickly enough, with Gerald claiming just two dances, both waltzes. Lucia danced with other gentlemen, but all felt wooden and stiff compared to Gerald's graceful movements and easy banter.

Near the end of the evening, the musicians began playing a polka. Lucia determined to sit this one out, as she'd never been comfortable with the fast-moving steps of the lively dance. Her plan was foiled however, when Gerald reached his hand out in invitation. She started to decline, but the combination of her mother's warning shake of the head, and his amused expression convinced her to try it.

They stood on the sidelines for only a moment before Gerald scooped her into the tricky steps of the dance, twirling her effortlessly between the other dancers, whirling around the room at a dizzying pace. Just when she thought she would swoon from all the spinning, he'd release her right hand and they'd continue dancing in an open position long enough for her dizziness to subside.

Then, he'd pull her back into closed position again and they'd whirled and twirled around again. By the time the dance was over, Lucia was gasping for breath, laughing so hard that her sides hurt. Gerald laughed just as hard as he led her back to her mother.

Bowing, he thanked her for the dance, and then thanked her mother for bringing her to grace his evening. As he walked away, Lucia's eyes followed him, her expression one of wonder and amusement. He was so suave, so cultured, yet so approachable and likable. Lucia didn't quite know what to think.

The ride home was quiet, each woman lost in her own thoughts. It wasn't until they reached home and were stepping into the house that Harriet spoke.

"I've given permission for Mr. Asher to call on you Sunday afternoon," she said without preamble.

"What? Mama, how could you? You know I'm engaged to Ronald." Lucia's mood changed from bemused to livid in that split second.

"That is no engagement, Lucia. That fop hasn't asked for my permission. He's a soldier, for heaven's sake. He has no future, and certainly none here in London. I won't permit it. You will allow Mr. Asher to court you, and if he so desires, you will marry him. He comes from a good line and his family is well set."

"No, no I will not!" Lucia's voice rose with each word. "I will not!"

But her protests were ignored as Harriet turned her back and ascended the stairs to her rooms.

Gritting her teeth, Lucia followed her up to her own rooms, seething at the high-handedness of this woman who was determined to marry her off to someone of her choosing, never mind what her daughter wanted.

Chapter Seventeen

Dearest Ronald,

My heart broke into a thousand pieces when I read your letter telling me you were not being released. I was certain you would be well enough to travel to London by now. I try not to imagine how much longer we must endure being apart, but my imagination runs away with me more frequently than I would like it to. When that happens, I try to ask myself, "What would my sergeant want me to do?" Most often, I imagine you would like me to sing, so I do.

Your sketch of the birthday cake was delightful. I look forward to next year's birthday card, especially if contains an original poem and is delivered in person.

I'm so sorry I missed your birthday. It's ironic that I asked just a week before. I hope you'll forgive me for not asking in time to send you something. I promise to make it up to you when we are together again.

Everything is going well at the hospital. There are a couple of nurses that I'd like to see taken to task for their lack of respect and concern for the patients. Sometimes they don't seem to have much patience for the patients. (Pun intended to make you laugh. Did it work?) However, I don't have the authority to chastise them myself.

So, I do my work and try to make the patients as comfortable as possible, letting them know that they are not alone. Let the other nurses do what they will. If the patients aren't endangered by their lack of professionalism, I'll try not to complain too much.

That soldier/singer you have there must be powerful because that kiss you sent on the ocean arrived today. Thank you. I wish you would tell me something about the fellows you know and more, if possible, what you do for entertainment.

Mama and I attended the last ball of the Season last week. It was as ornate and elegant as any I've attended. Everyone seemed to bring out their best attire, best accessories, and best manners for the event. The orchestra was excellent and I enjoyed the music very much. There were a few who asked me to dance, but none that compares with my sweet sergeant, so you have nothing to fear. I am yours and will be forever.

I'm having "cat troubles" again today. A little stray cat wandered in this morning and I've been watching it try to make up to Richard, my black cat. Poor Richard is so jealous that he won't come near me. When I pick up the little cat, he doesn't like it one little bit.

My dear, I pray each night it won't be long until you are here with me. Thank you again for your very sweet letters. I'll be looking for more, and will attempt to write letters as sweet as yours.

Always yours,
Lucia
August 22, 1855

"Lucia."

Her mother spoke before she entered the music room, which was uncharacteristic of her. Normally, her mother observed the protocol of knocking, entering when invited, and then speaking. That should have been Lucia's first clue that her mother was excited.

"Yes, Mama?"

"You have a caller waiting in the drawing room." She sounded almost gleeful.

Her brows furrowed, Lucia stood and crossed to the door. "A caller? Who?"

"Don't you remember? Mr. Asher asked to call on you today," Harriet chortled.

Lucia stopped and turned to face her mother. "Don't you remember? I told you I won't receive gentlemen callers. I'm engaged to be married, and it's not proper."

The gleeful look turned to one of rage and determination, but her mother's voice was lowered so as not to carry into the drawing room where Gerald was waiting.

"You are not engaged," she hissed. "You will receive this young man, and you will be on your best behavior. Do you understand?"

Gritting her teeth, Lucia didn't answer. She stared at her mother for what seemed like forever, but Mama wasn't going to back down.

Finally, without a word, Lucia turned on her heel and walked stiffly to the drawing room. She stopped just before entering and forced her mouth into a smile, willing her heart and breath to slow to a more normal pace. After all, it's not Mr. Asher's fault that he's not welcome to come calling.

As she entered the room, she saw Gerald standing dutifully in the center of the room, his eyes on his boots, obviously being careful not to stare at all the beautiful things Mama had collected over the years to accentuate her affluence. That would be rude, and Gerald Asher was not a rude man. He looked up and smiled, his eyes twinkling merrily.

"Miss Rix," he greeted her, "how lovely you look today."

Lucia nodded her acceptance of his compliment. "Won't you please sit down, Mr. Asher? Would you care for some refreshment?" Her voice was polite, but cold. She glanced at Mama who sat in a chair on the other side of the room. Mama's eyes narrowed her disapproval at Lucia's tone.

Gerald sat uncomfortably on the chair Lucia had indicated after she'd taken one close to it. He looked from Lucia to her mother and asked, "Is this a bad time?"

"Not at all, Mr. Asher," Harriet replied quickly. "You are welcome here." She looked pointedly at Lucia who stifled a sigh.

"Mama is right," she said, trying to moderate her tone and hide her irritation. "You are welcome here."

There was a long silence, then Gerald broke the silence, "It's been rather warm lately, hasn't it?"

"Yes, quite warm," Lucia replied, then fell silent again.

"Will you be attending the Bartholomew Fair?" he tried again.

Looking at her mother for confirmation, Lucia nodded. "Yes, it will be a nice finale to the Season. It's too bad it will be the last one."

"I agree. I always look forward to it. It's been a good Season this year, I think."

"Yes, quite nice."

Silence.

Finally, Mama intervened. "Will you be going to the country for hunting, Mr. Asher?"

"We had planned to, Mrs. Rix," he replied, sounding grateful for something to talk about, "but Mother hasn't been feeling well of late, and the doctor has recommended she remain in London for a few more weeks to recover."

"I'm sorry to hear your mother's been ill," Lucia spoke up. "I hope she recovers quickly."

"Thank you, I'm sure she will. What about you?" he asked. "Will you be leaving London this fall?"

"No, my work keeps me here most of the year, with only occasional holidays elsewhere," Lucia replied, ignoring her mother's glare.

"That's understandable. Patients don't stop being sick so nurses can go on holiday. How are things at the hospital?"

"Fine. Patients come and go, and we do what we can for them."

Gerald nodded. "It must be interesting work."

Lucia smiled. "It is. I wouldn't want to do anything else."

"I can see that about you," he smiled. "You love your work, don't you?"

"Yes, I do," she answered sincerely. "I love being able to help people who need help. It makes life worthwhile."

"We are planning to host a charity luncheon in a couple of weeks," her mother said, changing the subject. "I hope you'll consider attending, Mr. Asher."

"I'd be delighted, Mrs. Rix," he answered as Lucia's eyes narrowed at her mother's uncharacteristic rudeness.

Gerald glanced back and forth between the women one more time, then stood, "Thank you for having me, Mrs. Rix. It was wonderful to see you again, Miss Rix. May I call on you again?"

Lucia stood and walked with him towards the front door. "As I've told you, Mr. Asher, I am engaged to a sergeant who's fighting in Crimea. I don't think it would be proper while he's not able to defend his rights as my intended husband."

Gerald retrieved his hat from the rack and turned to face her. "You are absolutely right, Miss Rix. I believe we should limit our meetings to public events until his return. Don't you?"

Relieved that he understood, but disconcerted at his hint that he wanted to compete with Ronald for her attentions, she simply nodded. "Thank you for understanding, Mr. Asher."

He nodded his farewell first to her, then to her mother who was standing in the drawing room doorway. "I bid you a good afternoon, ladies."

Lucia turned to face her mother. The two women glared at each other for a moment, neither of them willing to back down. Finally, Harriet spoke.

"I don't understand you, Lucia."

"What don't you understand?" Lucia replied, ice in her voice.

"How you can turn away such a handsome, eligible young man who has been nothing but gracious since he laid eyes on you."

"Mr. Asher is gracious and charming," Lucia conceded, "and he's handsome, and rich, and everything you want for me, but he's not who I choose for myself, Mama. I've made my choice, and no amount of conniving, or scheming, or threats will change my mind, so I'll ask you once more, Mama. Stop trying to find me a husband. I already have one in mind."

"Now, Lucia…" Harriet began, but her daughter was already ascending the stairs, her back straight, her head held high.

Harriet closed her mouth and watched in fascination as she realized that the girl she'd been planning a future for had become a confident woman fully capable of planning her own future. She sighed. This was going to be more difficult than she thought. Her eyes narrowed speculatively. She would have to approach this more delicately next time. Yes, much more carefully next time.

"A note for you, Miss," Susan announced, holding out the folded paper as she entered Lucia's room.

"Thank you, Susan," Lucia smiled as she took the paper, then frowned a little when she didn't recognize the handwriting. She broke the seal and began to read.

Miss Rix,

Please, forgive my intrusion last Sunday. Your mother had invited me to call and I felt flattered by her invitation. However, I realize that I was quite out of line by calling on you without your express invitation. Although I enjoy our conversations, it was presumptuous of me to assume you would welcome my advances based solely on those experiences.

When you first told me of your engagement, I should have ceased my pursuit of you immediately, but when your mother invited me to call, I thought perhaps your engagement was not as set as I had first believed. However, now that you have set me straight, I shall be content to admire you from afar and leave you to wait for your intended. May I be so bold as to say, he is a very lucky man. Please, forgive my effrontery.

Sincerely,
Gerald Asher, Esq.

Lucia frowned. The note was intended as an apology, but the line about her mother's invitation bothered her. Something must be done about Mama's interference.

To my Only Darling,

Please excuse the shaky writing. I am writing to you from the back of a wagon on the way to Sevastopol. The doctors at the hospital finally declared that I was recovered enough to leave.

I was beside myself with joy, for I thought I would be on my way to my sweet London nurse, but that joy was soon dashed as they informed me that I was not being discharged from military service, but was being transferred to a regiment guarding Sevastopol.

You may have read in the newspaper the Sevastopol was bombarded on September 5, as I mentioned in my last letter. It was taken on September 8, and many good soldiers were lost and need to be replaced. Our unit is one assigned to guard it. So, rather than sending those of us who are mostly recovered home to our loved ones, the generals have declared that if we can carry a sword, we are to return to guard the city. I don't understand the generals' thinking. I believe that to become a general, you must pass a "no common sense" test.

Do not fret, my love. I promise to stay as far away from the enemy as my commanding officers will allow. For now, I have every reason to live and will not court my own death as I have in the past. I am hoping to be assigned to another cavalry unit to care for the horses. I cannot, as yet, ride for long, but I can muck out stalls and carry oats and water. I will write as often as I am able.

Say, can you read most of my writing? Personally, I don't think so, because I've just reread part of this letter and it appears to be a hell of a mess.

Darling, again, please don't worry about me! It's really a waste of whatever you waste when you worry. As my mother used to say, "They can knock you around a lot, but it'll take more than a few knocks to kill you."

Meanwhile, keep singing and smiling, for it warms my heart to picture you that way.

All my love to the sweetest girl in the world,
Ronald
September 13, 1855

Lucia lowered the letter into her lap with shaking hands. He was not coming to London. He was going back into the fighting. It was the worst possible news. Well, maybe not the worst, she chided herself. At least he's still alive.

Abruptly, she stood up and headed for the door to the gardens, nearly running into Susan on the way.

"I'm sorry, Susan," she apologized, and then continued, not hearing when Susan called after her.

As she made her way to the bench next to the hawthorn hedge, she was grateful for the shade it offered, and the solitude she found there. Her tears fell freely as her body wracked with sobs. After her tears were spent, she simply sat, allowing her disappointment to run its course.

"Be ye all right, Miss?"

She looked up, startled, then nodded. "I'm all right, George. Just feeling sad, is all."

"Missin' yer sergeant, then?" he asked kindly.

Again, she nodded. "Yes, and I just received bad news. He's been sent back to the fighting."

The old gardener shook his head. "That's frightful news, to be sure." He looked up at the leaves dancing in the welcome breeze. "Still, it means he's healed up proper, now doesn't it? And that's something to be glad of."

Lucia offered him a wan smile. "Yes, it is. Thank you for always reminding me to find the bright side of things."

He looked her in the eye, then. "Yer Papa always told me to be sure you never forgot that there's a bright side to any situation."

At the mention of her father, Lucia's smile faded. "I miss him, George."

"I know, Miss. I know." With a sad nod, he shuffled off.

Lucia watched him go and decided he was right. This was just a temporary setback, not a permanent situation. She would go on with her work and live her life, and continue to wait for the man she loved to return to her.

"Come take a walk with me," Harriet insisted. "The weather is beautiful, the autumn leaves are glorious, and I think the fresh air will do us both some good."

Lucia was puzzled. Her mother never wanted to go for walks. She was content to drive or ride wherever she wanted to go, so why was she being so insistent now?

"I really don't feel like walking, Mama," she answered.

"I'm worried about you, Lucia," her mother said, trying a new approach. "The past few days, you've hardly left the house. You spend all your time alone in your room. It's just not healthy."

"I go to work nearly every day, Mama. I have plenty of human interaction at the hospital. I'm fine."

"It's not the same!" Harriet argued. "Going to work is not recreational. Talking with sick people at the hospital is not a social activity. You need relaxing social interaction, Lucia."

"Mama, I'm fine. I'd rather not go, but thank you for asking."

"Please, Lucia," her mother's voice turned pleading, "I'd like your company. I'd like to spend some time with you. Let's walk. Please?"

When Mama turned on the child-like pleading tone, Lucia knew she had lost. She could not say no to that little girl voice. She sighed.

"All right, Mama. A short walk, then back home."

"Wonderful!" Her mother nearly danced with glee. That wasn't like her, either.

As they walked between the trees, Lucia had to admit that they were spectacular this year, and yes, she was glad she came. They talked about everything and nothing, but all superficial. Neither one mentioned the topic most on Lucia's mind... the fact that she hadn't heard from Ronald since his transfer.

Stepping around a cluster of bushes, Harriet's breath caught in a suspiciously fake gasp.

"Why, Lucia! Look over there. Isn't that Mrs. Beatrice Asher and her nephew?"

Suddenly it all became quite clear. Lucia glared at her mother. "Yes, it is. Did you know they would be here? Did you arrange to meet them, Mama?"

Her mother's face took on a shocked and almost hurt expression that Lucia knew was well practiced.

"I'm sure I don't know what you're talking about, Lucia," she whispered as the Ashers approached.

"How delightful to see you, Mrs. Asher!" Harriet's voice dripped like honey. "And you, as well, Mr. Asher," she nodded in his direction.

"Good morning, Mrs. Rix," Mrs. Asher's smile was genuine. "Isn't it a beautiful day?"

"It certainly is!" Harriet agreed. "May I present my daughter, Miss Lucia Rix?"

"How nice to meet you, dear," the sweet old lady smiled.

"The pleasure is mine," Lucia replied politely.

Harriet took control of the conversation at that point. "Have you seen the colors on the birch tree by the bridge?"

"Not yet," the older woman shook her head. "We were headed that way. Would you care to join us?"

"We'd be delighted," Mama gushed, taking Mrs. Asher's arm.

Lucia stood and watched as her mother and Gerald's aunt strolled back down the path, headed for the birch tree, apparently. She looked up at Gerald.

"Did you know about this?" she asked.

Looking all too innocent, he replied, "Know about what?"

Shaking her head, she sighed. "Never mind. We'd better follow them, in case your aunt needs rescuing."

Gerald laughed. "I'm sure Aunt Bea can hold her own against anyone, including your mother."

"Perhaps, but Mama can be difficult to handle sometimes."

"I'm sure she only has the best of intentions," he commented as they followed the older women.

"I won't argue that point," Lucia admitted, "but she doesn't take other people's feelings and ideas into account."

"Such as inviting me to court you when you're engaged to another man?" Gerald blurted out, then grinned.

Lucia looked at him, shocked at his bold directness. When she saw his grin, she relaxed, finally understanding that he truly did understand her situation.

"Exactly," she nodded.

"You don't need to worry, Miss Rix," Gerald reassured her. "I honor your engagement and will respect your wishes to keep my distance, but that doesn't mean we won't meet on occasion, accidently or otherwise. Can we be pleasant acquaintances at least?"

Lucia laughed. "Of course. Please, forgive my rudeness and suspicious nature. Mama brings that out in me, I'm afraid."

"I understand, and you are already forgiven," Gerald smiled. Lucia was grateful that the twinkle in his eyes was one of gentle humour and sincere understanding. While Mama may have her little schemes, it seemed Gerald Asher would not fall prey to them.

Chapter Eighteen

Dearest Ronald,

Yesterday, your letter arrived telling of your release and transfer. Need I tell you how very disappointed I was to learn you weren't being discharged? I really didn't expect such a thing to happen and I must admit it caused many tears.

However, darling, I know you are making the best of the situation, and I do admire you very much for the attitude you are taking. Every time I look at your letter, it makes a lump in my throat, because I was so positive you would be discharged and could come to London.

There is something I want to ask you that I have hesitated to before, but after reading your letter and the headlines in the paper, I can't help but worry. You said not to worry if I didn't hear from you. Then the papers are giving quite a detailed account of the fighting starting again in Sevastopol. Can you tell me if you are in any danger? If you were hurt or anything and unable to write to me, I'd have no way of knowing what happened.

I've felt so sad since reading your letter. Just can't help it, I guess. I'd surely be a happy person if this war could end soon. Please excuse the tear stains on this letter. They certainly do smear the words, but I can't seem to stop crying these days.

I'm too emotional, I guess, and that news really upset me. My thoughts are always with you, darling, and I will try to be patient until you can come to me.

I think I was especially emotional about your news because it came on the heels of an experience that just about broke my heart. Several days ago, I had a disagreement with Dell (you know he works at the hospital).

Well, Jean, his wife, happened to come into the hospital, and naturally she would take Dell's part in anything and I don't blame her. However, I do think she should have stayed out of it. We have had an agreement between us that anything that went wrong between Dell and his job would make absolutely no difference between us, because we have been such close friends for so long.

Well, this time our agreement hasn't held up well and she won't even recognize me. When she walked in with Dell yesterday, she sat down, and when I spoke, she just said hello, got up, and walked out.

Ronald, I don't think I have felt so bad about anything in a long, long time, because her friendship means so very much to me. I don't know what to do about it, but I know I'm going to have a talk with her about it tomorrow.

I didn't particularly like Dell when I first met him, but outside of this argument at work, I have treated him quite nicely just because of her, and he has received a lot of favors because of me. I've felt so bad about it yesterday and today that it has made me feel ill. I am going to try and straighten it out tomorrow, though, so I'll let you know what happens.

If I can't patch things up with her, I'll try not to dwell on what can't be, as my father used to say. Better to dwell on the good things to come, whenever they may happen.

So, I shall imagine a delightful prospect. As of this moment, I'll begin thinking about how we'll celebrate when you finally arrive in London. I'll have many happy moments imagining that, I'm sure.

I'm looking forward to reading some of your poetry. Do I have to wait until my next birthday? I missed the artwork on your last letter, but I understand it would have been difficult to draw while riding in a wagon.

Things are much quieter, now that the Season has ended. Frankly, I'm glad. I enjoy performing, but being social with people I don't really care about is exhausting. Please tell me we won't have to pay attention to such things when we're married? I'd love to have a little house in the country where the only socializing we must do is feed the horses and listen to the birds in the trees.

I started volunteering at the Middlesex Infirmary last week. Mama and I were having so many disagreements that it was miserable to stay at home with her when I wasn't working at the hospital. With fewer social events, we were spending far too much time together, I think.

Not much else happening here, except Mama has been feeling a bit ill. I wonder if her current "illness" has anything to do with my new pastime. I'm not certain if it's a true malady, or just her way of getting my attention. Either way, I'm trying to be understanding. I've spent more time with her in the past couple of days than in the past several weeks. She needs it, I suppose.

Speaking of Mama, she has sent for me, so I'll simply send my love and kisses on the ocean to you. I wish I could deliver them in person, though.

Ever yours,
Lucia
October 1, 1855

Lucia took the cloak and gloves Susan offered as she approached the front door.

"Will you be wantin' an umbrella, Miss?" Susan asked. "It looks like it might rain."

Lucia glanced out the window. "I don't think so, Susan. I won't be long, and I'm sure the rain will hold off until my return." She grinned at her maid who grinned back.

"So, you have that much influence on the weather, then?" she said, cheekily.

Lucia laughed. She and Susan had become good friends over the past months. She was glad her mother had hired her.

"No, but I'll take my chances," she replied, opening the door.

"Very well," Susan nodded, then grinned again and added, "Shall I have a hot bath waiting, just in case?"

"Not a bad idea," Lucia agreed.

She started down the walk, breathing in the chilly fall air. Looking at the sky, she wondered if Susan was right, but she wanted to talk with Jean and get this mess straightened out.

Upon reaching Jean and Dell's home, Lucia hesitated. What should she say? How should she approach it? It was all so very awkward. After a moment's hesitation, she knocked and waited. It wasn't but a minute until a young maid answered.

"Is Mrs. Lassiter available?" Lucia asked, putting on her best manners.

"Who may I say is calling?" the girl asked.

"Miss Rix," Lucia replied, handing the girl her mother's card with her name inscribed under her mother's.

The maid escorted her into the drawing room but she didn't have to wait long. Jean burst into the room with her arms open wide and practically ran into Lucia's arms.

"I'm so sorry…" both women began in unison, then laughed.

"Please, may I talk first?" Jean asked, leading Lucia to two chairs at the side of the simple but beautiful room.

Lucia nodded, and Jean began her apology.

"I don't know what got into me," she said, tears filling her eyes. "We have been friends for so long that I just can't imagine what made me treat you so coldly. I suppose it was that Dell spoke so angrily about the disagreement you had and I felt I had to take his side. But you'll never guess what happened at supper that night. Dell took your side! Can you believe it? He said he was wrong and that I ought not to treat you so rudely. He really gave me a tongue-lashing, which I richly deserved. He's planning to talk to you about it the next time you work together. Anyway, I hope you can forgive me, Lucia. I just couldn't live with myself if you didn't forgive me."

Tears welled up in Lucia's eyes as she listened to her friend's heart-felt apology. She reached over and pulled Jean into a tight hug.

"Of course, I forgive you," she assured her. "I'm sure I had my share of blame in all of this, so I certainly won't hold a grudge."

Jean sighed. "I'm glad I have my friend back."

They spent an hour chatting about nothing in particular. Then Lucia happened to glance out the window. Alarm filled her heart as she saw the first raindrops begin to fall.

"Oh my," she breathed. "It looks like a real deluge in the making. I'd best be off."

Her friend frowned. "It has turned nasty, hasn't it? Won't you let my man drive you home in our hansom?"

"No, but thank you for offering," Lucia smiled. "It's not far if I cut through the park. Besides, a little rain never hurt anyone."

Jean looked doubtful, but finally nodded. "All right, if you're sure."

Lucia assured her that she was indeed sure, and headed out the door. She decided her comment about cutting through the park was more true than not as it would cut several blocks off her journey. Hopefully, the weather would cooperate long enough for her to reach home.

She had rounded the second bend in the stream when she had her answer. The clouds opened up, and within three steps, she was drenched. She ducked under a tree, which gave her a little shelter, and shivered as she pulled the hood of her cloak back to brush her damp hair out of her face.

"Mind if I share your shelter?" a familiar voice asked.

"Not at all, Mr. Asher," she answered, looking up at a face that was more drenched than hers.

"It seems I've lost my hat," he laughed, wiping the rain from his face with a handkerchief that was nearly too wet to do any good at all.

Laughing, Lucia couldn't help but ask, "And how did you manage that?"

"I didn't duck down far enough when I ran under a tree back there. It grabbed my hat, and when I went to retrieve it, the wind picked it up and deposited it in the stream. It's halfway to the Thames by now."

"Oh dear!" Lucia cried, feigning distress over his plight. "Whatever shall you do?"

Considering his options, Gerald finally decided, "I suppose I'll just have to run home and obtain another."

Lucia giggled. "Good plan."

"What about you, good lady?" he asked. "Did your umbrella suffer the same fate?"

"Oh, nothing so dramatic as that," she chuckled. "It was a simple error in judgement that left me without protection from this downpour. I decided I didn't need it, so I left it home."

"Ah, a victim of your own short-sightedness, then. I'm afraid I can't feel very sorry for you in that case," he said forlornly.

"No need to feel sad about that, Mr. Asher," Lucia smiled up at him. "Why should you feel sorry for me when I don't feel sorry for myself?"

"Good point!" he exclaimed. "No pity for either of us, agreed?"

"Agreed." She peered out, looking at the sky. "It looks like it may be clearing up. Shall we make a dash for it?"

"Sounds like a grand adventure," Gerald agreed. "Shall I escort you home?"

"Perhaps that's best. I can't very well call on anyone else in this condition. I'm afraid I'd drip all over their rugs!"

They laughed together as they ventured out into the drizzle that continued to fall.

As they neared her home, she smiled at him. "Thank you for escorting me home, Mr. Asher. I'm sure if my mother saw us together, she'd get her hopes up again."

"That's probably not a good idea, is it?" he agreed. "I'll leave you to find your own way from here then. Thank you for sharing your tree with me."

"My pleasure, sir," she nodded formally, then grinned. "Don't get too wet."

"Too late," he called over his shoulder.

Chapter Nineteen

$\mathcal{D}$earest Lucia,

Last night, I felt quite homesick and lonesome. I thought about my boyhood days before my father got sick. Ah, me! If we could only turn back the hands of time. Then I decided I'd rather turn time ahead far enough that this war would be over and I could be with my sweet London nurse again.

It sometimes seems like an eternity between letters from you. I realize that the distance makes mail delivery slow, but there are days I wish it could be much faster. Wouldn't it be wonderful if we had a way to instantly send messages to each other and get a reply immediately? It might make us feel like we are nearer, maybe just in the next room.

I miss you so much that my heart aches sometimes and I can't breathe, can't eat, can't think straight. So, I re-read your previous letters and that helps some, but I still long for fresh news from my sweet Luscious.

Don't worry about the tear stains on your letters. They are part of you and I cherish each smeared word. Your letters seem to make the dullest day into the brightest since your last letter.

The only drawback is that my cribbage game suffers when your letters arrive. It seems as if the cards turn against me. I guess I'll have to give up cribbage and come to London. My friends are teasing me and asking why a great girl like you would waste her time with the likes of me. To be honest, I didn't have an answer. I'm just glad you do.

I'm sorry to hear that you were so sad. Many times, like last night, I have wished for a letter that hasn't arrived. It makes the whole day seem incomplete. I have spent many nights wondering what it will be like when I do come to London. Will I be able to speak when I see you again, I wonder? Your letters have filled a rather empty portion of my life. I shall always look forward to them.

When I read your latest letter, I was very sorry to hear about you and Jean. I can readily realize what her friendship means to you and how you must have felt. There was a time when I didn't like to discuss people behind their back, but as long as you've asked for it, here goes.

Do you remember in Scutari when you and I were having such a swell time? Jean seemed, to me, to be a bit resentful, if not slightly antagonistic. I am sure I will always feel that way in her presence. Of course, I know now, she was under quite a strain while there, but I don't think she should have shown her feelings so obviously.

I don't want you to feel that I want nothing to do with her, if you are still friends. I always say I can get along with anyone until I'm invited outside. After that, anything goes, no holds barred. Have I gone too far in expressing myself? If so, please forget it and let's get on to more pleasant subjects. Just remember that Father Time has healed the sorest spots in many people's lives.

Please, darling, try to be more cheerful. You know we'll meet again soon. Your worries, I'm sure, are more the product of your imagination than anything else. I could suggest that you stop reading the newspapers, and then you wouldn't think about the war, if no one mentioned it in your presence. However, if you can't avoid hearing or reading about the war, try not to worry. I'm staying as safe as I possibly can. When I say "don't worry", that's exactly what I mean.

As for your concern about not knowing if something's happened to me, I have it all worked out. If by any chance, or for any reason, I am unable to write to you, I have told my friends in the unit that you are to be informed as quickly as possible, so don't worry your pretty, dark head about that.

Any time you get an urge to deliver a kiss in person, come right ahead. You'll be more than welcome. I love 'em.

To be truthful, I haven't really concentrated on writing any poems. We are busier here than we were in Castle Hospital, so I can't show any results at present. I hope I have read your mind correctly and am not presuming too much. I shall enclose my efforts at the first opportunity.

Is your mother well again? It must be a wee bit difficult to be patient with her if she begins to feel ill when she just needs attention. You are an angel for trying to understand her, but I've known you were an angel since the first day you set foot in Ward B. I believe your volunteer work will bring you the respite you need from arguments with her. I'm sure the staff at the Middlesex Infirmary is grateful to have you.

Your description of your version of socializing sounds like a bit of heaven on earth. I wouldn't mind it one little bit. Especially if we were there together.

I must close now. Although I'm through writing, I shall be thinking of you always, Dearest One.

All my love,
Ronald
October 25, 1855

"Mama, how many times do I have to say no?" Lucia was at her wits end.

"It's just a fall fling, Lucia," her mother insisted. "Sort of an introduction to the holidays. You need to mingle with other people."

"Make myself available to be seen by eligible bachelors, you mean," Lucia's voice was bitter.

"That wouldn't hurt you at all," Harriet stated emphatically.

Lucia sighed. "I'll remind you again, Mama; I'm engaged to be married. It's not appropriate for me to be flaunted about with the single women of Society."

Her mother rolled her eyes. "I wish you would reconsider, Lucia. Your sergeant may never come to London. He's probably met some Crimean wench and hasn't thought of you in weeks."

"Mama!" Lucia was livid. "How dare you! I received a letter just three days ago and I have no doubt that he will come walking up that path just as soon as the war is over and he is discharged. I will not go to this fall fling, as you call it. I intend to stay true to my sergeant, and that's that."

Turning on her heel, Lucia left the dining room and had to restrain herself to keep from stomping up the stairs. Would her mother never understand?

Probably not until Ronald Ferguson was standing at the altar by her side, and they were being pronounced husband and wife, she thought wryly as she finished getting ready for work. Until then, I'll just have to be strong and pray for a quick end to this war.

Dearest Ronald,

I know you said I shouldn't read the newspapers, but I can't seem to help myself. I crave any information I can find on the war, hoping it will come to a swift end. However, not all the news is bad. I read a news article just this afternoon about how our letters to the soldiers in Crimea should be uplifting and happy. It said that you boys have enough to worry about without fretting over us here at home, so I'll try to be more cheerful in future letters. Your last letter started out so sad and lonely, I think the reporter may be right.

Just so you know how hard I'm trying, I wrote a long four-page letter yesterday. When I re-read it today, I crumpled it up and threw it away. The sad news far outweighed the happy news. I just couldn't send it and burden you further, so uplifting words is what you'll receive from me from now on.

I've thought about what you said, about your friends letting me know if something happens to you. I've decided that worrying about that is probably silly of me. My worrying won't stop anything, nor will it help if something happens, so I'm simply not going to worry about that anymore. I'm sorry if I caused you concern about it.

I didn't realize you played cribbage. I suppose it would be prudent to learn the game so we could enjoy quiet winter nights by the fire, playing cribbage. Or can you think of some other way to pass the time? You might tell your friends there that I'd love to tell them why I'm not wasting my time with a certain sergeant. If they send a stamped, self-addressed envelope, I'll be glad to tell them exactly what I see in you.

Say, how about a poem? Surely, you have finished one by now. Why don't you send a copy? I'd like very much to read one that you wrote, and you know you promised to send one as soon as it was ready. You asked me to be patient, but my curiosity gets the better of me, I'm afraid. I'm only teasing you, darling. I know you are busy. I am looking forward to reading whatever you write, whenever you have time.

I know I said I'd only write pleasant things, but this story has a happy ending so bear with me. Since my last writing to you, I have spent four days in bed with one very bad sore throat. I feel much better today, though, and very decidedly more rested. It is a very boring time for me when I can't do my nursing, or sing, or anything else I want to do. I have been off work, resting and trying to overcome this malady that's reared its ugly head.

The weather has turned terribly cold. I suppose it is either the cold weather, or something I have eaten. I'll no doubt live through it, but at present, I'm not much interested in working, eating, sleeping, or having fun. I'm feeling crotchety enough that you might decide to throw this letter into the fire and find yourself another dark-haired nurse to warm up with. Very poor attitude, don't you think?

I shouldn't complain, though. Mama is taking good care of me, and

Jean has been in twice to see if I need anything. She's been much nicer of late. I don't think I told you that I spoke to her after my last letter to you. We had a wonderful heart-felt conversation and are now on the best of terms again. I'm glad for it.

Not much else to say, except I love you. Again, I'll tell you I try not to worry about you. I say try, but darling, I won't say promise.

Ever yours,
Lucia
November 13, 1855

Lucia finished the last knot on the Christmas package she'd prepared for Ronald. She hoped it would arrive in time.

As she descended the stairs looking for Susan to post her package, she nearly ran into her mother.

"I'm sorry, Mama," she apologized breathlessly as they each caught a banister to keep from falling. "I didn't see you coming up."

"Apparently," her mother snapped. "Who's that for?"

Lucia smiled. "For Ronald, of course. Who else would I be sending packages to?"

Harriet sniffed. "Well, I'm sure I don't know. I wish you would just face reality and move on with your life, Lucia."

With that, she turned and continued up the stairs.

Lucia's eyes followed her, bewildered and hurt. She didn't understand her mother at all. Why couldn't she accept Ronald? Why did she have to treat Lucia like a new debutante who's fallen for the stable boy? Would anything change her mind and heart?

Dearest Lucia,

I don't really know how to start this letter. In a way, I want to give you a scolding, but then in another way, I don't want you to take it too seriously.

Yesterday, I received a letter from you. In regards to the first paragraph of your letter, I have always written to you to let you know exactly how I feel and think as far as I possibly could. I always felt that when you wrote you expressed your true feelings. Let's not change now because you read an article by some person who has nothing whatsoever to do with you and me.

Your last letter was a poor attempt at being cheerful. I could see right through it and knew you were missing me terribly. Darling, I want you to continue with the old form, as I like it much better. I'd much rather know what is truly happening in your life than get falsely cheerful letters that don't allow me to see the real Lucia Rix.

That being said, I was very sorry to hear about you feeling so sick. The next time you get sick, let me know about it ahead of time so I can come home and nurse you back to health. It would be a pleasure, I'm sure! In fact, you might get tired of having me around and tell your mother that you want to get rid of me, but you had better not try it.

Dearest, I do hope you aren't working too hard. After all, four or five days of rest doesn't mean you are ready to work seventy-two hours a week. You had better take it easy for a while. Doctor's orders.

It's too bad about your home being so cold. If I were there, I know one nurse I would enjoy keeping warm. Can I have the job? Perhaps it would be a good idea to think of all the coal you could save if I were there to keep you warm.

I'm very glad to hear you and Jean are back on peaceable terms. I hope nothing ever comes between you again. Does that sound confusing when compared to my last letter expressing my opinion about her? You have no need to worry. When I see her again, I will be friendly and give her another chance. I'm just thinking of you, and I don't like to see or hear about you worrying.

I'd give my bottom dollar to read those four pages you threw away. The ramblings of the mind are sometimes very interesting. For example, after you mentioned wanting to see some of my poetic ramblings, I have been working on a piece of poetry. The idea is lurking around, although I still can't find the words to fit the last verse. I know what I want to say, but the words don't fit.

I've even asked my friend, Art Hahn. He's very good with lyrics to the songs our band creates, but he wasn't much help. Someday, I'll have a wonderful idea and finish it fleet as a fox. Meanwhile, I shall enclose the completed portion as my Christmas gift to you and perhaps you'll have some suggestions or corrections.

"To Lucia
Tho'ts may come and tho'ts may go,
But none of them seem right.
The words I want, I cannot find
They're not in this brain tonight.

I dream of you at eventide
You haunt me in the day.
But when I wish to write to you
I can't find the words to say."

I wish I could send you more. A partially finished poem hardly seems a fitting Christmas gift for the love of my life. But perhaps you'll be patient and I'll make it up to you when we're together.

Meanwhile, why don't you go ahead and learn how to play cribbage? Although, we may not get through very many hands before I think of some other way to pass the cold winter evening. I like the way your mind thinks, by the way!

There isn't much other news at present that I can give you so I will end this with all my love.

Ever yours,
Ronald
December 4, 1855

Chapter Twenty

Dearest Ronald,

Happy Christmas, my love! I know you won't receive this until long after the holidays, but I am thinking of you and hope you are having the merriest Christmas possible. I've wondered what you would be doing today. Are you safe and warm in a farmhouse or barracks somewhere? Or are you fighting the wind and cold in a tent? Are you enjoying a day of peace and relaxation? Or are there enemy soldiers that you are battling with. I'm praying that you are warm and safe, and enjoying a day of peace and rest.

Thank you for setting me straight on falsely cheerful letters. I, too, would rather be open and honest as I write to you, but when I read that article, it made so much sense to protect our soldiers from further burdens that they can do nothing about. However, your comment about wanting to know the real Lucia Rix struck a chord in my heart. I promise always to write my feelings honestly to you from now on.

I was thinking the other day that I'd like to know more about your family. You shared a little with me when we were together, but I'd like to know more about your father and mother, and your grandparents. What were they like? What memories do you have of them?

As for me, Mama and I are alone. You may recall, my father died when I was twelve. I also had a twin brother who died as a baby.

Sometime, I'll tell you my life history. Would you be interested?

I believe you'll like my mother, although she likes to "mother" people, as in, she likes to tell them what to do. I'm sure that losing my brother so young and having only me to raise has made her a bit over-protective. It would have been nice to grow up with a twin brother. I'm so used to having my own way now, though, that my temper would most likely be rather hot.

Yes, I have a temper, even though I don't have your red hair. Is it true that all redheaded people have a temper? I'm sure you never show yours in front of people you love dearly, so I have nothing to worry about, right?

You said you would have liked to have read the letter I threw away. Yes, ramblings are interesting at times, however, those ramblings would have probably brought you more tears than laughs.

Speaking of letters, it occurs to me that I may be doing something that you won't agree with. I am saving all your letters in a little box that I keep in my drawer. I hope you don't mind. It helps when I am missing you. I can go back and re-read the old ones and feel a bit like you're here with me. Each letter is a little piece of you. I read them over and over and dream of the day we can be reunited.

Thank you, Dr. Ferguson for the orders on overworking, although I'm afraid I'm not going to be able to obey that order. Aren't I a terrible patient? I truly am feeling much better, so I have no excuse to lay around anymore. Although, I'd happily lay around if I had you here to keep me warm.

I am back at work and glad to be of use again. There is only so much laying around a person can do without going a little insane. I'm sure you can attest to that better than I.

Thank you for the partly completed poem you sent me for Christmas. It is such a thoughtful gift. I can't really explain how much it means to me. There is no other gift I would want, unless it was you in person. I can't suggest any corrections, and the ending is beyond me. In the first place, I can't write poetry, but I know what I'd like to have on the end.

Perhaps if you don't finish it before you come to London, I'll help you.

It would be so wonderful to share Christmas dinner with you by my side, but as it's Christmas Eve and I've had no word that you were coming, and no hint that you might surprise me, I'll not count on you being here for Christmas. Since you aren't here, I'll just imagine walking with you, enjoying the glitter of fallen snow, and savoring the moonlight in your arms. That's a lovely image to end with, isn't it?

All my love and kisses,
Lucia
December 24, 1856

Lucia was affixing the stamp to her letter to Ronald when Susan announced she had a caller. Taking the calling card from the silver tray she offered, Lucia frowned a bit and told her she would be down momentarily. What was her mother planning now?

She sealed her letter with a bit of wax, then took it with her downstairs. As she reached the bottom, she could hear her mother talking with someone in the drawing room. Sighing, she handed the letter to George and asked him to have it sent to the post office posthaste. He nodded his assent and disappeared through a side door leading to the servant's quarters.

Taking a deep breath, Lucia stepped into the drawing room and smiled. "Mr. Asher, how kind of you to call. Happy Christmas!"

Gerald grinned and stood to greet her. "Happy Christmas to you, too, Miss Rix. I hope you are having a wonderful holiday."

"I am, thank you. Please, won't you sit?"

She took her place on the settee and he sat back in the armchair by the window.

"Has your holiday been a good one?" she asked politely.

"It has, thank you. Oh, I brought you a little remembrance," he said as he pulled a box from his coat pocket.

"You shouldn't have," she protested politely, but accepted the box. Untying the string, she opened it to find several pieces of hard candy. The aroma of peppermint soon filled the room. "How delightful! Thank you, Mr. Asher. Look, Mama."

Lucia handed the box over to her mother, who looked inside and took a deep breath. "This smells heavenly, Mr. Asher. What a thoughtful gift."

"It's nothing," he replied. "Do you have plans this evening, ladies? Mother would enjoy having you drop over for dinner around seven, if that's convenient."

"We'd be honored," Harriet answered before Lucia could protest.

"Wonderful. I'll see you then." Gerald stood to leave. "I can see myself out."

"Thank you for calling on us, and Happy Christmas," Harriet called after him.

Lucia scowled at her mother. Obviously feigning innocence, Harriet looked at her daughter and smiled. "Won't it be lovely to join the Ashers for dinner? It's a perfect opportunity for you to wear the new gown I gave you. You'll look extra lovely in it, I'm sure."

With that, she turned and glided from the room, leaving Lucia wondering how she was going to get out of this one. As it turned out, she decided not to try. The more she thought about it, the more she realized she'd been backed into a corner. If she refused to go, Mr. Asher and his mother would be offended.

It wasn't their fault that her mother was conniving and sneaky and determined to marry her off to Gerald Asher. Besides, it was Christmas, and it really would be lovely to enjoy Christmas evening celebrating, instead of staying home and enduring another fight with Mama.

So, she donned the Christmas gown, arranged her hair in a simple, but attractive style, and picked up her fan as she left the room. She glanced down at it before she reached the stairs and frowned. No, she thought, there's no need to bring the fan tonight. I'm going to visit friends, not to flirt with Mr. Asher. Turning back, she placed the fan deliberately on her dressing table, then hurried downstairs to meet her mother.

Their carriage moved slowly down the street to avoid the people wassailing. Lucia loved this tradition. The less fortunate would take Christmas as an opportunity to bring a little extra income to their families. They'd carry wooden bowls filled with delicious wassail and go from door-to-door, hoping for donations of food, drink, or money as they invited those inside to share a drink from their wooden bowls.

When they came to the Rix home, Lucia would rush to open the door herself. Otherwise, Mama would chase them off. Of course, there were also other families who walked door to door, simply caroling to entertain their neighbors. That looks like fun, Lucia thought. I wish Mama would allow that, but Mama felt that anything done door-to-door was beneath the Rix family.

The Asher home was beautifully decorated. There were candles in each window, and greenery and ribbons above the doorway. Inside, the festivities were well underway. They were conducted to the drawing room, which was graced with a glorious Christmas tree, complete with candles, tinsel, beautiful ornaments made of colorful paper, and ribbons.

There were a few young children trying to reach baskets of candies hanging from the branches amid ropes of popcorn and cranberries that looped around the tree.

Lucia grinned as one little boy jumped as hard as he could and missed the basket he was aiming for, nearly falling into the tree as he came down. She moved quietly to the little group and motioned for them to follow her towards the back of the tree. She handed each child a basket with a wink and a finger to her lips. They giggled and ran off to enjoy their treats.

As she emerged from behind the tree, she nearly ran into Gerald, her breath catching as she realized he'd seen what she'd done.

"I'm…" she began, not knowing quite what to say. "I'm sorry. I just can't stand to see children frustrated on such a wonderful holiday."

He laughed merrily. "Me neither. I was about to do the same thing myself."

"You were?" her eyebrows rose in disbelief.

"Of course! Why do you think we put them there? Yes, they're pretty, but mostly they are for the nieces and nephews to enjoy."

She grinned. "Oh, I'm so glad you feel that way. Christmas is such fun for children. Why spoil it by not allowing them to enjoy it?"

"Absolutely," he agreed. "Would you care to join us in the dining room? Mother has announced that the table is laid and ready for us."

Lucia nodded her assent, and they moved to the elegant dining room, set with beautiful bone china and ornate goblets. As Gerald indicated her seat, he moved to join his mother at the end of the long table. Between each place setting sat a gaily-decorated Christmas cracker. Lucia was delighted. She hadn't enjoyed a Christmas cracker pull since she was a little girl. The small cardboard tubes were covered in brightly coloured twists of paper.

She looked to either side and grinned at her table companions, crossed her arms, and took one end of the cracker on each side. Her companions did the same. When all the guests were thus linked, Mrs. Asher called, "One, two, three, pull!"

Lucia pulled and jumped a bit as each cracker popped open, spilling tissue paper hats, narrow streamers, slips of paper that she knew had silly jokes on them, and a small gift. Looking at the ends she still held in her hand, she laughed when the right one had the larger remnant of the cracker.

"I win!" she cried, picking up the small blue box that had fallen from that cracker.

She opened it eagerly and found a tiny bell tied with a red ribbon. She turned to the woman on her right and asked her to tie it to her wrist, as was tradition. Once the bell was tied securely, Lucia shook her arm gently, laughing at the sweet tinkling of the bell. Then, she reached for the red tissue paper crown and placed it on her head.

Looking around, she saw everyone had done the same, including her mother who was sitting on the other side of the table. She seems to be enjoying herself, Lucia thought. I haven't seen her this happy in a very long time.

A larger bell was rung at the head of the table, drawing everyone's attention. Lucia stifled a giggle as she saw Gerald with a green paper crown sitting jauntily askew on his head. He stood and waited for everyone to quiet down. With great aplomb, he removed the little slip of paper from his cracker tube and flicked his wrists a bit as he settled the paper in front of him with a flourish. Clearing his throat, he began to read, "Where do fish wash?"

With one accord, the guests replied loudly, "Where?"

"In the river basin!" he replied. Everyone either groaned or laughed at the bad joke.

Gerald indicated his mother should be next. She stood and read her joke, "What lies in a pram and wobbles?" Again, everyone answered in unison, "What?"

"A jelly baby!" she read, and again everyone groaned and laughed.

One by one, each guest read the joke or limerick on their papers. They were all cliché and not very funny, but everyone groaned and laughed anyway, enjoying the silliness of the old party game. At last, the final joke was read and moaned over. Lucia's sides hurt from laughing so hard.

Mrs. Asher then rang the bell again, and a line of servants entered with silver trays laden with food of every description. Meats, cheeses, puddings, cakes, and of course, an enormous roast goose soon covered the table. Servants poured wine into each goblet in turn. Yet everyone sat with their hands in their laps, admiring, but not touching the feast before them.

When everything was laid out, Mr. Asher stood and announced, "We at Asher Manor welcome each of you to our Christmas table. As is tradition, I will begin with a toast." He raised his goblet and everyone followed suit.

"May this Christmas season find us all healthy and happy, grateful for what we have, and generous to those who have not. Our hearts and prayers go out to those who fight in the war, and the families they have left behind. May the coming year bring an end to the battles and a beginning to lasting peace."

"To peace," each guest repeated, raising their goblets and then taking a sip.

"Now, my friends, enjoy!" Mr. Asher proclaimed, and those at the table did just that.

After dinner, they all retired to the drawing room. It was customary in the Asher home that everyone participated in the evening's entertainment. Several shy children mumbled recitations and poems, then the older children and some of the adults performed short plays and scenes from history.

Lucia sang, of course, and Gerald's mother led everyone in singing favorite carols. It was a joyous occasion, and all that was missing for Lucia was Ronald by her side.

As she and her mother were preparing to leave, Gerald brought her a small package.

"Mr. Asher," Lucia protested. "You shouldn't have."

"It's not from me," he smiled. "It's from Aunt Bea. She insisted that I wait to give it to you until you were ready to leave."

Lucia untied the ribbon and opened the box. Inside was a tiny locket. As Lucia opened it, she was surprised to find it empty.

"There's a note," Gerald handed her a tiny piece of folded paper.

Dear Lucia,

I hope you will accept this small token of my esteem. The locket was given to me by my grandmother when I was about your age. Over the years, it has held locks of hair from each person I've loved and lost. I hope you will cherish it and use it to remember your loved ones as the years go by and death takes its toll. I also hope you don't have to use it for many, many years! It has brought me much comfort and I hope it will do the same for you.

Happy Christmas.
Aunt Bea

Lucia shuddered. Although the gift was meant as a token of friendship, she couldn't help but wonder if Mrs. Asher's insight would prove to be too true too soon.

"Please tell your aunt thank you, and I'll be calling on her soon."

Gerald smiled. "I will. Goodnight."

For some reason, the cold night air seemed just a bit colder to Lucia as they made their way home. Harriet was blessedly silent for a change.

As they entered the house, Lucia suddenly turned and hugged her mother. "Happy Christmas, Mama," she said through unexpected tears.

Harriet hugged her daughter tightly, then answered, her own voice thick with emotion. "Happy Christmas, Lucia."

"But I've already told them you'd sing!" Harriet fairly yelled. "You can't embarrass me by not going."

"Mama, you should ask me before agreeing to these events. I am working New Year's Eve and New Year's Day. I need to sleep between those shifts, not attend an all-night party."

"Fine, I'll tell them you can't come. No, I'll tell them you won't come," her mother pouted.

Lucia looked at the ceiling and silently prayed for strength. Looking back at her mother, she sighed. "I'll go, Mama, but only long enough to perform. Then I'm going home to bed."

"Wonderful!" Harriet crowed. "It will be such fun."

Why do I do this to myself, Lucia wondered. Why do I let her do this to me?

Lucia was gorgeous in a blue satin gown she knew Mama would approve of. It was certainly better than the ugly gray one she picked when I was twelve, Lucia thought as she examined herself in the looking glass.

As they entered the Wingate's ballroom, Lucia found herself feeling lighter and happier than she thought she would. The fatigue of a twelve-hour shift at the hospital seemed to fade away with the music and gaiety of the crowd.

"Miss Rix, how wonderful to see you." Gerald approached her with a huge smile on his face. "May I presume to ask for the first dance?"

"Mr. Asher, we've only just arrived and…" Lucia began, but Harriet interrupted.

"She'd love to, Mr. Asher. How good of you to ask." Her mother gave her a little shove toward him.

Lucia started to protest, then shook her head and gave in.

As Gerald whisked her off onto the dance floor, he winked at her. Her eyebrows shot up at his boldness.

"No need to look shocked," he grinned. "I thought I'd save you from all of those eligible bachelors your mother is bound to parade in front of you tonight."

Lucia relaxed and laughed. "That's a heroic gesture, good sir."

When the music stopped, he escorted her to the refreshment room where he offered her a glass of punch. As they sipped their punch, they talked amiably. Lucia felt quite comfortable with him, she noticed. Perhaps because he'd made it quite clear he would not pursue her without her consent. That made him safe.

And since her mother seemed to think he was perfect for her, she would not object to the two of them being seen together at gatherings such as this. It seemed to be a win-win, except something niggled at the back of her mind.

"Mr. Asher," she began, "if I may be so bold, you've made it clear that you'll honor my desire to remain true to my fiancé. Yet you deprive yourself of other feminine companionship by rescuing me from other would-be pursuers. May I ask why?"

He smiled down at her, his eyes twinkling. "Quite simply, Miss Rix, because I find you relaxing."

"Relaxing?" she asked, puzzled.

"Yes. Other... how did you put it... feminine companionship requires a certain amount of chasing, and flirting, and surface adherence to propriety while expecting propriety to fly out the window when we find ourselves alone, but you and I have an understanding. I can relax, knowing that I don't need to be on my guard for unwelcome feminine advances, or be coerced into advancing a relationship that has no future. I'm not ready to settle down, but I'm quite bored with the expectation that I should be looking for someone to settle down with right this very minute. You see, our objectives are quite compatible."

Lucia nodded and smiled. She understood perfectly.

"I am grateful for your company, Mr. Asher. And even more grateful that it doesn't come with strings attached."

"Indeed, Miss Rix. Shall we take another spin around the dance floor?" She smiled up at him and took his proffered arm, ready to fool the world, or more accurately, her mother, into thinking they might truly be a couple.

Darling,

I've started to write five times and I've had so many interruptions you may never get this missive. I've been thinking about our first meeting in Scutari. My first impression of you was that you were quite the tough nurse who wasn't going to allow me to wallow in the pit of self-pity I'd buried myself in. It didn't take long for you to wiggle into my heart, either! I'm very grateful for the storm that forced our evacuation from the tent hospital to the Barracks Hospital at Scutari. The timing was perfect and I had the best nurse in the place.

I would dearly love to hear your life history, my dear! I'm ready to learn all about my sweet London nurse. Of course, hearing it in person would be much better than a letter. I can't wait for this war to finally be over. I'm sure I'll kiss the first square foot of good old British soil as soon as we land. I'm getting very tired of being away from you for so long. When I arrive, would you want time to prepare which also would give you time to be nervous and anxious? Or would you prefer to be surprised and perhaps be caught unprepared for my arrival?

How is your mother getting along? Fine, I hope. I look forward to meeting her and hope she will like me as much as you believe I will like her. Mothers are often protective of their children, you know, so we may have an uphill battle of it at first. But I promise to be on my best behavior and perhaps I can wiggle my way into her heart just a wee bit.

I remember you mentioned once your mother being frustrated with your hair. Personally, I think your long dark hair is wonderful. I'll bet it is beautiful when it's brushed out nice and long. I should like very much to see it that way. Putting you under it makes for perfection.

As for you choosing a certain red-haired sergeant, aren't you a lucky girl? Because that sergeant has given his whole heart to you, as well.

You? Are you telling me that you have a temper? I don't believe it. Well, maybe just a little when patients don't follow your instructions. Remember when you refused to let anyone wait on me so I'd have to get off my bed and walk? Or the time you told the private next to me that if he didn't start cooperating, you were going to roll him off his bed and around the floor of the ward just to get some circulation going? You sounded quite angry to me that time! Still, most of the time, your sweet disposition can't be matched by anyone, anywhere.

Besides, I don't think hair color has anything to do with temper. I, for one, have red hair and have absolutely no temper at all. In all honesty. None at all. Despite the rumors you may have heard from the enlisted soldiers, I am an even-tempered, well-mannered gentleman who would never think of raising his voice or hand to nary a soul, man nor beast. Do you believe me?

I don't mind you saving my letters. In fact, I do the same. But I ought to insist that you don't show them to your grandchildren about forty years from now.

I promise that if anything ever happens to me, you shall know about it as soon as possible. I promise you will get word. I know you think about all those soldiers lying in the hospital at Scutari and imagine that I might end up there again. But I promise you I am keeping my head down and staying as safe as I possibly can. Just keep waiting and hoping. It won't be very long now. That's a lot of promises, isn't it? And I mean to keep every one of them.

Lovingly yours,
Ronald
January 18, 1856

Chapter Twenty-One

Dearest Ronald,

Your last letter was very sweet, and I have read it many times. You mentioned my hair and that you'd like to see it after it's brushed. That made me think to really look at it when I brushed it that night. I'm glad I have my father's hair, thick and dark. I think you'll like it when you see it that way.

Although, Mama gets frustrated with it. Because it's so thick, it won't hold the style she thinks an eligible young lady should wear. Personally, I prefer either pulled back out of the way for work, or brushed out loose.

Of course, the hair fashions today are much more elaborate than that, which is Mama's point exactly. In her words, "You can't expect to attract an eligible young man if you insist on looking like a frumpy spinster or some kind of gypsy!" What she doesn't accept is that I am not looking for an eligible young man. I've already chosen the young man I want to marry. A certain red-haired sergeant has captured my heart and I have no interest in anyone else.

I have no doubt that you will be able to wiggle your way into Mama's heart. Remember what happened to me when I first looked at you, lying so still and angry back in Scutari? I fell head over heels, and haven't been the same since. I'm sure, in time, Mama will love you, too.

I think you should know that I have an ally in my battle with Mama. One Mr. Gerald Asher is Mama's odd-on favorite for my husband-to-be. However, as he and I have talked, he has made it clear that he respects our engagement and honors my desire to wait for you. We have agreed to be seen together at social events. It should appease Mama's desire to find me a husband if she believes I'm keeping company with Mr. Asher.

For his part, he's expressed the desire to seem "off the market" as well, for different reasons. I hope you won't mind, darling, but it seems the most reasonable way to handle Mama while I await your arrival.

What a tough choice you've given me! To be surprised or have time to anticipate your arrival. Each option has its merits. If I knew when you were coming, I could get dressed in my finest apparel and meet you at the dock. It would be wonderful to see you walking down that gangplank in your uniform. I can just imagine us running toward each other, my hair flying, your sword clanging at your side. What a picture we'd make!

On the other hand, it would be such a lovely surprise to have you knock at my door unannounced. I don't know if I'd throw myself into your arms or faint from the shock of it. I suppose I'll just have to let you make that decision for me. I just can't choose.

You? No temper? I'm sorry, my love, but while your temper is usually under control, I wouldn't go as far as to say you have none. That's not a bad thing, mind you. If someone were to accost me, for example, I'd expect and desire you to let your temper flare in my defense, but let's make a pact to keep our tempers in check unless it's in defense of another person or creature.

I will allow you to kiss the first square foot of British soil, if I get the second kiss. And the third, fourth, fifth, etc. I miss you, too, darling! If those kisses happened to be on my birthday, that would make my birthday so wonderful. I wouldn't want any other gifts at all, just you in my arms. I'm sorry if I keep repeating myself on that point, but that's truly all I can think about these days.

That, and a pen that writes better than this one. Its tip is worn to a nub so it barely holds the ink at all. It doesn't help that the ink runs on this thin paper. To add to the difficulty, my tears are smearing the ink again. I hope you can read this scribble. If not, I'm sorry. I'll try to get a better pen, better paper, and fewer tears when I write again.

You mentioned a fellow by the name of Art Hahn. That is really an unusual name and I used to know a family in London by that name. They moved here from Brighton three years ago. Could he, by any chance, be from my favorite city? I'd surely like to visit that beautiful place again this summer, and it would be even better if you could come with me. I'd love to show you all my favorite places.

What? You don't want our grandchildren to see what we've written to each other? I'm surprised that you'd be that shy, my darling. Wouldn't it be ironic if someday, one of our children or grandchildren decided to write a book based on our letters? I don't know what future generations would find so very interesting in them, though, so I supposed we don't need to worry about that.

You asked me to try and recreate the four-page letter I threw out. I don't think I can recall all of it, but there are two stories I do remember writing about.

The first was about a young boy at the hospital with tuberculosis. Sadly, he died, but that wasn't the whole of the story. I was with him near the end. His mother had stepped out for a moment and I was alone with him.

As I was bathing his forehead, he reached up and touched my arm. He thanked me for helping him, for making him comfortable. His eyes held such gratitude that I was moved to tears. All I could do was smile and tell him that it was my honor to serve him.

Throughout my shift, I watched as he did the same thing for each staff member who interacted with him. It was as if he knew he wouldn't last long and he wanted to be sure to thank each person who'd helped him. Oh, that we all could be so grateful for the kindnesses we are shown!

The second story came to my mind one evening when I came in from work. I was chilled from a winter storm and was trying to think of warm things to take my mind off my frozen fingers and toes. The one I recalled happened last summer.

Mama and I were walking under the trees, near the stream, trying to get a little relief from the scorching sun. I noticed a group of children playing downstream. They were floating paper boats in the water. One little girl, maybe three or four years of age, was watching from a little way off. She looked so forlorn as a woman, I assume it was her nanny, held her hand tightly. I'm sure she'd been forbidden to go near the water. I felt sad for her, because the water did look inviting.

We walked a bit further, and I saw the nanny let go of her hand and bend over the pram she was pushing. I watched the little girl look up with a surprised expression, then look at the water, then back at her nanny, then back at the water. I nearly giggled when her expression changed to one of great determination. She took one step away from the nanny, then another, then one more.

Finally, she turned and broke away, racing toward the water as fast as her little legs would carry her. What's more, she didn't stop until she was knee-deep in the stream, laughing and giggling with such joy and abandon that I wished I was four years old again so I could splash with her. The nanny retrieved her shortly, scolding her for getting wet, but the look on the little girl's face was one of pure joy, and I'm certain she felt it was worth it.

I, for one, will not restrain our children from playing in the water on a hot August day. There's too much joy in it, and how can I deny them whatever joy they can capture in their lives?

Oh, my love, how I miss you! I think of you constantly, and I hope you are honoring your word and keeping your head down when the fighting gets too close. I want you to come to me soon and safe.

Meanwhile, I'll continue imagining what it will be like when you step off the boat and rush into my arms. That is, unless you forget me after all this time has passed. That thought is just too horrible! Please, don't forget me, as I will never, ever forget you.

I don't think I ever told you, but the night I left, we ran into a storm in the middle of the night. The ship was rocking so hard, I couldn't stay in my bunk. I ended up curled on the floor, clinging to the leg of the bunk with both arms and legs, but the storm outside didn't compare to the storm raging in my heart. The mixture of grief, rage, and torment were almost more than I could bear.

The only thing that kept me sane at all was the memory of that last kiss with you. That kiss held the promise of a future that could not be seen. A future filled with love, peace, and joy. There are nights when I still must cling to that promise. Please, hurry back to me and fulfill that promise!

I think of you constantly, and the past few days I've been so worried that something has happened and I won't ever know about it. I know you told me not to worry, that you'd arranged for me to hear if something happened, but what if something happened to you and all your friends? What if your entire unit was ambushed and killed? How would I ever know?

I'm sorry, dear. I don't mean to go on about it, but today has been one of those days when I have thought of you so much I've started to worry again. Darling, if you have been hurt or you are ill, I think I'd have a collapse the minute I learned of it. You say not to worry, but I can't help it. I will, however, try to keep my worry to a minimum for your sake.

Ever yours,
Lucia
February 8, 1856

Lucia cursed the heavy front door. It would have been so satisfying to slam it closed, and it wouldn't matter that her mother would have one more reason to be angry with her. This fight had been especially terrible, with her mother insisting that she allow Mr. Asher to call, while Lucia insisted that it wouldn't be appropriate. It had escalated from there, and finally, Lucia couldn't stay in the house one minute longer.

She pulled her heavy cloak around her, wishing she'd brought a heavier scarf against the bitter wind. Trudging down the path, she felt a snowflake on her nose.

"Great," she muttered aloud. "Just great."

She hadn't gone very far when a hansom cab pulled up beside her.

"May we give you a lift?" Gerald's voice was muffled in the falling snow.

Lucia looked up and saw that he was with his aunt, but shook her head.

"No, thank you. I'm just trying to clear my head."

Mrs. Asher leaned over her nephew. "Nonsense, dear. You'll only clog it up in this cold night air. At least come in and warm yourself. Then we can drop you home when you're sufficiently clear-headed."

Lucia smiled despite the anger that still seethed in her heart.

As Gerald helped her into the cab, she slid into the seat next to his aunt, who patted her knee and said, "Now that you're not being turned into a snow-woman, tell us what's troubling you," she demanded kindly.

Again, Lucia smiled but shook her head. "It's nothing, really."

The older woman cocked her head. "Doesn't look like nothing to me. It might help to talk about it."

Lucia considered this grand lady who looked so kind, then looked into Gerald's eyes, which mirrored the kindness in his aunt's. She took a deep breath and began, telling them all about the fight with Mama.

When she was finished, Mrs. Asher nodded sagely. "I think I know what the problem is."

"Oh?" Lucia was curious now.

"Neither you, nor your mother are considering how the other feels."

Stung, Lucia started to protest, but the older woman held up a hand to stop her.

"Let me finish, dear," she said sweetly.

"You are very much in love with your sergeant, right?"

Lucia nodded.

"Your mother loves you very much. Would you agree?"

Lucia nodded again, slower this time.

"Would you agree that she wants to see you happy?"

"Yes, but…"

"The problem is your idea of what will make you happy is different than hers. She only knows your sergeant by what you have told her. She doesn't know him for herself. She sees eligible young bachelors from good families that look like they would make you good husbands, and in her mind, that's what you should be aiming for. On your end, you're so focused on your sergeant that you're not seeing things from your mother's perspective.

"It's like a poor man who's been promised roast beef tomorrow if he'll give up his gruel today. All he's ever had is gruel that doesn't ever fill him up, so he can't even imagine what roast beef would taste like, let alone that it might leave him feeling satisfied like he's never been satisfied in his life. Your mother can't imagine anyone she doesn't know making you happy or providing a good life for you. If you take a moment to think from her perspective, perhaps you'll be able to better understand her need to… how did you put it?"

"Parade you in front of every young dandy this side of the Thames," Gerald filled in helpfully and his aunt nodded.

"So, if I understand her perspective, how does that change the situation?" Lucia asked, still frustrated.

"It doesn't," Mrs. Asher stated flatly, "but it might help you handle her differently. Instead of coming at her head on like two prize bulls, why don't you share more with her? Perhaps read her some of your letters from him. Let her get to know him through his letters. That might give her a taste of your perspective, and perhaps she'll decide to leave off and let things happen as they are intended to."

Lucia nodded. Share her letters. She'd never thought of that. Perhaps that would work.

"Thank you, Mrs. Asher. You're a wise woman."

Beatrice Asher smiled and hugged her. "That's what us old biddies are good for; wise words. Now, let us take you home so you can change into some warm, dry clothes."

Chapter Twenty-Two

Lucia woke with a start as someone knocked on her bedroom door.

"Yes?" she called.

"Miss Rix, there's a letter for you," her maid responded softly. "Shall I slide it under the door?"

"Yes, please, Susan. Thank you."

She tumbled out of bed and threw on her dressing gown, nearly tripping on the sash as she dashed to retrieve the letter. She didn't bother to read the front, but carefully broke the seal and unfolded the precious, long-awaited letter.

Dear Miss Rix,

You don't know me, except perhaps by name. I have been a friend of Sergeant Ronald Ferguson. He…

Lucia blinked twice, then re-read the first line. Her breath caught and she re-read it again. Closing her eyes against the tears that already threatened to fall, she took a deep, shaky breath, and forced herself to read on.

…joined my unit in 1842 as a young private. I've worked by his side through many battles and numerous injuries. We were both injured in

the battle at Balaclava, but I was sent to the General Hospital before he was evacuated to Scutari. We reunited here in Sevastopol after it was taken last September. Some months ago, he charged me with a task, which task I now sadly perform.

Two days ago, Russian guns bombarded the city. Our unit was hit hard. We had many casualties. I regret to report that Sergeant Ferguson was killed...

A scream of horror erupted from her throat as she dropped to the floor, clutching the letter to her breast. Sobs wracked her body, and she was unaware of her mother bursting into the room. She didn't notice her mother pause, then cross the short distance to sink to the floor beside her. She didn't feel her mother's arms wrap around her, or hear her crooning softly as they rocked back and forth together. She didn't notice Susan peek in, and didn't see her back away quietly when Harriet frowned at her.

Nearly an hour later, Lucia's tears were spent, yet she continued clutching the letter and rocking back and forth, still unaware of anything but the broken heart still unreasonably beating in her chest. Another hour passed and her rocking slowed, and then stopped. Harriet slowly sat up and released her hold on Lucia, but kept one arm around her shoulders.

"Would you like me to read the letter to you?" she asked softly.

Dully, Lucia looked up, her eyes red and swollen from weeping. She nodded and handed the rumpled letter into her mother's waiting hand.

Harriet glanced over it briefly, then started reading from the beginning, pausing from time to time to be sure Lucia was still listening.

Dear Miss Rix,

You don't know me, except perhaps by name. I have been a friend of Sergeant Ronald Ferguson. He joined my unit in 1842 as a young private. I've worked by his side through many battles and numerous injuries. *We were both injured in the battle at Balaclava, but I was sent to the General Hospital before he was evacuated to Scutari. We reunited here in Sevastopol after it was taken last September. Some months ago, he charged me with a task, which task I now sadly perform.*

Two days ago, Russian guns bombarded the city. Our unit was hit hard. We had many casualties. I regret to report that Sergeant Ferguson was killed.

It was a surprise attack, as we had been told the Russians were pulling back and the war would soon be over. Apparently, someone forgot to tell this Russian unit.

Perhaps it would help to know the circumstances surrounding his death. As I said, we took Sevastopol last fall and have been defending it ever since. On the evening of January 28, the sergeant and I were on guard duty when we spotted movement just outside of town. He ordered me to keep watch while he went to report to the general.

Try as I might, I couldn't pinpoint the movement we'd just seen, but I kept my eyes open anyway. When the sergeant came back, he told me the general was passing the word to stay alert, but our orders were not to attempt to engage the enemy should we spot them, but to retire and give the alarm.

Around five in the morning, we were relieved, and I went to my tent to sleep. As was his normal routine, Sergeant Ferguson went to care for the captain's horse, feeding, watering, and currying her in the corral before turning in himself. I fell asleep quickly with full assurance that those on watch would warn us if anything happened.

We have a good sprinkling of the right sort of stuff with us; old soldiers, men that have smelt powder on many a hard-contested field, men that know well how to do their duty and are no strangers to a musket ball whistling past their heads, who understand well the sound of a live shell in the air and know within a little where it will drop. One feels much more comfortable with such men than with three times their number who have never smelt powder.

The attack happened as we were eating breakfast. Even though we thought the Russians were out there, no alarm was sounded, so were unprepared. When the cannonballs started flying, we scrambled to the walls, under tables and behind crates and anything else that might afford an illusion of shelter. Unfortunately, not everyone made it to safety.

When the bombardment began, the sergeant managed to move a couple of the horses close to a wall where they'd be relatively safe. I had found some safety behind a stack of crates near a window, and could see him and a couple of other groups of soldiers clumped together near the wall.

The Russian fire was very heavy. They had more guns in position than we knew. Imagine some hundreds of guns and mortars firing in salvoes. For a time, the guns would stop, to allow them to get a little cool, then they would burst forth again, the thunder being enough to shake the earth to its very centre; and this lasted for hours. Still, the barrage went on and death was raining fast around. It seemed something like a hell upon earth.

The shells were exploding all around us, and we could hear screams from somewhere to the right of our building. When I glanced out the window again, I saw the sergeant's head turning this way and that, and knew he was accounting for his men, as he did every time we were attacked. I figured there was someone missing when he stood up and looked around again, fixing on one doorway across from us.

I glanced in the direction he was looking and saw our newest recruit dash across the open area, clearly panicking. He stopped, and the expression on his face was one of utter terror. He looked back at the doorway, then at one group of men near the wall, then at our doorway, then back to his own again. He seemed frozen with fear. I heard the sergeant holler for him to go back inside, but I don't think the private heard him.

Finally, Sergeant Ferguson dashed out, grabbed the young man, and started back for the relative safety of the building. Zig-zagging as they ran, they finally dove through the doorway, and I felt relief that they'd found some protection.

Those of us in my building had a very narrow escape from a huge shell that came right through the roof and into the midst of us; we had just enough time to throw ourselves down when it exploded and sent tables, chairs, and our breakfast flying in all directions. Before long, we were covered with smoke, dust, stones, and food. The cannonballs were still coming fast and furious, so I ducked my head and stayed low until the barrage stopped.

When it was quiet again, I looked up and was shocked to see our building was still standing, but it had several large holes in the roof. I looked out the window, and the building the sergeant had taken shelter in was flattened and burning.

Several of us ran to try and rescue the sergeant and anyone else trapped under there. We were having some success pulling boards and planks away, and finding several injured men. Then we saw his leg under the debris. It was bent strangely and not moving. I repositioned myself to begin pulling boards away from where I thought his head should be.

After a few minutes, I saw his red uniform. I hollered for help and kept pulling boards away. Two privates that I don't know came to help. A few more planks, and I could see his face. There wasn't much left of it, so I knew he couldn't have survived.

I kept pulling at boards, thinking the least I could do was give him a decent burial, but a captain ran by and ordered the lot of us to help rebuild the barricade on the north side. When I returned, the area had been cleared. I don't know where they put his body. Probably in an unmarked grave with the other poor souls who died that day. When all the casualties were counted, we found that we had lost nineteen men, two corporals, and Sergeant Ferguson out of thirty in our unit.

I'm sorry. I know this must be a terrible shock to you. I hope you can remember that he died doing what he always did, looking after his men first. He was a great man, an excellent leader, and the best friend I've ever had. I shall miss him.

If there's ever anything you need, I know he'd want me to do my best to help you. I've enclosed a ring he had in his belongings. He bought

*it several months ago, and was planning to give it to you when he came
to London. I'm certain it was going to be your wedding ring. I know he'd
want you to have it.*

Respectfully yours,
Corporal Art Hahn
January 31, 1856

Lucia never moved throughout the reading, but sat staring
straight ahead. When the last words were read, Harriet carefully
folded the letter, then placed it and the ring in her daughter's hand.
She stood and urged Lucia to stand, as well.

After a moment, Lucia responded and allowed herself to be led
to the bed where her mother gently helped her lie down. Harriet
covered her with the blankets, brushed her hair from her face, kissed
her forehead, and said, "I have a few things to take care of. You rest
and I'll return in a few minutes."

Not waiting for a response, she left the room, closing the door
behind her.

The next week passed in a daze for Lucia. She was barely aware
of the rising and setting of the sun. She never left her room and ate
but a nibble here and there. She allowed herself to be bathed and
dressed in the black crepe gown her mother provided, but did nothing
to aid in caring for herself. Day after day, she sat in a chair by the
window, staring out at nothing.

Well into week three, Harriet entered her room unannounced. If
Lucia had been aware, she would have noticed the firm expression on
her mother's face and the determined way she walked across the
room. She would have known her mother had something up her
sleeve.

"Lucia?" Harriet gently shook her arm. "Lucia, you need to come
with me."

No response.

"Lucia," Harriet's voice was more firm, this time. "Get up. You have callers."

Still no response.

"Lucia Grace Rix! You are being quite rude. You must get up and greet your callers."

Taking a deep breath and stirring as if from a long slumber, Lucia slowly looked up into her mother's eyes, a dazed bewildered expression on her face.

"Callers?"

"Yes, callers," her mother stated flatly. "I know you are in mourning, but even in mourning there are protocols of etiquette that must be observed. You have callers, and it's time to greet them."

Allowing herself to be pulled to a standing position, she followed her mother slowly out the door and down the stairs. As they approached the drawing room, Lucia paused, becoming more aware of what was happening.

"I don't really feel like greeting callers, Mama," she said, her voice dull.

"That doesn't matter, Lucia," her mother instructed. "You will greet them, and you will be polite."

As her mother opened the door, Lucia dutifully followed her into the drawing room. In deference to her mourning, the heavy drapes had been left closed and the lamps lent a soft glow to the room.

"May we extend our deepest condolences, Miss Rix?" a sweet, somewhat familiar voice spoke.

It was joined by a deeper, more familiar voice. "Yes, please accept our condolences."

She looked up into the warm grey eyes of Gerald Asher, his face somber for once. Turning her gaze to his left, she saw his mother looking at her, quite concerned. "How can we help?" she asked.

"Thank you," she answered softly, tears filling her eyes. "There's nothing to be done, but I appreciate your sympathy."

"Won't you sit down?" Harriet invited.

"Thank you, no," Mrs. Asher replied. "We know it's a difficult time and we only wanted to see if you needed anything. Please don't hesitate to send word if there is something we can do to help."

As Harriet and Mrs. Asher moved toward the door, Gerald touched Lucia's arm. "I'm truly sorry, Miss Rix. I know your heart must be breaking right now. If you need someone to talk to, or if you need a distraction, please allow me to help."

Lucia looked into the eyes of this man that she knew only briefly, grateful that he seemed so understanding. "I will, Mr. Asher. Your offer is most kind."

She walked with him to the front door. No more words were spoken, but Lucia felt surprisingly comforted by the visit.

As the door closed, her mother turned to her. "That wasn't so bad, now was it?"

Lucia shook her head and tried a half-smile. "No, Mama. It wasn't so bad."

Three days later, the maid brought Lucia a note. "From Mr. Asher, Miss. He said no answer is required."

She closed the door behind her and Lucia unfolded the small piece of paper. The first thing Lucia noticed was that the penmanship was exquisite. It was so different from her Ronald's haphazard scrawl. She smiled, then frowned as the pain of his death hit her again. She closed her eyes and took a deep breath, willing the tears not to fall.

After a moment, she opened her eyes and tried to focus on the note.

Dear Miss Rix,

Thank you for seeing Mother and I on Tuesday. I was honored that you took the time to greet us.

Mother is hosting a tea at five in the afternoon in honor of my birthday on Saturday. We would be pleased if you and your mother would join us.

I understand you are in mourning, so please don't feel pressured to accept this invitation. Mother and I will understand.

Sincerely,
Gerald Asher, Esq.

Lucia sighed. She certainly didn't feel like going out, and it was rather insensitive of them to invite her and Mama when they knew she was in mourning.

Shaking her head, she sighed again. Mama. Mama had been very patient with her. In fact, Mama hadn't left the house since that fateful letter, either. She said it was her duty to stand vigil, to be there just in case her daughter needed her. Maybe we should go for Mama's sake, Lucia thought, standing up to go and find her mother.

Harriet was in the music room, playing a simple piece on the piano. Lucia stood in the doorway and listened. Her mother often played, but had never achieved her daughter's level of proficiency. When the piece was finished, Harriet sighed, placed her hands in her lap, and sat with bowed head.

"Mama?" Lucia's voice showed her concern.

Harriet looked up, startled. "Lucia! I didn't hear you come in."

"Are you all right, Mama?"

Her mother smiled. "I'm fine. I'm happy to see you venturing out of your room."

Looking at the invitation in her hand, Lucia took a deep breath. "The Ashers have invited us to tea next Saturday."

"How delightful," her mother's response was enthusiastic, but almost immediately, her expression became concerned. "Do you feel up to going?"

Lucia nodded. Harriet's first reaction showed how much she needed this social interaction. "Yes. Although I can't understand why they invited us. They were so polite to call and extend their condolences the other day. Then to extend an invitation to a social event seems rather... indelicate... doesn't it?"

"Wonderful! Perhaps you could wear the flowered silk morning dress. It's very flattering."

Sighing, Lucia realized her mother wasn't listening, again. "No, Mama. I'm in mourning. I'll wear the black crepe."

"What?" her mother seemed genuinely shocked. "That dress washes out your complexion and makes you look like an old spinster. I wish you'd wear the flowered silk."

"Mama," Lucia was trying to be patient. "You and I both know that I am to remain in black for two full years. That's only proper."

"Two years!" Harriet's voice rose. "That's ludicrous. Two years is required when your spouse dies, not some soldier you barely knew."

"Mama," Lucia was losing her battle with patience, "Ronald was my fiancé. That's as close as a spouse, according to *The Queen* and *Cassel's* manuals. I intend to observe the full mourning period."

"Well, it's your choice, of course, but I do think you're carrying this mourning period too far. It's just not warranted under these circumstances," her mother's voice was determined, and Lucia recognized that the next two years were going to be long and hard. She stood up and turned to go.

"Lucia," Harriet began.

"No more, Mama. I'm going upstairs to lie down."

She ascended the stairs slowly, sorry she'd even thought of accepting the Asher's invitation.

Chapter Twenty-Three

Saturday morning dawned with a sparkling sunrise, made even more brilliant by the gentle rain that had fallen the night before. The grass was wet, the flowers bedazzled with raindrops, and the air smelled wonderful. Lucia had tossed and turned most of the night, but the gentle rainfall had soothed her to sleep in the wee hours of the morning.

As the sun peeked in her bedroom window, kissing her eyelids with gentle warmth, she took a deep breath and stretched. Blinking the sleep from her eyes, she opened them and watched the leaves rustling on the trees just outside her window.

She stretched again, then sat up. Her toes wiggled of their own accord in the thick rug at her feet. She stood up and crossed the room, pushing the window open to breathe in the fresh air. It was going to be a beautiful day.

Then she stopped. A beautiful day? Where was the heavy grief she'd been suffering? She allowed her mind to tentatively touch the memory of her sweet Ronald. Oh. There it is. A rush of sadness filled her heart, as her eyes filled with tears. She allowed them to flow freely, even as her lungs filled with the rain-scented air that now filled her room. So strange to feel both sadness and peace at the same time, she thought.

There was a soft knock on her door.

"Yes?" she called.

"Miss Rix, would you be wantin' a bath this morning?" the maid asked through the closed door.

Lucia thought for only a moment. "Yes, please, Susan. I'll be ready in half an hour."

"Very good, Miss."

Lucia allowed herself to luxuriate in the warm bath, Susan adding more warm water as it cooled. From time to time, the pain of her loss overcame her again and she allowed herself to feel the grief even as her body relaxed in the water. When she was finished, she put on a dressing gown and went to find her mother.

Harriet was sitting at her dressing table, as her maid was arranging her hair in an elaborate style.

"Good morning, Mama," Lucia greeted her.

"Ah, Lucia. Good morning to you, too," her mother smiled at her. "Are you looking forward to tea this afternoon?"

"Yes, the Ashers are good people. It should be a very nice tea," Lucia replied sincerely.

"Oh good. Don't overdo this morning, and plan on a nap this afternoon. We want you well rested, don't we?"

Stifling a sigh, Lucia simply nodded, then made her way back to her own room. So much for enjoying the relaxed feelings today. Mama was returning to her controlling ways, it seemed.

The day passed uneventfully, and as Lucia donned the black crepe gown, she steeled herself for what was sure to be a tirade from her mother as she descended the stairs, but to her surprise, Harriet, dressed in deep green satin, only raised one eyebrow and handed Lucia her fan.

By the time they reached the Asher home, the sun was low in the western sky, lending an almost mysterious golden light to the upstairs windows. One might think the house was ablaze, Lucia thought. Before her thoughts could ramble any more, the front door opened and Gerald's mother greeted them enthusiastically.

"I'm so glad you could come," she gushed. "It's simply delightful to have you here."

They were ushered into the drawing room, which somehow seemed larger without the huge Christmas tree that had graced the front window the last time they'd been here. It was elegantly decorated, however, and Lucia was relieved that there were only a few guests, most of whom she knew.

They visited briefly before a butler announced that tea was served. As the guests made their way to a small dining room, Gerald stepped up beside Lucia.

"I'm glad you came," he said.

"Thank you for inviting us." Lucia decided to ignore the inappropriateness of the invitation. "Mama really needs the diversion. She's kept faithful vigil with me these past few weeks, so it's good for her to get out among good people again."

As they entered the room, it was evident that Gerald's mother paid as much attention to detail in her tea presentation as she had the Christmas dinner a few months before. Each place setting was exquisite and placed just so. There were delicacies of many descriptions, and sweetmeats besides.

Taking her place, Lucia found herself between two women she didn't know well. However, they were polite and expressed their condolences for her grief, even though Lucia was certain neither woman knew who had died.

After tea, Mrs. Asher invited them back into the drawing room for a bit of entertainment. Her niece had prepared several pieces on her harp, which seemed to have magically appeared while they were enjoying the tea. Lucia took a chair near the door and settled in to listen.

The first piece was slow and haunting, reflecting the sadness in Lucia's heart. She lowered her head and let the tears fall, dabbing at them with her handkerchief. When it was over, she was surprised to see Gerald sitting in the chair next to her.

"Aunt Bea has asked me to escort her to her sitting room. She tires easily, but doesn't wish to be alone until she's ready to sleep. We would be honored if you'd join us, unless you'd rather stay and listen," he whispered softly.

"Thank you, I'd like to join you," Lucia answered.

He smiled and nodded, then stepped over to offer his arm to the same elderly woman she'd met twice before. Lucia followed and offered her arm, as well. The woman smiled warmly and accepted. They helped her rise, then moved slowly into the hall, then one slow step at a time, they ascended the stairs into an airy room just off the landing. It was lit with soft lamps, decorated with delicate bric-a-brac, lace doilies, and smelled sweetly of lavender.

They helped her sit in an armchair with needlepointed roses on the seat. They took chairs on either side of her.

"Are you comfortable, Aunt Bea? Do you need anything?" Gerald asked.

"No, no, dear," she answered in a quivery voice. "Just keep me company for a while."

She turned to Lucia and asked, "What does your father do, dear?"

Gerald's eyes grew wide as he started to answer for her, but Lucia smiled a bit and shook her head to stop him.

"My father passed some years ago, Mrs. Asher."

"Oh dear, I'm sorry. Please forgive an old lady's *faux pas*."

"Of course. He was a merchant who transported goods from Sardinia to England and back. His ship went down in a storm. He was quite successful and assured we were well provided for."

"I'm glad he thought ahead, but it's so sad to lose someone you love. I still miss my sweet William and he's been gone nigh onto thirty years now."

"I'm sorry. Does the grief get easier as time goes on?"

The old woman pursed her lips. "I don't know about easier, child. It gets different. Some days are sunny, and some are not. Some days I feel his loss deeply, and other days he is like a pleasant memory that I cherish. Perhaps it's fair to say some days are easier than others."

"I think I understand," Lucia commented softly.

Aunt Beatrice looked at her sharply. "Oh? How old were you when your father died?

"Twelve," was her soft reply.

Nodding, Beatrice pursed her lips. "Twelve is old enough to understand grief a bit, but until you've lost a husband, you won't really have a true understanding of deep grief."

"If I may be so bold, I believe I do understand," Lucia ventured.

"Oh? Who of such importance could you have lost at so young an age?" the old woman pried.

"Aunt Bea!" Gerald was aghast at his aunt's brashness.

"Hush, boy," she instructed. "Let her answer."

"The sergeant I told you about the day you found me walking in the snow."

Beatrice nodded. "Oh, dear. Again, please forgive me. Gerald told me of his passing, but my memory isn't what it used to be. Please, tell me about him."

Lucia found herself telling this audacious woman all about Ronald, how they met, how they fell in love, how they met in secret, how she'd been sent home, how they'd written letters faithfully, their love growing with each one, and how the final letter from his friend had sent her world into despair. The telling was filled with tears, smiles, and even a few laughs.

When she was finished, Beatrice reached over and patted her hand. "You have every reason to mourn, my dear. Take your time, but don't deny yourself the possibility of happiness in the future. I don't believe your Ronald would have wanted that for you."

She shifted in her chair, then announced. "I believe I am ready to retire for the night. If you children will excuse me, and please send in my maid."

"Of course, Aunt Bea," Gerald replied, standing.

Lucia followed suit, then on an impulse, leaned down and kissed the old woman on the forehead. "Thank you for listening."

Beatrice smiled up at her. "It was my pleasure, child. It's not often I get to hear a real love story. I thank you for keeping an old woman company, and I hope to see you again."

As they left the room, Gerald motioned towards a young maid waiting at the end of the hallway. She nodded and they made their way down the stairs back to the drawing room.

"I must apologize for our insensitivity, Miss Rix," Gerald said quietly as they descended. "My mother doesn't always follow proper etiquette. We should not have intruded on your grief by inviting you today."

Lucia looked up at him. "Thank you for your apology. You are forgiven. The music was beautiful and I am honored to have spent time with your aunt. She's a wise woman, isn't she?"

"Yes, she is," he smiled.

The drawing room was deserted, except for Harriet and Gerald's mother talking softly in a corner.

"I'm sorry, Mama. Have I kept you too late?"

"Not at all, Lucia. Did you get Mrs. Asher settled?"

Lucia smiled. "Yes. We had a wonderful visit before she grew too tired to talk anymore."

Harriet stood and extended her hand to Gerald's mother. "Thank you for a delightful evening. I haven't enjoyed myself this much since your lovely Christmas party."

"Thank you for coming, Mrs. Rix. I hope you will join us again."

Lucia turned to Gerald, "Best wishes on your birthday, Mr. Asher, and many happy returns."

"Thank you, Miss Rix," Gerald offered a slight bow in acknowledgement.

Both women were quiet on the walk home, each lost in her own thoughts. As they entered their home and handed their wraps to the maid, Harriet turned to her daughter.

"I'm glad you accepted the Asher's invitation, Lucia. I find Mrs. Asher quite pleasant, and her son seems a gentleman through and through. I was especially impressed with how he cared for his elderly aunt."

Lucia smiled softly. "Yes, that impressed me, as well. He's very thoughtful." She paused, then continued, "I hope you don't mind, but I think I'll skip dinner tonight and go straight up to bed. I'm not at all hungry, but am rather tired."

"It was a lavish tea, wasn't it? I believe I'll follow your example and skip dinner, as well. Good night, Lucia."

Harriet smiled as she watched as her daughter ascended the stairs. With a contented sigh, she went to find the cook to cancel dinner. It's a good beginning, she thought. Yes, a very good beginning.

"I've made an appointment with the dress-maker for tomorrow afternoon," Harriet announced at breakfast.

"Are you getting a new gown made, Mama?" her daughter asked, afraid she already knew the answer and hoping she was wrong.

"No, you are."

Lucia frowned. She wasn't wrong. "I don't need a new gown. I have enough black in my wardrobe to last two lifetimes."

"Exactly. It's time to incorporate some grey and lavender, maybe even something in mauve. What do you think?"

"Mama, you know that deep mourning is observed for two years. The black gowns I have will be sufficient."

"Now, Lucia," Harriet's voice took on a pleading tone. "How will it look for you to be seen in deep mourning at the events this Season? That's certainly not the way to attract a husband."

"I won't be attending any events this Season, Mama. I've already told you that I intend to observe the full two years of mourning to which I am entitled. I am simply not ready for social functions. I need time."

"But you attended tea at the Ashers last Saturday. How is that different?"

Lucia's voice rose in anger. "I made an exception when we went to tea at the Ashers out of respect for you. You've been holding vigil with me and I could see you needed time away, but that doesn't mean I'm throwing away all etiquette and decorum."

Her mother went on as if she hadn't heard. "The Browns are hosting a pre-Season luncheon next Tuesday. I've already accepted. With any luck, you'll have your new gown by then. Won't that be lovely?" Harriet was obviously determined to have her way.

"I hope you have a lovely time, Mama. I'm not going," Lucia's lips were turning white with barely concealed rage.

"You've already attended one Society function, which obligates you to any that I see fit to accept," Harriet seemed not to notice the effect her words were having on her daughter.

"It was not a Society function, Mama. It was a small, private tea."

"Not so private. There were several people there with whom I was not acquainted." Her mother sounded reasonable, but Lucia knew she'd dug her heels in and would not be swayed.

"That's beside the point. I have no intention of parading around any Society events this Season. I'm in deep mourning and I wish you would respect that."

"How can you be in deep mourning? You hardly knew the boy."

Harriet sounded irritated. "By all rights and proper protocols, you shouldn't be in mourning at all."

"I loved him! We were engaged to be married! Why can't you accept that?" Lucia wanted to scream, but she kept her voice low which actually served to accentuate the depth of her emotions. Or it would have, if Harriet had been listening.

"Because I think you are a silly girl who needs to find a husband before you are labeled a spinster. I also think you have become enamored of a mistaken notion that this so-called mourning will get you out of your social obligation to find a husband this year." Harriet was adamant.

Silence. Lucia could not think of one thing to say that would not come out as hateful and hurtful. Finally, she chose to simply leave the room.

Harriet watched her go, and almost regretted her last comment. Almost. If it woke her daughter up to the desperation of the situation, then it would be worth the hurt look on her face. She's still quite young. She'll get over it and thank me later, she thought.

Chapter Twenty-Four

"Where did that lovely morning go?" Lucia wondered aloud. "Just last week, I remember feeling a bit of peace in my heart. Now, I can't seem to see the sun when it's staring me in the face."

"Are you speaking to me?" Jean asked.

They were sitting together in Lucia's garden. It was unusually warm for late March, so the two had decided to spend the afternoon outdoors. Jean had brought her embroidery, prompting Lucia to dig hers out of the drawer it was hiding in, but Lucia's project lay untouched in her lap. She stared at the crocuses bravely poking their heads up through the dirt, but she didn't really see them.

"Not really," was Lucia's answer. "I was just thinking out loud."

"Something about a bit of peace?" Jean prompted.

"Yes. Last week, we attended a birthday tea for Gerald Asher."

That caught Jean's attention and she deliberately set her embroidery aside. "You did? You didn't tell me that. I want details, Miss Rix, intimate details."

Looking at her friend, Lucia just shook her head. "It wasn't a big event, and nothing earth-shattering happened. We just had tea, listened to his cousin play the harp, and then escorted his great-aunt to her sitting room."

"We? We as in you and Mr. Asher?" Jean pressed.

"Well, there were several guests for the tea and recital," Lucia recalled. "Then Mr. Asher and I were with his aunt for a while."

"Just the two of you?" There was excitement in her friend's voice.

"No, Jean. We were with his aunt the entire time. In fact, Mr. Asher didn't say much at all. Mrs. Asher and I had a lovely conversation about grief and true love."

Looking puzzled, Jean frowned. "Grief and true love? That's an unlikely combination for a conversation."

Lucia looked back at the unseen crocuses. "It didn't seem so at the time."

"Still," Jean picked up her embroidery again, "if he wanted you to visit with his great-aunt, that sends a message, don't you think?"

Opening her mouth to answer, Lucia stopped when she saw Susan approaching them.

"Miss Rix?" the maid began. "The Missus asked me to fetch you to the drawing room. You have a guest."

Eyebrows raised, Lucia replied, "But I already have a guest, Susan. Doesn't Mama know that Mrs. Lassiter is here?"

"Yes, Miss, but she says to tell you that Mrs. Lassiter can come back tomorrow. This is important."

"How very rude!" Lucia exclaimed.

"And that's not like your mother, is it?" Jean asked sarcastically. "That's all right, Lucia, the light is beginning to fade out here anyway. I'll come back tomorrow afternoon and you can tell me all about this important caller of yours."

Gathering her things, she called over her shoulder, "I'll let myself out through the side gate. Have fun."

Lucia put her abandoned embroidery in its silk bag, then followed Susan into the house. She had no intention of confronting her mother about her rudeness in front of guests, but she would have to confront her at some point. As she approached the drawing room door, she handed her embroidery to Susan, took a deep breath, and held her head high as she entered.

Gerald stood up as she came into the room, then crossed and gently took her hand, smiling.

Eyes wide and eyebrows raised, Lucia couldn't help but comment, "Why, Mr. Asher, this is a pleasant surprise. What brings you calling this afternoon?"

She heard her mother's quick intake of breath at her breach of protocol. Lucia knew it was impolite to inquire about a caller's intentions without first observing the niceties of greeting and chitchat, but today she didn't care.

Gerald's smile broadened as he led her to a chair. "Very forthright, Miss Rix. Straight to business. That's one of the things I enjoy about you."

Nodding slightly, Lucia acknowledged the compliment, but she wasn't going to let him skirt the question. "I thank you for that, but you haven't told me why you're here."

"Lucia," her mother scolded, but Gerald raised a hand to stop her.

"No need to rebuke her, Mrs. Rix. I'll get right to the point."

He knelt on one knee in front of her and reached into his breast pocket, pulling out a small box. "Miss Rix, to follow your lead, let me speak plainly. I think you are beautiful, talented, and charming. I admire your intelligence, your desire to help others, and your tenacity in following your heart. I would be honored if you would consent to be my wife."

He opened the box to reveal a stunning ring with rubies and pearls. Reaching inside, he drew it out and placed the box on the floor beside him. Holding his hand out to accept hers, he waited.

She couldn't help it. Her jaw dropped as her hand flew away from his to rest at her throat.

"What?" was all she could manage to croak.

"Did I really take you by surprise?" Gerald laughed. "I thought you might have expected it after the lovely time we had with Aunt Bea."

His laughter did much to ease Lucia's shock, but not her confusion. "Why would that lead me to expect a proposal of marriage from you?"

"It's customary in my family to introduce any prospective spouses to the matriarch of the family and gain her approval. In this case, that would be Aunt Bea."

Lucia shook her head slowly. "How would I know the customs of your family, Mr. Asher?"

That took him aback a bit. "Isn't that tradition in all families, Miss Rix?"

Sighing, Lucia replied. "I'm not familiar with other families' traditions, so I couldn't answer that. In reference to your proposal, perhaps you've forgotten that I'm in mourning? It would not be proper for me to even consider courting until the two years of deep mourning have passed. Then at least another year before any kind of proposal would be acceptable."

Gerald sat back on his heels. "But, your mother said…" His voice trailed off.

"Lucia," her mother began.

Looking at her mother pointedly, Lucia interrupted. "We will discuss this later, Mama."

She stood and nodded at Gerald. "Thank you for your offer, Mr. Asher, but it's far too soon for me to even consider it. Good day."

As she left the drawing room, she heard her mother offering profuse apologies to their guest. Sparks would fly once he'd gone, no doubt. No matter. Mama needed to understand and stop pushing, she thought as she entered her room and shut the door behind her.

Surprisingly, Harriet left Lucia alone, and Lucia chose to avoid her mother by not coming down to tea or dinner that night.

The next morning, however, Susan came in to announce, "Mrs. Rix requests your company for breakfast this morning."

Frowning, Lucia considered it. The fact that it was a formal request meant that her mother meant business. The fact that she'd left her alone last night could mean anything. She sighed. She couldn't avoid Mama forever. Might as well face the music now.

"Tell Mama I'll be with her shortly," she told her maid.

After taking her time to dress, she made her way down to the small dining room. Her mother was already seated and enjoying a cup of tea. Looking up, she smiled.

"Good morning, Lucia," her voice was cheery. Not at all what Lucia expected. "I trust you slept well?"

"Not particularly," Lucia grumbled, partly to see if her mother would really listen.

"That's nice, dear," Harriet replied absently.

So much for Mama listening, Lucia thought, sitting down and pouring herself a cup of tea.

"I was thinking about the wedding," her mother began. "I'm thinking a relatively short engagement. Even though you and Mr. Asher don't know each other well, yet, your age is definitely a factor. We don't want to wait so long that you won't be able to have children, now do we?"

Lucia stared at her mother aghast. "What did you say?"

"The wedding, dear. We must make preparations, you know."

"Didn't you hear what I told Mr. Asher yesterday? I am in mourning, Mama. It's not…"

"Nonsense," her mother interrupted. "You have mourned more than sufficiently for a young man you hardly knew. It's time to get on with life, and for you, that means a wedding. Isn't it exciting?"

"No, Mama. Not exciting. Ridiculous!" Lucia exploded. "You have no idea what I am feeling, how I loved Ronald. You can't fathom what it's like to have your true love ripped from you with no warning. You have no idea what it's like to love and lose that love." Lucia's voice rose with each word, becoming almost hysterical in tone, heedless of her mother's reaction.

If she'd paid attention, she might have seen Harriet turn ashen white, then beet red as her lips pressed tightly together. She might have noticed the tears well up in her mother's eyes, then disappear as she furiously blinked them back. She might have chosen her words more carefully if she'd witnessed the quiver of Harriet's chin, or the clenching of her fingers around her teacup. She might have been surprised that for once Mama didn't fight back.

Instead, Harriet allowed her daughter to rant and rave for nearly five minutes before placing her napkin carefully by her plate, standing with her back straight, her head erect, her eyes blazing, and her lips tight.

In a cold tone, she finally replied, "I have heard quite enough, Lucia Grace Rix. You are my daughter. I want only what's best for you. As your mother, I have decided that being a spinster is not what's best when you have a perfectly good offer of marriage at hand. As long as you live in my household, you will follow what I deem best. I have given you much latitude in your choices, Lucia, allowing you to study nursing, allowing you to go to that damnable war, allowing you to wallow in this senseless mourning for a boy you were never going to be allowed to marry anyway." She paused, then continued.

"Perhaps I've been too lenient with you to make up for you not having a father growing up. It's given you a diminished sense of duty and honor. Either way, I have told Mr. Asher that you will be ready to marry at his discretion, although why he'd want to marry you after your rudeness yesterday, I'll never know. Still, he has indicated that he intends to have you, so have you, he will."

Harriet moved deliberately around the table, putting it between her daughter and herself. As she approached the doorway, she paused, then turned around, her face pale again. "As for not knowing love, you have no right to speak to me of love. I loved your father more than you will ever know. When we received word that he'd died, I died, too. There is never a day goes by that I don't mourn him. Never a day that I don't wish he were here with us... with me. But life goes on, Lucia, and we must move on with it no matter how we hurt inside."

With that, she turned and left the room. Lucia stared after her for a few moments, then placed her head in her hands, feeling like she had just been slapped. She had no idea her mother felt so deeply. No idea why Harriet had been so stern with her, or why she was insisting on this marriage.

It was more understandable now, but it didn't change anything. She was still in mourning and jumping into a marriage with someone she barely knew just didn't make sense, no matter that Mama thought she was losing her best childbearing years. No matter that she might be considered a spinster. No matter that Gerald Asher might not wait for her to be ready for such a huge step.

Slowly, Lucia stood up and wandered to the garden. It was chilly this morning, but she didn't feel the cold. She sat next to the hawthorn hedge and tried to think. She felt ashamed that she'd lost her temper so completely, bewildered at the revelation that her mother had real feelings too, confused about what to do next.

Over and over, she rehearsed the entire conversation in her mind, trying to find a clue, a hint, anything to help her with her next decision. But try as she might, she could find no answer.

If the days and nights were long before, they paled in comparison to the ones that followed. Lucia puzzled and stewed and worried and mourned in a random pattern of self-doubt, confusion, and grief. She rarely ate more than a bite of food. Her sleep was restless, and she spent many nights staring at the stars, tears falling unheeded down her face.

She began losing weight, and in only a few days, her eyes had dark circles under them. In a week, her normally compassionate bedside manner began to deteriorate into a cold and clinical approach to both patients and staff.

Finally, after watching her friend decline so quickly, Jean pulled her aside. "What's wrong with you, Lucia? That patient didn't deserve the harsh reprimand you just gave him."

"He's refusing his medication. He needed to be told that was unacceptable," Lucia answered tersely.

"That medication makes him dizzy! I wouldn't want to take it either."

"But the doctor prescribed it, so he must take it," Lucia was adamant.

"Yes, but he deserves compassion, not a rebuke. What's gotten into you? I've never seen you like this."

"Nothing. I'm fine."

"You are not fine. You look like death, and act as if you've got one foot in the grave already. Talk to me."

Lucia looked at her friend and sighed. "There's nothing to talk about, but thank you for caring."

She walked away, leaving Jean shaking her head and wondering if she'd lost her mind.

Still, the conversation had an effect on Lucia. She began noticing her own actions and became concerned. Was she really losing her mind? Did she look as bad as Jean seemed to think?

The rest of the day, she tried to keep her temper in check and pay attention to the patients more than their charts. When she arrived home, she went straight upstairs and looked hard into the little mirror on her dressing table. Jean was right. She did look like death was ready to claim her, but what was she to do? She was caught between her mother's desire to see that she married well, and the still-overwhelming grief that haunted her.

That night, Lucia slept deeper than she had in weeks. So deep that her dreams seemed real. In one, she was standing on the dock, looking out to sea. A ship was coming in, and her heart raced when she recognized her beloved Ronald on the deck waving at her.

She waved back, but the ship stopped and didn't approach any closer.

"What's wrong?" she called, yelling above the wind. "Why aren't you coming in to dock?"

"I can't come to you," Ronald yelled back. "You need to see Mrs. Asher. She has the answer."

"What?" Lucia yelled again. "Who shall I see?"

"Mrs. Asher," Ronald called as his ship began retreating towards the horizon.

"No!" Lucia screamed. "I can't lose you again, I can't!"

She awoke at that point, realized it was only a dream, and turned over, sobbing into her already wet pillow. The rest of the night was much like the ones before. Only this night was spent wondering if she should really talk with Mrs. Asher, or if that was just an unimportant part of an overemotional dream.

By the time she was ready to leave for work, she decided it wouldn't hurt to consult with the dear old lady. She seemed wise and compassionate. Yes, it was time to get some help with this, Lucia thought. I'm just making a mess of things, trying to do it on my own, and I certainly can't talk to Mama.

After checking in at the infirmary, she told the doctor on duty that she had some personal business to take care of and asked if could she be excused for the evening. There were very few patients, so he agreed.

She raced home and changed out of her uniform, putting on the black crepe gown she'd grown so accustomed to wearing. Luckily, she didn't run into her mother, so she didn't have to explain.

As she approached the Asher home, she began to have second thoughts. Mrs. Asher is Gerald Asher's great-aunt, she thought. She's going to insist that I either marry her great-nephew, or forever stay out of his life. How can she be objective when it comes to a family member?

She'd just decided to turn around and forget the whole thing, when the front door opened. Gerald stepped out and turned to shut the door behind himself. Quickly, Lucia decided to take the bull by the horns and cleared her throat, getting his attention.

"Why, Miss Rix, what a pleasant surprise," he smiled. "What brings you to my humble home this fine afternoon?"

Lucia nodded at his deliberate use of her own tactless words. "I apologize for calling unannounced, Mr. Asher. I was hoping to visit with your aunt for a little while. Is she up to having a caller?"

Apparently not holding a grudge, Gerald grinned. "I'm sure she is, but let me announce you."

"Oh, I completely forgot to grab a calling card!" Lucia exclaimed.

Laughing aloud, Gerald opened the door for her. "No matter. I'm sure she'll remember you."

Showing her into the drawing room, he left her alone for a few moments. She stood in the center of the room, trying not to be rude by staring at the lovely décor. His mother has exquisite taste, she thought, glancing around quickly, then choosing to look out the window at the gardens beyond.

"Mrs. Asher will see you now," Gerald announced formally, bowed, then gestured toward the stairs. Then he stood tall and sported a grin that accentuated his impish nature.

Matching his formality, Lucia easily fell into his play-acting, despite the serious nature of her call. "Why, thank you, Mr. Asher. If you would be so good as to show me the way?"

He laughed again and she couldn't help but smile a little as they ascended the stairs. Once they reached the landing, he knocked, then opened the doors to his aunt's rooms. He didn't follow her in, but nodded to his aunt and discreetly left them alone.

"What a nice surprise," Mrs. Asher greeted her.

Lucia smiled in return. "That's exactly what your nephew said."

"Where do you think he learned it?" the older woman quipped as she motioned towards a chair near hers. "Shall I ring for tea?"

"Tea would be lovely," said Lucia, realizing suddenly that she was hungry.

After arranging for the tea, they sat and chatted about unimportant matters until it arrived. Once it was settled and they were each served, the older woman suddenly became serious.

"So, my dear," she began. "What brings you to visit an old woman on such a beautiful afternoon?"

Lucia looked at her hands, unsure where to begin. She knew that Beatrice Asher had a reputation as a patient woman, and appreciated that she held her peace so she could gather her thoughts. She didn't know if Mrs. Asher knew why she had come, but she didn't pry, which allowed Lucia to find her own words.

Finally, Lucia looked up, tears in her eyes and whispered, "I'm so confused, Mrs. Asher. I just don't know what to do."

"Please, child, call me Aunt Bea. Why don't you just dive in and tell me what's troubling you?"

Once again, Lucia found herself baring her soul. She told her about Gerald's proposal, Mama's conniving, the argument with her last week, the confusion about her mother's feelings and intentions, and the way it was all affecting her work, her health and her relationships with her friends and coworkers. She shared with her how much she missed Ronald, and how it felt like she'd be unfaithful to his memory if she didn't give herself time to properly mourn him, everything, all of it, nothing held back.

Aunt Bea sat quietly, watching her face, nodding her understanding and sympathy.

When Lucia finished with the same question, "What do I do, Mrs... Aunt Bea? What do I do?"

"Unfortunately, child, I can't answer that for you," she began. Holding up a hand to forestall Lucia's objections, she continued. "What I can do is give you a recommendation. I recommend that you need time and space to think things through without interruption. You need a break from your mother, my nephew, your friends, and your work. You need to get away and give yourself permission to make this decision all on your own. You need a place that is both secluded and restful."

"I must admit, that sounds like a heavenly idea, but I have nowhere to go that would afford me such privacy," Lucia's voice was sad and heavy.

"It just so happens that I do," Aunt Bea announced with a nod of her head. "I have been thinking of going to the beach house, but no one here is available to accompany me. Would you consider going as my companion for a week or two? I will pay you for your time, and will give you as much privacy as you require."

Lucia's eyebrows rose. "Please tell me you are serious. I would be honored to accompany you to your beach house."

"Then it's settled," the old woman declared. "You go home and pack, and I'll see you here promptly at ten in the morning."

"Thank you, Mrs... Aunt Bea. I don't know how to thank you."

"No thanks are necessary, dear. Just run along. We both have much to do this evening."

As Lucia fairly flew home, her heart was lighter than it had been in weeks. Oh, the problems were still there, she knew, but at least now she'd have a chance to gain some perspective on them. Her mother wasn't home, which was unusual, but Lucia took a few moments and wrote a quick note to each of her employers stating her intention to be away for a couple of weeks, then had Susan deliver them.

While Susan was gone, she packed a few things, then wrote a note to her mother, in case she didn't see her before she left. She almost hoped she wouldn't. It would make leaving easier.

Chapter Twenty-Five

Lucia was up before the sun rose, too excited and anxious to sleep any longer. She put her last-minute toiletry items in her bag, checked that her appearance was acceptable, then went down to see if breakfast was ready. It was.

She sat down and poured herself a cup of tea, then nibbled on a piece of toast, wondering if she'd see her mother or not. Last night she was hoping she wouldn't, but this morning, she thought she might like to say goodbye. After all, you never know when a goodbye will be the last, she thought with a frown.

She was nearly finished when Harriet entered the dining room.

"Good morning, Mama," Lucia greeted her.

Harriet raised one eyebrow and replied, "Good morning, Lucia. I trust you slept well?"

"Fair. You?"

"Fair." Harriet took her place and poured her tea.

They ate in silence for a few minutes. Lucia drained the last drop of her tea, then sat uncomfortably, not knowing how to approach her mother about her plans.

Harriet took the burden off her, however. "I noticed your bag in the hallway. Are you going somewhere?"

Oh, my! Lucia nearly panicked. She'd forgotten that she'd asked for it to be brought down.

She took a deep breath and plunged in. "Yes. Mrs. Asher has asked that I accompany her to the beach house for a week or two. No one in her household is able to go and she's craving a bit of sea air."

Harriet nodded. "I see. So Mr. Asher isn't going?"

Cocking her head, Lucia studied her mother intently. "No. If he were, she wouldn't need me, would she?"

"I suppose not," her mother replied not looking up.

"Mama... I..." Lucia stammered, then stopped.

Taking a deep breath, Harriet finally looked her daughter in the eye. "There's no need to apologize, Lucia. We both said things we regret. It's hard for you, I'm sure, to reconcile yourself to the fact that the young man is dead. It's hard for me to see you in such pain. I still feel that Mr. Asher could help you move on with your life. He'll make a great husband and a good father. I want to know that you are happily settled before I die, and if there are little ones, I'll be even happier. I hope while you're gone, you'll give that some thought."

Lucia shook her head. "Die? What are you talking about, Mama?"

"It's nothing, dear," her mother brushed her concerns aside. "The doctor says I have a touch of lung fever, and if it gets worse, I could die, but at this point it's nothing to worry about."

"Maybe I shouldn't go, then," Lucia said, knowing she didn't really mean it.

Harriet waved her hand dismissively, "No, no. You need time away from this place... and me, I'm sure. I'll be fine. The servants are here if I need anything. You go and don't give me another thought."

She punctuated the last with a long sigh, followed by a brief coughing fit.

Scowling now, Lucia stood up. "All right then, I'll be off. I'll see you in a week or two, Mama."

Unexpectedly, she stepped over and bent to kiss her mother's forehead. "I love you, Mama."

Harriet looked up, her face showing her surprise. "Why, I love you, too, Lucia."

But Lucia was already halfway to the door. As she reached it, she turned, hesitated, and then waved. "Goodbye, Mama."

Then Harriet found herself alone, staring at the closed door. Two lonely tears crept down her cheeks.

"Mama! Mama! Are you home?" Lucia yelled up the stairs and down the hallway, quite unrepentant that she was breaking an important rule of the house; no yelling.

"Lucia!" her mother appeared at the top of the stairs, her tone scolding. "Is that how we speak in this house?"

"No, Mama, but I'm glad to see you." Lucia grinned as she bounded the stairs to hug her surprised mother.

"I'm glad to see you, too, but why this sudden exuberance?" Harriet looked truly perplexed.

Lucia sighed a contented sigh. "No real reason, I suppose. I'm just glad to be home."

Harriet cocked her head. "You've come to a decision, then?"

Her daughter nodded. "Yes, but it wouldn't be appropriate to tell you first, now would it?" she teased.

"I don't suppose it would. Still, a mother can hope, can't she?"

Lucia simply hugged her tightly, then went to change out of her travel clothes.

The next day was beautiful. As Lucia and her mother finished breakfast, she turned her face to the open window and took a deep breath of the cool, spring air.

"You look content," Harriet commented.

"Content?" Lucia looked at her mother and considered that word. "Perhaps more content than I was a week ago. At least now, I can enjoy the breeze, whereas last week I didn't even notice it."

"That's an improvement, I suppose. Still no hints as to your decision?" she asked hopefully.

Shaking her head, Lucia smiled a secret little smile, "No. No hints. I'm planning to call on the Ashers this afternoon. Would you like to join me?"

Looking shocked and pleased at the same time, Harriet could only nod her agreement.

The afternoon brought more sunshine as the morning haze had drifted away, which suited Lucia beautifully. She and her mother walked side by side to the Asher home, neither woman speaking. As they approached the door, Harriet suddenly turned and touched Lucia's arm causing her to stop.

"What is it, Mama?" Lucia asked, concerned.

Instead of answering, Harriet stepped up and embraced her daughter tightly. When she released her, she looked into her face for a long moment, then smiled. "Shall we?" she invited, gesturing toward the house.

Puzzled, Lucia followed her mother to the door.

A maid answered their knock and saw them into the drawing room. It wasn't long before Gerald and his mother joined them.

"How wonderful of you to call," Mrs. Asher gushed. "May we offer you some tea?"

They graciously accepted, and Mrs. Asher instructed the maid to serve it in the back gardens. "It's such a beautiful day, I think we should enjoy it," she said by way of explanation.

"I agree," Harriet nodded.

As they enjoyed their tea and sweetmeats, Harriet and Mrs. Asher chatted about the weather, the upcoming events of the Season, and which debutantes were to be presented to the Queen this year. Gerald and Lucia listened, but did not add much to the conversation.

When they were finished with their tea, Gerald waited patiently for a lull in the conversation, which took a while. When it presented itself, however, he jumped in, "Mother, I'd like to show Miss Rix your lilies. May we be excused?"

"Of course, dear," his mother answered, then plunged into another favorite topic, the latest fashions.

Gerald helped Lucia with her chair, and they wandered down the path a short distance, far enough away that their mothers wouldn't overhear them, but close enough that they could be seen, thus answering the requirements of propriety.

Lucia made a show of bending down to admire the beautiful tiger lilies, then stood and faced him.

"Mr. Asher," she began.

"Don't say it, Miss Rix." Gerald smiled gently. "I can see by your face that you have something to say that you don't think I'm going to like."

Lucia bent her head, then looked up and started again, "Please let me say what I have to say. I've spent the past week pondering and thinking, and trying to decide what I should do. You have offered me a generous future. You are a kind, decent man with a heart as big as all England. Any woman would be lucky to be your wife. I've truly considered what it would mean to be Mrs. Gerald Asher." She hesitated.

"But…" Gerald prompted.

"But my heart still belongs to Ronald Ferguson. It would be unfair of me to marry you when I am still grieving his loss. You deserve a woman who can love you for you, not as a substitute for someone else. You deserve a woman who is as head-over-heels in love with you as I am in love with Ronald. I can't… won't do you the disservice of tying you down to a woman who will never love you that way. I'm sorry. I hope you can find your perfect match soon."

She searched Gerald's eyes and found only compassion there.

"I understand," he replied kindly. "I think we could have been happy together, but I appreciate your candor and will honor your wishes by not pursuing you further. I'll tell you what, though. If I haven't found my perfect match by the time you are ready to consider marriage, I'll happily renew my proposal. How does that sound?"

Lucia smiled. "That's fair."

Gerald reached down, took her gloved hand, and kissed the back of it gently. "Until then, Miss Rix, I wish you all the best."

"And I you, Mr. Asher," she replied.

On the way home, her mother could handle the suspense no longer.

"Well?" she prodded. "Do I get to know your decision now?"

Lucia stopped and turned to face her. "Yes. I've decided not to marry Mr. Asher."

Harriet's face fell. "Oh."

"I'm sorry, Mama. I know you wanted me to agree to this marriage so you wouldn't have to worry about me anymore, but it wouldn't be fair to him to have a wife who was still pining for a lost love. He deserves a wife who adores him, and I don't. He's a good man, and I'm sure he'll be a good husband, but I still love Ronald. Until that fades enough to make room for someone else in my heart, it's not fair of me to marry."

Harriet nodded, then spoke softly. "It's the same reason I won't marry again. I love your father too much to make room in my heart for another."

She turned and began walking again with Lucia beside her. "Perhaps, in time, you'll be able to move on with your life, Lucia. I hope so. I certainly don't wish the spinster life for you!"

Lucia took her mother's arm. "I know, Mama. I know."

Chapter Twenty-Six

The weeks that followed were relatively calm. Harriet didn't really sulk as much as Lucia thought she might. She was quiet and sad, but there were none of the usual manipulations and machinations. She didn't even ask if Lucia wanted to go to any of the opening Society events. Quite unusual, but Lucia was grateful. While it was a relief to not have to fight Mama on that front, it did leave her more time to think about her lost love, and that was bittersweet.

Although the weather was still a bit chilly in the mornings, Lucia began taking long walks along the docks. There was something soothing about the ocean breeze, the comings and goings of the ships, and the hustle and bustle of the people. In the afternoons, she'd stay close to home and walk in the gardens. The flowers were blooming happily, and she found herself gazing at their bright colors which were a perfect counterpoint to the sadness in her heart.

The nights were the hardest. There was nothing to soothe her mind in the darkness. The stars were cold and far away. The moon was distant as well. It made her remember the few moonlit nights she'd enjoyed with Ronald. Many tears fell in the wee hours of the morning. When sleep came, it was either restless or filled with dreams, mostly nightmares where she lost him all over again. Mornings after the nightmare nights were generally spent in seclusion.

She managed to continue her work, although she seemed more distant to staff and patient alike. Jean noticed that she wasn't as grumpy, though she seemed sadder. No matter what her friend tried to do to cheer her up, Lucia would smile a sad little smile and thank her for her efforts.

Five weeks after her final refusal of Gerald's proposal, there was a Saturday night that was especially bad. The nightmares were filled with soldiers, guns, swords, cannonballs, and her in her nightdress calling and calling for her sweet Ronald. She awoke shivering with fright and grief.

When Susan came to inquire whether she would be attending church, she declined, saying she was suffering from a headache. An hour or so later, her mother came in to check on her. Still in bed, Lucia thanked her for her concern, but assured her that the headache would pass and that she should go on without her.

Lunchtime came and went with Lucia remaining in bed, alternating between tears and fitful sleep.

Finally, mid-afternoon, Lucia woke up feeling a bit better. The fear was finally gone and her grief had subsided to a manageable level, so she decided to get up and maybe take a walk in the garden.

The crepe gown felt extra itchy, and she considered for a moment replacing it with a softer black one, but the itchiness seemed to match her mood, so she put it on anyway. Brushing her hair back into a simple bun, she sighed. Why does life have to be so hard, she wondered.

The weather was pleasant, if a trifle cool. Her shawl kept her warm enough for her to enjoy the walk. There were flowers covering the hawthorn bush and Lucia reached over to caress its petals.

"Are you trying to tell me something, little flowers?" she asked it. "Are you trying to tell me that spring is here, even though it still feels cold in my heart?"

Tears welled up in her eyes as she stood up and took a deep breath. She turned to walk back up the path toward the house and noticed someone coming down the path toward her. Puzzled, she stopped.

Who was this person calling unannounced?

As the man grew closer, things began to register… uniform, red coat, red hair, sergeant's stripes.

It couldn't be! He was dead.

She shook her head to rid herself of the hurtful illusion, but when she opened her eyes, the apparition was drawing closer.

"Lucia!" The deep voice calling her name made her heart beat rapidly. Her breath caught and she reacted without thinking.

"Ronald!" she cried, racing toward the man in the red sergeant's uniform, who was running toward her with his arms outstretched.

As they met, he caught her up in his arms and hugged her tightly. She returned his hug, tears streaming down her face.

"Oh, my sweet Ronald," she cried, "are you really here?"

Looking down at her, his own cheeks damp with tears, he replied, "I'm really here, my Luscious. You are as beautiful as I remember."

"I can't believe it's really you," she whispered. "I want to feel your arms around me, hear your voice in my ears, see your eyes and lips and hair. I want to take each part of you in and know that you are not some dream-created apparition that's going to disappear when I open my eyes."

She stroked his face softly, marveling at the length of his red hair, the inviting curve of his ears, the strong line of his nose, the firmness of his jawline, and the prickly stubble on his chin. Even with all her senses telling her he was real, she still could not comprehend that he was truly here in her arms.

"It's really me," he chuckled. "In all my Scottish glory." He drew her in for another embrace.

"But how?" she whispered even as she returned his hug. "You're dead. Is this a dream? Another nightmare come to haunt me?"

"Does this feel like a nightmare?" he asked, his voice a bit teasing.

She looked into his smiling face and shook her head. "No, but…"

Ronald cocked his head and grinned. "Is this face an illusion? Is this hand connected to a dream figure? How can I convince you that I'm real?"

Without warning, she pinched his arm.

"Ow!" he cried. "What was that for?"

"To see if you're real," she giggled, then leaned in to kiss his arm where she'd pinched it. "Is that better?"

"That's not how this works." He tried to look stern, failing terribly. "If you're dreaming, then I'm supposed to pinch you."

"Oh, no…" she started to protest, but before she could wriggle away, he'd pinched her arm firmly.

"Ow!" she complained, then grinned. "I guess neither of us is dreaming."

"I guess not," he whispered, his voice husky. His hand slid down to cup her chin, lifting her face. "But just to be sure, is this kiss the stuff of nightmares?"

Leaning in, his lips met hers, gently at first, then more firmly as his arms tightened around her, drawing her closer. Her body thrilled to the touch of his lips against hers. She moaned and returned his kiss, her arms sliding around his neck pulling him down to her. Feeling her response, his kiss became more ardent. Her heart pounded in her chest as she gave herself up to the moment.

As the long kiss ended, Ronald stroked her hair, tucking a stray lock behind her ear.

She continued to gaze at him in wonder, unwilling to question the miracle before her, but her brain was beginning to function now and the question must be asked. "How are you here? You are... were... dead."

"I nearly was," he nodded, leading her to the bench next to the hawthorn hedge. "What were you told?"

Frowning, Lucia recited the horrible letter she'd received telling of his death. She had it all but memorized, having read and re-read it so often.

Ronald listened carefully. When she was finished, he took her in his arms. "There is so much more to the story, my love. Are you feeling up to hearing it?"

She looked up into his eyes and thought a moment. "I don't think so. Not just yet. Let's just enjoy being together for a while. There will be plenty of time for stories later."

He smiled. "As you wish, my love."

Bending down, he kissed her sweetly and held her close enough that she could hear his heart beating in his chest. She reveled in the sound, closing her eyes, and feeling safe in his arms.

Time passed, but they were not aware of it. They spoke little, preferring to enjoy the reunion without words or further questions. Instead, they enjoyed sweet kisses, warm embraces, and soft touches, which sent shivers of delight that contrasted sharply with the dark grief Lucia had felt the past two months.

While they were unaware of the passing of time, the sun continued in its appointed round, drawing ever nearer to the horizon, casting longer and longer shadows, then finally sliding silently out of sight.

When the last of its rays had gone and the night air became too chilly to ignore, only then did Lucia sigh and pull away.

"I suppose we should find Mama and tell her the good news," she whispered reluctantly, not quite willing to end this dream, if that's what it was, with what was sure to be a disappointing, if not harsh, awakening.

Ronald gazed down at her and agreed. "I suppose we should."

Making their way toward the house, they were still surrounded by the surreal haze of the moment. Still drinking in the sight of him, Lucia walked slowly with her arm in his, gazing into his eyes, not paying the least bit of attention to where she was going, until her mother's voice broke the spell.

"What is this?" she accused from the garden doorway. "Lucia Grace, who is this… man?"

Allowing herself to separate a bit from the dream to face reality, she answered without taking her eyes off the face of her beloved.

"Mama," her voice was thick with emotion, "may I present Sergeant Ronald Ferguson, newly returned from the dead."

There was silence from her mother, which made her look over. Harriet's face was dark with anger.

"Mama, what's wrong?" Lucia was suddenly reminded how formidable her mother could be.

"I want you to come into the house, Lucia, at once." There was no arguing with Mama when she took that tone, but Lucia tried anyway.

"Mama…"

"At once!" Harriet snapped sharply.

Lucia frowned but took two steps out of habit before realizing what she was doing. She stopped and faced her mother.

"No, Mama," her voice was firm now, with no trace left of the little girl she once was. "This man is going to be my husband as soon as we can arrange it, and I won't have you trying to run him off."

"There will be no trying," Harriet's voice was deadly calm now. "He will go and not return to this house again."

Ronald tried to break in. "Lucia…" he began.

"No, Ronald, I won't let her do it." Lucia was adamant. She stepped back and linked her arm in his. "Mama, if Ronald goes, I go with him."

"You'll do no such thing, young lady!" Harriet's voice rose.

"I'm no longer a young lady, Mama," Lucia pointed out, her voice calm. She vaguely recognized that her mother no long intimidated her. "I'm a full-grown woman and can make my own decisions."

"Not when they are clearly foolish and threaten your future."

Ronald looked down at Lucia. "My sweet, one of two things must happen here and now. Either I must leave so you can resolve this with your mother, or you must leave so I can."

"No, I'm not leaving your side again," Tears came unbidden to Lucia's eyes, rolling down her face unheeded.

He took her shoulders and gently turned her to face him. "We'll be together forever soon, my love. For now, I think you need to talk with your mother. I won't be far, and I promise I'll come back later this evening. There is so much more to tell you, and I have some business to take care of before we can be married. After all, it's going to be difficult to marry a dead man, isn't it?"

Lucia's eyes widened as the impending challenges of his rise from the dead finally sank in. "Oh," her voice was meek. "I didn't think about that. Of course. Why don't you join Mama and I for dinner at eight?"

"Perfect," he agreed.

After he left, Lucia steeled herself for the impending argument with her mother. When she turned around, Harriet was watching her, an unreadable expression on her face.

"Mama," Lucia began, but her mother raised a hand to stop her.

"Don't say anything, Lucia," she instructed. "We have both had quite a shock and need time to adjust. You have invited him to dinner, so there are preparations to be made. I will take care of them while you take time to really think about what this all means. We can talk later."

With that, she marched back into the house, back straight, head tall, every bit the matron of the house that she'd always been.

Frowning, Lucia followed her. This did not bode well. If her mother wouldn't even allow a discussion, that meant she'd made up her mind and no amount of arguing would dissuade her. Somehow, Lucia had to find a way to penetrate her mother's armor, for that's what it was; armor, meant to protect her.

But protect her from what? From pain, obviously, but what pain was she afraid of? The pain of losing Lucia to marriage? No, that couldn't be it. She'd been trying to marry Lucia off for years, so that wasn't logical. The pain of not maintaining her standing in Society? Maybe, but she had enough money to keep that standing if she chose. The pain of Lucia not maintaining that standing? Maybe, but it's my life, thought Lucia, and I don't care about what Society thinks or does, so why should that matter to Mama? No, I think it must be something else.

Wandering around the house, Lucia was restive and worried. She just couldn't figure it out. Why was Mama being so stubborn about this?

Without realizing it, Lucia found herself walking by her father's study. The door was open, which was unusual, except when the maid was dusting the room. Lucia peeked in to find her mother sitting in her father's favorite chair with his pipe in her hands. She was talking softly and Lucia had to strain to hear what she was saying.

"...wish you were here, Roberto. I simply don't know what to do. I want her to have the good life we planned for her. I want her to be happy, but how can she be happy if she must fight for every penny? You and I both know that a military man won't earn enough to secure her future. Besides, military men are rarely home and often in danger. How is that a happy life for her? I've seen how she pined for him when she thought he was dead. How much more anguish will she have to endure if he leaves for battle again? I want her to marry a nice, safe Society gentleman so she'll have everything we want for her. I don't want her to suffer alone the way I've suffered without you."

Harriet clasped the pipe to her chest and leaned her head back to rest on the back of the chair. Lucia saw the tear stains on her face and knew that she'd been crying long before Lucia saw her.

Stepping away from the door, Lucia's heart was heavy. How could she hurt her mother by marrying Ronald? How could she hurt Ronald by not marrying him? How could she put her own wants and needs ahead of her mother's happiness... or Ronald's? She rubbed her forehead to ease the headache that was forming behind her eyes. Swallowing hard, she walked quietly down the stairs, took her cape and hat from the rack, then called back up the stairs.

"I'm going for a walk, Mama. I'll be back soon."

Walking aimlessly, her mind whirled round and round from one choice to the other with no relief in sight. It just wasn't fair. She'd thought Ronald was dead, and Mama had seemed sympathetic to her grief, finally, but now that he was back in her life, Mama seemed set on thwarting their plans to marry.

She soon found herself in front of the Asher's home and an idea began to form. Aunt Bea. Aunt Bea would know how to handle this.

She turned up the walk and stepped to the door. A maid answered and told her that Mrs. Asher was out and was not expected until after dinner that evening.

Disappointed, Lucia turned for home. She couldn't talk to the wise old woman, maybe she could figure out what Aunt Bea would have said.

First, she would listen carefully to all sides of the problem. That was certain. Then, she'd ask some pertinent questions so she could be sure she understood the situation. Then, she'd say... what would she say?

"She'd say I need to think this through and follow my heart," Lucia said aloud. "So what does my heart say?"

The answer was immediate. "My heart says to marry Ronald and Mama will see in time that he's exactly what I need for a happy life."

She smiled and sighed. "Mama just needs to see how happy I am with Ronald, and she'll realize that I have to marry him to be happy. It's perfectly simple."

Decision made, she entered the house with a lighter heart, and went upstairs to dress for dinner.

Chapter Twenty-Seven

Dinner was surprisingly calm, if a bit awkward. Harriet played her role as hostess well, seeing that Ronald was comfortable and well-fed. She kept the conversation light, avoiding the difficult discussion that must inevitably follow the oh-so-polite meal.

Never let it be said that Harriet Rix was outright rude to a guest at dinner, Lucia thought, even one she obviously disapproved of.

After dinner, they retired to the drawing room, where Ronald convinced Lucia to sing a bit. She was sure he was stalling, but it didn't take much convincing since her heart was soaring. Her sweet Ronald was there and had asked her to sing.

For his part, Ronald sat and applauded loudly as each song ended. The grin on his face was as proud as a peacock strutting before his mate. When her voice started to feel strained, she took a chair near Ronald as Harriet signaled the maids to bring in coffee. At last, all that was left was the huge, unresolved situation between Ronald, Lucia, and Harriet.

Lucia looked at Ronald, reached over and took his hand, then faced her mother.

"Mama, it's time to talk," she announced, unnecessarily. "Ronald and I are going to be married. I wish you would be happy for us and join in our celebration, but we are getting married with or without your blessing."

She felt Ronald stir beside her and looked over at him. He was watching her closely, a solemn look on his face.

"Lucia," his voice was soft. "Let's allow your mother to express her concerns before we go any further. Maybe we can address them to her satisfaction. Then we can all enjoy making plans together."

Puzzled, Lucia hesitated, then nodded.

"Thank you, Sergeant," Harriet said formally. "I appreciate your thoughtfulness. My concerns are these, and I hope you'll forgive me for what I'm about to say. First, Sergeant, your so-called death has put my daughter through terrible torment. Who is to say that won't happen again? I have been through my own torment with my husband's death so many years ago, so I understand what she was feeling. I don't want her to ever experience that again. With you in the... cavalry, is it?... there is no guarantee that it won't happen again."

"Mama," Lucia began to protest, but Ronald shook his head. She frowned, but closed her mouth.

"Second, even if you never have to face that kind of danger again, a sergeant doesn't make much in wages, I'll warrant. My daughter deserves the best, as I'm sure you'll agree. Unfortunately, Sergeant, you can't provide her with the kind of financial security she deserves." Lucia squirmed under her mother's calm, but relentless arguments.

"Third, you are from Scotland, are you not?"

Ronald nodded, "I am."

"Where were you thinking of living? Were you planning to take my precious daughter away from me to live in some far-off hamlet where I would never see her again? Or were you thinking you could just slip seamlessly into London Society where she truly belongs? If that was your plan, Sergeant," her voice was beginning to rise in intensity, if not volume, "you can just forget it. Lucia Grace Rix is a name to be reckoned with here, and I won't have her wasting away in Scotland where she would be a nobody in a nowhere place."

Lucia gritted her teeth and gripped the arms of her chair, trying to keep her anger under control. She looked over at Ronald, who looked for all the world as if he was listening to a most interesting lecture, rather than an irate matriarch who was determined to keep them from marrying.

Harriet took a deep breath, and then continued, a bit calmer. "Furthermore, she has a perfectly valid proposal from one Gerald Asher who is well suited to her station and will provide everything she wants or needs. I'm sure you wouldn't want her to give up such a promising future, now would you?"

That was it. Lucia could take no more.

"Mama, that's quite enough!" she exploded, starting to rise. "You know perfectly well that I refused Mr. Asher's proposal long before Ronald returned to my arms. As for your other reasons…"

"Lucia," Ronald's hand on her arm was gentle, but firm, "may I speak first?"

Taken aback, Lucia settled back into her chair and waited to hear what he had to say.

He turned back to Harriet and began. "I understand each of your concerns, Mrs. Rix, and appreciate your position. I cannot hope to sway you tonight with only my words to defend me. You do not know me, nor have you had sufficient time to see what your daughter and I mean to each other. She is my light, my life, my everything.

"I know Lucia received a letter telling her I was dead. The truth was, I was taken prisoner by the Russians. They held me in a small cell with several other soldiers until the peace treaty was signed.

"During my imprisonment, it was her face in my mind that kept me sane. It was the memory of her voice urging me to live, that gave me reason to hope. It was her sweetness, her beauty, her compassion, that provided me the incentive to keep breathing, even when the torment was greatest. I love your daughter and cannot deny that.

"However, I understand and honor your concern for her well-being. May I propose that you allow us to court properly for a time, under your supervision, of course. Observe for yourself my behavior, my intentions, and my love for your daughter. If, after an appropriate time, you decide I am unworthy of her, I will leave quietly and never darken your door again."

"Ronald!" Lucia exclaimed, her eyes filling with tears, unable to bear the thought of him leaving her again.

Squeezing her hand gently, he looked over and smiled at her. That smile she knew so well had a different message this time. It seemed to say, "Trust me, sweet Luscious". Surprisingly, her shock, fear, and anger at his proposal melted and she found she did trust him, implicitly. He knew what he was doing and she would follow his lead.

The next few weeks were heaven, as far as Lucia was concerned. Ronald called on her as often as possible, which was nearly every day. Some days, he'd invite them to ride with him in the park. Other days were spent walking in the garden. Evenings were nearly always spent in the drawing room with Lucia singing and Ronald listening with rapt attention, adoring every note that came out of her throat.

Always there was Mama, sitting nearby, looking quite conspicuous in her attempts to look inconspicuous. The happy couple didn't mind, however. They knew that as long as Harriet was willing to let them spend time together, there was hope that she'd eventually agree to let them marry.

Nearly a month after Ronald's unexpected return to life, they had their answer.

It was a beautiful June evening, the flowers were in full bloom, brightening every corner of the garden. Ronald and Lucia were sitting in their favorite spot, next to the hawthorn hedge while Harriet pretended to work on some embroidery nearby.

Lucia knew she was pretending, because her needle did not have the rhythmic precision which punctuated Mama's usual embroidery technique. Instead, her mother poked the needle in, drew the thread partway through, paused, drew it a little more, paused, drew it a bit further, paused, and finally finished the stitch.

All the while, Harriet kept her eyes studiously on her work, except when she thought they weren't looking. Then she'd watch them through lowered eyelashes.

It made Lucia want to laugh. Mama was trying so hard not to look like she was chaperoning them, but she was fooling no one. She was taking her supervisory role very seriously. The more Lucia thought about it, the more grateful she felt that her mother was giving them a chance... giving Ronald a chance... to prove their love was real.

The sun was just beginning to set when Harriet stood abruptly, dropping her embroidery in the silk bag she carried it in.

"Enough," she announced. "I've seen enough."

"Mama?" Lucia suddenly felt her mouth grow dry and her heart dropped into her shoes.

"I've made my decision."

Lucia's voice trembled. "After just a month?"

"Yes. I've seen all I need to see." Harriet's tone was matter-of-fact and unemotional, which Lucia was sure didn't bode well.

She gulped, afraid of the answer. "What have you decided, Mama?"

Harriet took three steps toward them and held out her hand to Ronald. "Welcome to the family, Sergeant Ferguson," she said bluntly, then her face softened into a smile like Lucia hadn't seen in years. "Welcome to the family... Ronald."

The man addressed didn't hesitate. He grinned widely, then stepped up to clasp Harriet's hand in his own. He turned it palm down and kissed the back of it gently. "Thank you, Mrs. Rix. Thank you."

Lucia was still in shock. "Really, Mama? You'll approve our marriage?"

Her mother opened her arms and drew her daughter in. "Yes, Lucia. I approve."

Hugging her mother tightly, Lucia couldn't stop the tears from flowing freely down her face. "Oh, Mama," she cried. "Thank you."

Later that evening, in the drawing room, Lucia's curiosity finally got the better of her.

"Mama, may I ask what changed your mind about Ronald and me?"

Harriet smiled. "I've watched closely this past month, trying to find any reason I could use to put a stop to this marriage. I looked for impropriety, deviousness, even a bit of rudeness would have sufficed."

She turned to Ronald, her face suddenly serious. "What I saw in your behavior, your attitude, and your attentions to my daughter was a perfect gentleman attending to the woman he loves with all his heart, mind, and soul. In addition, you have treated me with utmost respect and dignity, even when I've been unfriendly and aloof. I even thought about being rude to you, to drive you away, but I couldn't bring myself to go that far."

With that, Harriet grinned in a way that left Lucia a bit bewildered. This was not the mother she'd grown up with. This was an entirely different woman. A woman who was friendly, warm, caring, and reasonable.

Ronald stood and crossed the room, taking Harriet's hand in his, kissing the back of it as he had earlier that afternoon.

"Thank you, Mrs. Rix," he said softly.

Harriet cocked her head with a mischievous twinkle in her eye. "I think Mrs. Rix is a bit formal under the circumstances, don't you?"

"What would you prefer I call you?" Ronald asked sincerely.

"Mama will do nicely," she replied.

"You truly have no reservations now, Mama?" Lucia asked, still wondering if her mother was truly convinced or just setting up another machination, hoping to sabotage their marriage.

Harriet thought for a moment. "I have no reservations about Ronald's love for you, nor yours for him. I still worry about how you will live on a sergeant's wages, and what will happen if he's called back into battle, but you have proven you are two responsible adults who love each other. As important as the rest may seem, that's really all that matters, isn't it?"

"Didn't I tell you?" Ronald looked surprised. "I've given up my commission. I couldn't bear the thought of being called up and leaving my sweet Lucia again, so I have resigned from the cavalry."

Frowning, Harriet once again had the look of a mother bear trying to decide if the man before her was putting her cub in danger.

"So, you won't even have your sergeant's wages?" Her voice was once again cold.

Lucia's face showed surprise, too, but she quickly recovered.

"There's no need to fret about that," she reassured her mother. "I'll simply take extra shifts at the hospital to make up the difference."

Turning to Ronald, she had an idea. "Perhaps you could find a livery stable where you could work with horses? I know you'd enjoy that type of work, and between us, we will do just fine."

As she looked into her sweetheart's face, she noticed a strange twinkle in his eyes, one she hadn't seen before.

"Wait, have you already arranged something like that?" she asked, both accusing and hoping it was true.

"Not exactly," he hedged. "Are you ladies in the mood for a story?"

Both women nodded in unison, so he sat back down, looked first at his feet, then at his hands, then seemed to peer out the window.

"Well?" Lucia prompted.

He looked at her and winked. "Patience, my love. This story will take a bit of telling and I must be sure I start at the beginning."

His face took on a faraway look as he stood and walked to the window. He paused, then turned back, looking at Harriet earnestly.

"I'd like you to understand my background and my upbringing before I relate my tale, with your permission, of course."

Harriet nodded, curiosity on her face.

Ronald told his life story without apology or dramatics. He told of his life as a child, moving from one relative to another after his father's death. He told the story of the ducklings, the story of his mother's fading health, the story of his grandmother's death and his subsequent apprenticeship to first the farmer, then the blacksmith.

He told how he found himself joining the cavalry, and how he used his skill with horses to gain a position that used his talents with animals. He told about how he was wounded, and the evacuation to Scutari hospital. He told of meeting Lucia, and how their love had blossomed even under the strict eye of Florence Nightingale.

Ronald told of the heartache he'd suffered as distance, war, and generals kept them apart. He told of the precious nature of each of Lucia's letters to him. Then, he told of the battle at Sevastopol where he supposedly died.

"While the cannonballs were flying, all I could think about was keeping myself and my men safe. There was a young man who was newly recruited, who panicked. He ran out of the building he'd been sheltering in, then stopped in the open like a frightened rabbit. He didn't hear me when I yelled for him to take cover. I didn't think, I just ran. Pulling him back into the building, I felt we were safe. At least, safer than out in the open like that.

"But he had other ideas. No sooner did I let him go, than he bolted and ran out the back door heading for the wall and the nearest gate. I just couldn't let him be killed, so I followed him, calling to him, urging him to come back in where it was safe. I couldn't hear my own voice for the noise all around us, so I kept running.

"The cannonballs were still flying, and I kept my head down as much as I could," he looked at Lucia, "just like I promised you." He smiled, then returned to his story.

"He managed to reach the gate before I did. I followed him outside the wall. We'd only gone a short distance when I caught up and threw myself at him, rolling with him into one of the trenches dug to protect our riflemen.

"Once again, I thought I was relatively safe, but then the world exploded around me. I remember a glimpse of a black uniform as my head felt like it had been split in two. I don't remember anything after that until I woke up in a small prison cell.

"I had no idea where we were, and the private wasn't any help. He said he saw the Cossack hit me, but didn't have time to fight or run before he was captured, too. He said we were trussed up, thrown in the back of a wagon, covered with a blanket, and rode long into the night before being thrown into that cell. All we really knew was that there were black-uniformed guards outside the cell, and we could hear them speaking in Russian. We were prisoners.

"It wasn't long after I regained consciousness that they began hammering me with questions. Who was I? Which unit did I belong to? What did I know about British troop movements?

"I couldn't tell them anything, because I didn't know anything. The entire attack was a surprise. We'd been told that the Tsar had accepted the Austrian demands and that the war would soon be over."

Lucia was puzzled. "But if you were a prisoner of the Russians, why did Corporal Hahn report that he'd found you dead under a pile of rubble?"

"I'm not sure," Ronald frowned and shook his head. "All I can think is that there must have been another sergeant who'd taken refuge in that building. Apparently, Corporal Hahn thought it was me and reported me dead."

"So how did you escape?" Harriet asked, fully involved in the story.

"I didn't exactly escape," he smiled. "Apparently, when they heard the Treaty of Paris was signed, the officers who'd kept us prisoner decided to let us go. One morning, they stormed into our cell, tied our hands behind our backs, covered our faces, and marched us outside.

"We were thrown into a wagon with some other prisoners and taken outside the city. They removed the ropes, uncovered our faces, and then literally tossed us out as they drove away. After picking ourselves up and making sure none of us were badly injured, we decided that since Russia was north of Crimea, we'd be safest walking south. It took us a couple of days to reach Sevastopol, as we were all weak and some were still recovering from previous injuries.

"So, when you reached Sevastopol, why didn't you contact me?" Lucia accused.

"I planned to. I spent a couple of days in the hospital so the doctors could check me over. The second day, I was writing the letter to tell you about what had happened when another soldier pointed out an article in a London newspaper. He'd read an article about a London socialite named Lucia Rix. It hinted at an upcoming marriage."

"I never!" Lucia protested, looking accusingly at her mother, who looked genuinely puzzled.

"I didn't tell the reporter you were engaged," she said, defending herself. "I told them that Mr. Asher was considering a proposal. That's all."

Lucia glared at her mother, then at Ronald. "So? Go on."

"I didn't know what to do. You had obviously moved on with your life and who was I to interfere with your future? I stewed about it for a couple of weeks. Then decided I would try to move on with my own life and let you live yours."

Harriet cocked her head. "But you are here. What changed your mind?"

Ronald smiled at her. "Something my *seinmheir* told me."

"I'm confused," Lucia interrupted. "Isn't she dead? Or is she just pretending, too?"

Ronald ignored her sarcasm and continued. "When they released me from the hospital, I went back to my unit. A couple of weeks later, my unit was disbanded. We were assigned to other units, but I asked for a leave of absence. I needed time to decide what to do with my life. I was tired of war and killing, but I didn't have another direction in mind. With my leave papers in hand, I made my way back to Scotland. I didn't have a plan, just needed to touch home soil again.

"One day, a few weeks ago, I found myself kneeling beside *Seinmheir's* grave. I don't know why, but I poured my soul out to her as if she was there. I ended with a question. What should I do now?"

"And she answered you?" Lucia was incredulous.

"In a manner of speaking." Ronald's voice was soft with emotion. "I looked up and saw two birds flying together. They darted this way and that, as if they were dancing. Finally, they lighted on a tree branch above my head and one of them started singing. It was the most beautiful song I'd ever heard in nature. When it was finished, the other bird hopped close and the two of them cuddled like I've never seen birds cuddle. It was beautiful, and I'm not ashamed to tell you I shed a few tears watching them.

"As I stood to go, I remembered something *Seinmheir* had told me once. *'S ionnan tosd is aideachadh.'"

"What does that mean?" Lucia asked.

"Those who raise no objection to something said or done are assumed to agree." Ronald knelt in front of Lucia, his expression earnest.

"I knew if I didn't come back and let you know how I felt, I'd forever regret it. Then, when you greeted me with such warmth and obvious affection, I was certain you felt the same way. I am grateful you turned down Mr. Asher's proposal before I came back. Otherwise, I might have wondered if you were marrying me out of pity or a sense of obligation because of what we shared in Scutari. Now, I no longer doubt that you love me."

He stood and addressed Harriet formally, "Mrs. Rix, I've told my story to the best of my ability. Now I ask you, may I have your daughter's hand in marriage?"

Harriet stared at him for what seemed like years, but was in reality only a few moments. "You have told a pretty story, but you haven't answered all of my concerns, Sergeant."

Lucia groaned. Would her mother never quit?

"I apologize. I did get carried away with the tale, didn't I?" Ronald grinned. "Let me see if I can remember the order in which you presented them.

"First, I've already stated that I am no longer in the cavalry, so there's no concern there."

"Second," Ronald's eyes grew wide and he slapped his palm to his forehead, "I do believe I've neglected an important part of the story. After I left the cemetery, I stopped by my former employer, the farmer I told you about. He was pleased to see me, but not just because he liked me, I'm happy to say.

"Apparently, he and his wife were clearing out *Seinmheir's* cottage after her death, and they found an old wooden chest. He was under strict orders to save it for me until I was of age, but if you'll recall, I ran away from the blacksmith before I came of age, so they held onto it all these years.

"When I opened it, I found a deed to a castle owned by James Ferguson, who was the third Laird of Pitfour. He was my great-uncle, or some such relation. He died in 1820 and left his estate to my father's father. However, because of a family dispute long before I was born, my grandfather refused to take up residence there, and my father honored his father's wishes and ignored the inheritance as well."

"So you're a Laird..." Harriet stumbled on the Scottish word, "in Scotland?"

"So it seems. But I don't want to take my Lucia away from her mother and friends here," he continued. He turned to Lucia. "That was one of the items of business I needed to complete that first afternoon, my love. I began the process of selling off a portion of the Pitfour land and buying the Windemere estate. I may not have a proper English title, my love, but we will be well set for the rest of our lives. And if we are wise, our children will inherit a sizable sum upon our demise."

"So, you plan to live in London?" Harriet's voice was hopeful.

"Of course," he answered. "And I plan to have the castle in Scotland repaired, as well. We can summer there. Of course, Mrs...I mean, Mama, you will be welcome to join us whenever you like. I believe that answers your second and third concerns. As for the fourth…"

"That's already been answered, hasn't it, Mama?" Lucia broke in with a huge smile illuminating her face.

Harriet looked from one to the other, and smiled. "Yes, Lucia. It has."

The following afternoon, Ronald escorted Lucia to the bench next to the hawthorn hedge, which was still full of fragrant blossoms. She breathed deeply and sighed with contentment.

"I just love the smell of hawthorn blossoms, don't you?" she asked.

He breathed in the scent and replied, "Yes, but I'd rather be sitting next to you and smelling your hair. It's twice as lovely as any flower scent could be."

She laughed. "Now you're just trying to butter me up. What is it you want, you scoundrel?"

Smiling, he bent to one knee beside her. He took her hand and looked deeply into her eyes. When he spoke, his voice was soft, sweet, and warm, like molasses on a summer day.

"I've been working on this for months now, and I think I've finally got it right. Tell me what you think.

"To Lucia
Tho'ts may come and tho'ts may go,
But none of them seem right.
The words I want, I cannot find,
They're not in this brain tonight.

I dream of you at eventide,
You haunt me in the day.
But when I wish to write to you,

I can't find the words to say.

Perhaps this poem is not enough,
To show you how I feel,
Please take my hand and listen close,
As on one knee I kneel,

My Luscious one, I love you so,
You are my light and life,
I pray that you will honor me,
And say you'll be my wife."

Lucia's eyes filled with tears as she slid from the bench to kneel beside him. Her arms, of their own accord, wrapped around his neck. Her forehead touched his and she whispered, "You finished it. You finished my poem."

Chuckling softly, he pulled her close and whispered into her ear, "Yes, but what is your answer, my dearest Luscious?"

"Answer?" she nuzzled his neck and kissed his ear, her breath tickling him.

He pulled away just a bit and tweaked her nose. "Yes, darling. I've just asked you to marry me and all you can do is blow in my ear?"

"Marry you?" her eyes widened as she realized what he had just asked. "Marry you? Why you silly goose, of course I'll marry you. I've just been waiting for you to ask me in person."

He laughed aloud, then, and drew her into a long, sweet kiss.

After a moment, he pulled back, looking a bit forlorn.

"Why the sad face, my love?" Lucia asked, concerned. "Didn't you want me to say yes?"

Ronald shook his head. "Of course, I did. But I have lost the ring I intended to give you upon our official engagement."

Laughing, Lucia unclasped a delicate chain from around her neck freeing the ring she had hung on it. "Do you mean this ring? Corporal Hahn sent it from your belongings when he thought you dead."

Grinning widely, Ronald took the ring from her and placed it on her finger, then pulled her into yet another tender embrace.

Chapter Twenty-Eight

Lucia was stunning in her gown. She was still amazed that her mother's dress fit her, and even more that Mama seemed pleased that she'd want to wear it. Although it was certainly not "fashionable", Lucia felt it suited her beautifully.

The cream-colored silk was soft to the touch and felt quite elegant. The sleeves were short, but immensely wide and were gigot-shaped. The skirt had full, pointed flounces with beautiful ornaments at the top. The skirt was a full twenty yards of silk, which Lucia decided was something she could live with to please her mother.

She waited patiently for Jean to finish fastening all the buttons down the back. Unexpectedly, she began to giggle.

"What's so amusing?" Harriet asked as she handed her daughter her bouquet.

"I was just imagining how Ronald is going to feel about unbuttoning all of those buttons tonight."

Her mother looked shocked, but when Jean joined Lucia's giggles, she allowed herself a little smirk, hesitated, then said, "Who says he'll actually unbutton them?"

Now it was Lucia's turn to look shocked. "Mama!"

"What?" Harriet pretended confusion. "You started it."

Laughing, the beautiful bride hugged her mother. "I'm so glad you and Ronald are getting along so well. It means a lot to me."

Harriet hugged her back and replied, "All I've ever really wanted was to see you happy and well cared for. The past few weeks have shown me that Ronald can and will do both."

At that point, Susan poked her head in and announced that it was time.

One last hug all around, and the women made their way to stand by the heavy chapel doors.

Ronald adjusted his cravat for the hundredth time.

"Stop fussing with it," Dell Lassiter instructed with a laugh. "You'll mess it up. You'd think you were a fainting bride or something."

"Just a nervous bridegroom," Ronald answered, deliberately stuffing his gloved hands in his pockets.

"Nothing to be nervous about, Sergeant," Dell retorted. "Just let your love and nature take its course. You'll be just fine. How are things with Mrs. Rix? I heard they were a bit rocky for a while."

Ronald smiled. "Everything's worked out famously, actually. Once she realized that I had every intention of taking care of her precious girl, she simmered down and has been quite cooperative."

"I'm glad. My own mother-in-law leaves something to be desired in that category."

"Oh? How so?"

He didn't have a chance to answer, however. The priest knocked and informed them that it was time to begin.

Ronald followed Dell, who followed the priest through a side door into the chapel. As he took his place, he looked around, surprised at how many guests were present. He'd expected a small wedding, but apparently, his new mother-in-law decided it was to be a grand affair after all.

He looked down the aisle at the large wooden doors, closed at the far end of the chapel. That's where his sweet Luscious would appear in her wedding finery. He found his heart beating fast and his breathing was shallow.

Dell leaned over and whispered, "Easy there, big boy. Take a deep breath. You're going to be fine."

He tried to take a deep breath as he looked down at his feet. He was only partially successful, because just at that moment, the organ began to play. He looked up and saw the doors open. This was it!

Lucia watched as her flower girl and bridesmaids took their places at the chapel doors. She smiled at each in turn. Jean, her matron of honor, hugged her one last time.

"You look beautiful, Lucia. Ronald is one lucky man."

Laughing, Lucia answered, "Thank you. I think Dell is pretty lucky, too."

Finally, she turned to her uncle, who would escort her down the aisle.

"Thank you, Uncle Edward, for making this day special for me," she whispered.

"It's my pleasure, Lucia. I know your father would be proud of the choices you've made, and he'd bust his buttons to able to escort you on your wedding day. I'm honored that you asked me to stand in for him."

Lucia hugged him, then looked down to brush an imaginary fleck of dust off her dress for the hundredth time, mostly to hide the tears that welled up in her eyes. She seemed to be doing that a lot lately. Mostly tears of joy, though. She imagined her father's face smiling down at her, offering her his arm, and wished he'd lived to escort her down the aisle. But Uncle Edward was right. He'd be proud of her, and he'd welcome Ronald with open arms.

"Don't you have a groom waiting at the altar?" Uncle Edward prompted her.

"Oh my, yes!" Lucia exclaimed, just as the doors opened and the music wafted into the antechamber. Her flower girl marched resolutely down the aisle throwing flower petals as she went. Each bridesmaid followed one by one in measured steps.

Finally, Lucia and Edward were standing at the chapel entrance. The happy bride looked up into her uncle's face. He grinned down at her, then lifted his arm in perfect escort position. She laid her hand on his, eyes sparkling, smiling so hard her cheeks should have hurt, but she couldn't think of anything except the man waiting for her at the end of the aisle.

As the music changed, they stepped out. Halfway down the aisle, she noticed several familiar faces. Aunt Bea dabbed at tears in her eyes with a lacy white handkerchief. Behind her, Gerald's mother also dabbed her eyes. Towering over his mother, Gerald grinned and winked. Lucia almost giggled at his playful impropriety, but she kept her steps measured and only allowed her smile to broaden a bit.

A few more steps and Lucia could see her mother, who also had tears in her eyes and a smile on her face. She was glad Mama had finally recognized what Lucia had known all along… that Ronald was her one and only true love.

"Who gives this woman in holy matrimony?" the priest began when they finally reached him.

"As proxy for her father, I do," Edward responded.

He lifted Lucia's veil enough to kiss her on both cheeks, then lowered it again and the ceremony progressed.

When the final vows were said and the priest gave his permission, Ronald lifted Lucia's veil, smiling tenderly into her eyes. "May I kiss the bride, Mrs. Ferguson?"

Lucia nodded happily, and they enjoyed a sweet, tender kiss that held great promise for a passionate wedding night.

Later that afternoon, Ronald carried his bride over the threshold of their new home. She laughed at how easily he lifted her. It was a heady sensation to be lifted and carried like that.

He set her down in the entryway, tucked a stray curl behind her ear, and leaned in to kiss her. Gently at first, it grew in passion as she returned his kiss. She felt his hands fumbling with the buttons on the back of her dress and couldn't help but giggle.

He pulled back and looked at her with mock disapproval.

"You laugh in the face of my troubles?" he growled.

"Mama said you might not have patience enough to unfasten each button," she grinned.

His growl deepened as he tried once again, then gave up. "She's right."

His hands grasped the top of the gown and pulled. She felt the buttons pop off one by one, flying everywhere. She threw back her head and laughed.

Oh yes, she thought. It was going to be a beautiful life.

Epilogue

"Mama, Mama!" The little three-year-old's curly red hair bounced as she ran. Her five-year-old brother ran behind her, a little bit more carefully, with something cupped in his hands.

Lucia smiled as her children reached her. "What is it, Mary? What's happened?"

"Andrew has a squirrel and it's hurt bad!" she exclaimed. "We have to help it, right?"

"Of course, we do," Lucia assured her.

"What have we here?" Ronald came up behind her and squatted down beside his son. "What have you found, Andrew?"

"A squirrel, Papa. It has a hurt leg. Can we help it?"

The proud papa ruffled his son's hair. "That's what we do, isn't it?"

The four of them walked around back to a small building behind the house. As they walked in, a cacophony of animal noises greeted them. Birds of many kinds filled cages along one wall. The other side held cages, too, but these were filled with dogs, cats, mice, and other four-legged creatures. Each occupant of the "animal clinic" had been hurt in some way, and was receiving the best of care from the Ferguson family.

Mary danced from cage to cage, greeting each occupant, telling them how beautiful they were and how they would soon be all better and ready to go home.

Andrew was too concerned about his latest patient to notice the others just now. He and his father took the frightened squirrel to a table at one end of the clinic, with Lucia close behind.

"Now, now, gentlemen," she chided softly, "make way so the professional can do her job."

"Yes, Mama," the little boy replied, and obediently stepped back to make room for her.

She examined the creature and smiled reassuringly at her son. "He's going to be just fine. We'll splint his leg, and once it's healed, he'll be racing up trees with his friends in no time. Want to help me with the splints?"

The youngster's face lit up like a new morning sun. "Oh yes, please, mama!"

Watching his wife work, Ronald nodded his approval. "You haven't lost your touch, Luscious. You're still as skillful as that nurse who saved me in Scutari."

Lucia glanced up. "Why thank you, Sergeant. What do I owe you for that compliment?"

His eyes sparkled with mischief. "Why don't we just leave it on the books for now? Meanwhile, you keep working, and I'll get these children cleaned up."

"Aww!" Mary grumbled. "I like being dirty."

Her parents laughed and Ronald tousled her hair. "But when our new patient is settled, we're supposed to go and have tea with Grandmama Harriet. How does that sound? Worth getting cleaned up for?"

"Oh yes, Papa!" the children agreed.

"And maybe Mama will sing for us?" Mary added excitedly.

Lucia grinned. "Only if you will sing for me, too."

Mary's red curls bobbed with her agreement and both children ran toward the house.

"One request, sweet Luscious," Ronald said as he took her in his arms.

"What's that?"

"No sad songs. No laments, ever. Agreed?"

Lucia looked deeply into the sparkling eyes of her husband, listened to the happy chatter of her children outside, and smiled.

"Agreed," she whispered softly as she kissed her soldier. She couldn't think of a single reason to lament ever again.

Coming Soon

A Song for a Soldier

"When life has neither rhyme nor reason, sing until it does."

by

EMILY DANIELS

CPSIA information can be obtained
at www.ICGtesting.com
Printed in the USA
LVOW10s2117160917
548706LV00001B/1/P